The Fear

'Listen, Carl, and listen good. He made a mistake and I've come down hard on him. All right?' Bobby tried to smile away the threat.

'Is that all yer have to say?'

'Well . . . yeah. Just wanted to let yer know that.'

'Why does everybody disappoint me?' Carl snapped, as he began to back away. 'Bye-bye, Mr Chalker.'

'I'm warning yer, son. You go away and think about yer wife and kids. I know 'bout you.'

'I've upped me insurance, Mr Chalker,' said Carl, his shadow disappearing into the fog.

'You leave the little prat alone!'

Carl's voice came echoing and ghostly. 'It's too late, Mr Chalker. A debt is a debt.'

'I'll deal with you! I can.'

'Old man. Old man. Who are you talking to?'

The Fear

PAUL HINES

A Thames Methuen Paperback

For my sisters

THE FEAR

First published in Great Britain 1988
by Methuen London Ltd
11 New Fetter Lane, London EC4P 4EE
in association with
Thames Television International Ltd
149 Tottenham Court Road, London W1P 9LL
Copyright © 1988 Paul Hines

Printed and bound in Great Britain
by Richard Clay Ltd, Bungay, Suffolk

British Library Cataloguing in Publication Data

Hines, Paul
   The Fear.
   I. Title
   823'.914[F]   PR6058.I528

ISBN 0-423-02290-3

One

Across the top of the white façade of Islington Town Hall, a white banner, marked in red with the number of unemployed in the borough, hung in a huge, untidy swathe. In the persistent drizzle and fading light of that afternoon in April, few passers-by noticed the sodden statistic. A breath of wind took pity on the banner, raising it in one last shout for attention before Happy Hour, and the rainwater which had collected in the folds of the material showered down on the milky marble steps below. A labour councillor looked up and cursed the unemployed.

The bad-tempered councillor slouched down the steps of the Town Hall and crossed Upper Street, weaving his way through the line of traffic which was slowing to its rush-hour crawl up to Highbury Corner. He dodged the tide of bowed heads and lethal umbrellas, sweeping up the pavement to the tube. Wiping the droplets of water from his shoulder, he entered the Hare and Hounds public house, where a large Scotch and soda would warm away the homeless, the unemployed, the criminal, and the Opposition.

From the street, the Hare and Hounds looked an unlikely place to seek solace. The front of the building was dark and unwelcoming, squatting beneath Edwardian flats. Two oak-framed bay windows guarded the entrance, and through their frosted glass the clientele inside were only shadows against a dingy, mustard light. A forbidding, cobbled alley stretched down one side of the pub, separating it from a redeveloped mansion block. On the other side, fine metal grilles protected the front window of a feminist bookshop. The Hare and Hounds was one of the islands of antiquity which punctuated the gentrification of Upper Street.

In the deepening shadows of the alley beside the pub, Carl Galton looked out to the street where his car was parked on a double yellow line. The gold Mazda RX7 was a sharp, metallic flash in the gloom. A young traffic warden circled the car, admired its sleek lines, noted the number, noted the time.

Carl turned, unconcerned at the prospect of a ticket, and continued to meander up the alley towards a pool of light which spilled onto the cobbles from the open back door of the pub. He moved noiselessly and smoothly into the light, glanced briefly through the doorway at a cramped, dingy lobby, and then fixed his stare on his own reflection in the glass panel of the door. He smoothed down the jacket lapels of the ink-blue linen suit, and gently kicked out the trousers until they sat symmetrically across the tongues of a pair of classic black brogues. He took a step backwards and surveyed the hang of the suit on his tall, slim frame. The image in the glass seemed to disappoint him. Not one of his better ones. Only four or five hundred quid. Just a 'business' suit.

He moved close to the glass again, and stared intently into his own face. At twenty-five, no line interrupted the smooth contours of his skin; no blemish detracted from his sharp, angular features. He ran one hand through his short-cropped, dark-blond hair, smiled slightly, and then began to whistle the theme from *The Third Man*.

The tune was cut short by a tinny blast of Buddy Holly

6

from the pub juke-box, as the door to the public bar opened. Two figures moved into the sticky yellow light of the lobby. The landlord of the Hare and Hounds took a purposeful stride towards Carl. He was a squat, decaying man in his late forties; his face was stained with beer and nicotine.

'What comic d'you spring out of then?' he snapped dismissively.

Carl cast a brief look at the second figure in the lobby and said: 'I don't think we need an audience, Freddie.'

Freddie eased shut the door to the public bar and then leaned against it. He was two years younger than Carl, but it was impossible to tell that from looking at him. His open, round face sat on a granite plinth of a jaw. The cut of his suit rivalled Carl's, but its fullness could not disguise the heavy expanse of Freddie's body.

Carl returned his attention to the landlord. 'One of my colleagues fortunately heard that a certain gentleman had mouthed you out to the pigs. Now we've done you a valuable service by . . .' He paused; not groping for the word, but increasing the threat. '. . . by dealing with that gentleman.'

The landlord's face broke into a smile and he nodded. 'Proper Youth Opportunities scheme, ain't yer?'

'We don't expect you to write us a cheque,' Carl continued. 'Just know that you . . . owe us.'

'Owe you what? Now look, lads, stick to running errands for other people, will yer?'

He barely had time to turn his head before Carl's hand clamped onto the front of his shirt and forced him back against the frame of the door. The expression of poise and charm drained from Carl's face. He bowed his head slightly and the line of his brow cast a dark menace over his eyes. He jerked the older man back into the lobby, and with his free hand reached behind to close the back

7

door after them. As the door swung to, the landlord, breathless and sweating, raised his arms in a gesture of surrender.

Five minutes later, the gold Mazda had gone from outside the Hare and Hounds, and in the gutter, near where it had stood, the rainwater was beginning to seep through the clear plastic wrapper of a parking ticket.

Six more 'visits' to make that damp night for Carl and Freddie. The Thursday routine was as familiar to them as a paper-round is to a young boy. Between four o'clock and five o'clock they worked exclusively for themselves. The 'insurance' payments from about a dozen restaurants, shops, and pubs were usually effortless, accepted. They allowed five minutes for each pick-up; long enough to be civil, even warm, if they were greeted with warmth. Long enough for Freddie to block out the light, and for Carl to take that one, long, deliberate step towards any proprietor who might appear to be hesitant, grudging, or thankless.

From six o'clock onwards, their schedule was more flexible: they called in 'favours', or let people know they were owed; they freelanced for others; they ventured to the outposts of their territory to recce the lie of the land; they spread goodwill.

They spoke little as they drove against the flow of traffic in Southgate Road on the eastern edge of Islington. They passed the shops selling stripped pine and earthenware, futons and wholemeal bread. They silently noted the landmarks of their youth, transformed and tagged with the words 'exquisite', 'exceptional' and 'luxury', as the estate agents and developers extended the boundaries of affluence. Islington was familiar to them.

At nine o'clock, the Mazda swung round the triangular island of Islington Green and pulled into the only available parking space, opposite the canopied entrance to

Camden Passage. The two boys got out of the car and began to walk back down Essex Road.

'The posh are all out tonight,' said Carl, frustrated by the walk. 'What's the movie at the Screen?'

'Dunno. Some crap about Nicaragua,' Freddie replied, uninterested and uninformed. They reached the row of shops at the end of the Green.

At first glance, Fiorelli's seemed to advertise itself obviously: the red, white and green sign above the façade indicated it was offering something Italian. But the clues became more obscure after that. The plate glass windows were plastered with posters and scraps of paper, informing passers-by of opening hours, specials, set menus, and the fact that part-time help was wanted: 'No time-wasters.'

The long, narrow interior of the restaurant bore witness to the inefficiency of the local health inspector. The Formica-panelled walls were heavy with a film of grease and nicotine, and the row of orange vinyl bench seats and pine tables showed the grime of twenty years' use. A wrought-iron shelf hung insecurely over the serving counter. Mrs Fiorelli thought the display of carnival glass brightened up the place, but a coating of dust had long since dulled its lustre.

Mario Fiorelli leaned against the counter and gazed dreamily at the couple who sat at the table just inside the door. A young woman in a tight, white cotton dress sucked hard on a cigarette and stared at the clock. A picked-at dish of lasagne had been abandoned to one side of the table. The late-middle-aged man opposite her sucked hard on his last, over-ambitious forkful of pasta. He compounded his vulgarity by trying to laugh at it. The woman began to recount the professional encouragement she had had for her modelling career.

Mario ran a hand through his thick mop of black curls and sighed. He had heard it all before. He decided the

9

tricks could not be up to much if this was the only place she could persuade them to bring her. Frederick's was only a spit away down the passage, with its pink tablecloths and fifty-pound menu. But then he noticed how the side seam of the woman's dress had been repeatedly repaired, and how her fingers had roughened where she bleached away the nicotine, and he concluded that she had probably settled to her level.

The man raised a hand and clicked his fingers. 'Bill,' he demanded. Mario glared at him, snatched the bill from a pad and a saucer from below the counter. For a moment he considered tossing it the ten feet to the table, but then he realized the crash would drag his dozing parents away from the news. He marched his sinewy, compact body round the counter and up to the table. He dropped the saucer and the hand-written bill from a good three inches.

Mario's bored expression lightened when Carl and Freddie strode into the spaghetti house. 'Eh, Mario! All right?' said Carl exuberantly.

'All right, Carl? Freddie?'

Freddie nodded and walked down to the far table. He sat and began to lay out a number of small slips of paper before him. He reached into the jacket pocket of his suit, worked a cigarette from a Marlboro packet, flicked it up into the air and caught it between his lips. He looked up and smiled at his own skill.

Carl moved to the end of the counter and lifted the phone from the shelf. 'Need to make a call, Mar,' he said. He cast a glance towards the couple as they got up to leave. He looked the woman up and down, decided she was unworthy of closer inspection and began to dial. He clapped his hand down and postponed the call when he saw Marty enter through the front door. 'Nice gear,' Carl whistled. Freddie and Mario turned to size up Marty's new black leather jacket.

10

The compliment illuminated Marty's face with a smile. He was a boy of Carl's age. If anything, he was more conventionally attractive than his best friend. His build was solid and he had strong, well-set features. A shock of dark hair had been shaved at the back and gelled on top. His deep, violet eyes twinkled with child-like mischief.

Marty looked bashful and embarrassed as Freddie and Mario began to applaud his walk down the room. 'Leave off, will yer! S'just a jacket.' Carl began to dial again as Marty approached. Marty said: 'I caught Gilmour as he was locking up. He's gonna drop that welding gear off tomorrow. No problem.'

'The boys down Holloway Motors was promised it last week. We better watch out or we lose our commission,' Carl warned. 'Where d'yer go after that?'

'Quick drink,' Marty replied casually.

'On yer own, little boy?' quipped Carl. 'Give him Murray's slip, Freddie. You can take care of that, can't yer, Mart?'

Carl pushed the receiver close to his mouth as his call was answered. 'S'me,' he announced down the phone. 'You heard from Mark? . . . Well, I ain't gonna be big brother to him all me life, Linda . . .'

Marty left Carl remonstrating with his wife and wandered over to sit next to Freddie. He cast an eye over the array of slips: pick-ups of stolen goods, addresses and dates for car repos, protection and intimidation, each catalogued individually in a scrawling, unsteady hand. Marty looked up when he heard the creak of the louvred saloon doors which led to the kitchen.

Jo Jo picked his way gingerly down the two small steps to the restaurant floor. His spiky, mousy-coloured hair was too short to appear dishevelled, but the rest of him did not look so hot. The cream blouson jacket he was wearing was at least two sizes too big, and beneath it

11

every bone of his short, scrawny body seemed to be creaking out in pain. One hand was clamped over his right eye, and his little terrier's face was screwed up and puffy.

Freddie let out an enormous guffaw. 'Look at the state of the runt,' he roared. He and Jo Jo had baited each other for years. They snapped and taunted, played practical jokes and never held back in their public criticism of each other. In reality, diminutive Jo Jo swam close to Freddie's powerful jaws, like a pilot fish accompanies a shark. Everyone knew there was affection lurking beneath the gloss of scathing animosity.

Jo Jo scowled at Freddie and lowered his hand from his face. Freddie's amusement increased when he saw the swollen, purplish-black bruise which was beginning to hem in Jo Jo's pale green eye. Marty, too, found it hard to stifle a laugh.

'Someone chuck a chapati at yer?' asked Freddie, incredulous.

Jo Jo looked sour. 'No one told me they was so bloody vicious in that take-away! It was a bit difficult actually, fatty. But I SAS-ed it, din't I?'

Marty shook his head. 'The old woman's sixty, Jo Jo. Her son's on crutches.'

'Don't I know it!' the boy cried. 'He come at me with one.'

Carl's phone call had begun to bore him. 'We'll be down Cheers 'bout eleven . . . yeah, yeah, yeah. OK . . . 'Bye.' He put down the receiver and caught Mario's 'tut, tut' glance.

'Well, I gotta check she's not having it away with some fat, greasy Italian,' said Carl.

Mario said: 'You looking for Mark? He was in earlier, with Barry and a violin.'

'A what?' Carl queried.

12

'Barry's brother nicked it from school. Barry said he was gonna flog it. He's got a screw loose, that one. They went out East. Mile End, Whitechapel, I dunno. Some drinking club.'

Carl rolled his eyes up to the ceiling and clenched his fists. 'I told Mark enough times not to mess with trash in the boonies. Some ignorant East End maniac'll do for him one of these days.' He forced his attention away from the meanderings of his younger brother and back to the other boys. 'And that is the worst filing system I have ever seen, Freddie. Get one them Filofaxes. Gotta change, man. See yer in a bit, lads.'

Marty rose to leave with Carl. Carl paused by the door and turned back to Freddie. 'Where's Russell?'

Freddie looked up from his slips. 'Doing the repo on that Ford. One what Micky's bird had off Theo.'

Carl drew his breath in sharply. 'Oh Christ,' he murmured. 'Keep yer heads down, lads. Micky don't like his lady messed with. And what is that old coat yer got on, Jo Jo?'

'The bloke down Reiss told me it was the latest thing in,' Jo Jo protested loudly.

'Yeah,' Carl muttered as he walked out of the door. 'Cleaner took it off and forgot it.'

Mark and Barry left the bright oasis of Mile End tube station and set off into the tangled network of narrow streets which straggled up to Globe Town.

Mark strode confidently through the hostile environment. At twenty, he already had much of the self-assured composure of his brother. He turned his vigorous, youthful face to his companion, and gave a slight laugh and shake of the head. Barry clutched the violin case to him, like a little boy with a teddy bear. He peered down the streets anxiously, desperately inseparable from Mark,

13

frightened of the night and of exposure to the easy cruelty of others. Mark protected him, guided him, and cushioned him from the harshness of a world that Barry perceived through child-like eyes.

'Is Kev gonna be there?' Barry questioned.

'I hope so, man. It was his idea.'

'Carl'll kill us, Mark. He said. You know he said.'

'He's me brother, Bal, not me mother. Come on.'

Mark tugged at Barry's sleeve and diverted him down another anonymous side-street. After they had gone about a hundred yards Mark stopped by a faceless two-storey building with a plain black door. 'I guess this is it,' he said, unsure. '148.' Barry shrugged his uncertainty as Mark tapped on the door. A bolt was drawn and a crack of light squeezed out from the interior. A grim-faced doorman peered out suspiciously. Mark and Barry smiled hopefully. The door was opened without comment and they stepped inside.

The two boys followed a steep, dimly lit staircase down to the basement. At the foot of the stairs were two doors, leading to ladies' and gents' toilets. They walked on down a red flock wallpapered passage, through an open door and into the main bar of the drinking club.

The sprawling, low-ceilinged basement had changed little since the Krays visited it for 'afters' in the sixties. An antique juke-box was still trying to sparkle in one corner; the copper-faced clock, decorated with an etching of *The Golden Hind*, still clung for dear life to a nail on the wall. A random selection of chairs and tables were dotted about the place. The bar stretched along one wall. The stock was desultory. There were a couple of shelves of wildly varying glasses, a few crates of beer, and a row of optics. The dusty shelf behind the bottles was backed by square mirror tiles, and held the usual bizarre collection of paraphernalia: postcards of the Costa del Sol, fancy glass, donkeys in sombreros, flamenco dolls, the Guinness Toucan and the Babycham deer, a signed photo of Helen Shapiro.

Bobby Chalker sat enthroned at a table near the door of his club. He was in his late fifties, breathless and overweight. He felt uncomfortably restricted in the suit he had bought in 1970, and his face glowed jaundiced in the yellow light thrown by the fluorescent tube over the bar. He surveyed the room. Not a bad crowd in. Few faces were under forty, and most bore the weary marks of a lifetime, lost to late nights and cheap liquor.

Bobby turned to the door and greeted an acquaintance. 'Welcome, welcome. Have that drink with yer later, old son.' He looked round to the large, ponderous man at his side and hissed: 'I can't stand that bleeder.'

'Come on, Dad!' The vacillation of his father was beginning to aggravate Jimmy Chalker. Bobby looked up at his son's podgy, demanding face and sneered. 'I ain't your bleedin' bank. Get 'em in, Toddy.'

Toddy groaned slightly as he heaved his large frame from the chair. At fifty, even the ex-heavyweight boxer's body was beginning to surrender to arthritis. 'Motty's in,' he remarked in a gravelly voice.

'The bird's waiting for a drink, Dad. Gi's a note,' Jimmy demanded.

'G't out! Yer pissed away fifty already tonight.'

Jimmy dropped his lip as far as it would go. 'Don't see why I've gotta pay in your place,' he said.

'I hate you when yer whine. Give prat face a tenner, Toddy.' Jimmy snatched the note from Toddy and took his weasly body back to the bar.

Bobby looked up expectantly as Motty approached. The accountant sat in the chair opposite the boss. His thin, weary face looked even more troubled than usual.

'Wos the damage?' Bobby asked.

15

''Bout a grand at the Oak. Monkey down Mary's.'

'Jesus!' Bobby breathed. 'I don't put money in shirt-lifter joints to have 'em break the places up! Wos happening with the world?'

'Queers ain't what they used to be, Bobby.'

Bobby took a pill from a small bottle on the table. He popped it in his mouth and swilled it down with a mouthful of vodka. Motty looked at him doubtfully. 'You shouldn't take those things with alcohol, Bobby,' he warned.

'S'acid,' Bobby countered. 'Breaks 'em up quicker.'

All was not right in Bobby Chalker's world.

The girl with the pink miniskirt stretched tight across her thighs was living up to her reputation. Jimmy always said Lorraine would talk to a dead caterpillar, as long as it did not answer back. She edged along the bar and smiled at Mark. 'I din't think I'd seen yer before. I can remember a face.'

Barry eased past Mark and offered his face for inspection too. 'Ever seen me?'

'No . . . no. A musical man, you. See, I'd remember something like that.' Mark smiled his appreciation of her friendliness.

'Excuse me,' Jimmy barked as he jabbed roughly at Barry's shoulder. Barry looked round, confused, nervous as usual that he might have done something wrong. 'Shift it, pillock,' ordered Jimmy.

Barry slid out of Jimmy's position next to Lorraine. Jimmy called for the attention of the barman, and then cast a stern glance towards the two newcomers. Lorraine patted at her chaotic bush of home-permed hair and whispered: 'They ain't done nothing, Jimmy.'

'I bet.' The barman took the ten-pound note off Jimmy. 'Sorry mate. I was a bit short.'

'Bit ugly too,' muttered Barry under his breath. Mark dug Barry sharply in the ribs, well aware that Jimmy was in no mood to be baited. But his hopes that the remark would go unnoticed were not fulfilled.

Jimmy rounded angrily on Barry. 'Whad'yer say?'

'Nothing,' Barry murmured.

'Din't sound like nothing.'

'Here we go again.' Lorraine sighed and looked away.

'Come on, clever boy. Whad'yer say?'

'Nothing,' Barry repeated, becoming slightly distressed now.

'He din't mean it,' Mark interjected.

Jimmy's face still held its leer. 'Who are you? His bleedin' boyfriend?'

'No.'

Lorraine had obviously suffered this performance before. 'Don't start here, Jimmy,' she pleaded. 'No one meant nothing. No one said nothing.'

'Whad'you know 'bout it, yer stupid soddin' cow,' he shouted.

'Don't talk to me like that, you foul-mouthed rude git!'

For a moment the focus seemed to have shifted from Barry. The respite did not last as Jimmy bit back. 'You need him to change yer nappies?'

'No,' said Barry weakly.

Mark tried to defuse the situation again. 'He don't understand sometimes, that's all.'

'What is he? Spastic?'

'No, he just – '

'Hey lads,' Jimmy called out to the rest of the crowd, 'we got a bleedin' spastic in.'

'You're drunk,' said Lorraine.

Mark reached over and tapped Jimmy on the arm. 'Leave off, eh?'

Jimmy was in no mood to stop. 'Anyone wanna see

17

what a genuine spas looks like? I got one here.' He grabbed Barry by the back of the collar and pulled him up onto his toes. 'Here's one. I got one!' Barry's arm flailed out to Mark for help and his eyes filled with tears. Mark wrenched Jimmy's grip from Barry's shirt and said threateningly: 'Why don't you shut yer big mouth.'

Jimmy pressed his grinning face close to Mark. 'Why don't you make me?'

Barry broke the growing tension between the two boys. 'Can we go to Cheers now?' he said quietly.

Mark released Jimmy's arm and eased back. 'Finish yer drink first, Bal.'

Barry's face twitched with embarrassed distress. 'I'm sorry.'

'Surprised a spastic can get it in his mouth,' Jimmy snarled.

'Finish yer drink,' Mark repeated.

Barry lifted the glass of beer to his mouth, but before he could take a sip, Jimmy jolted his elbow. The glass slipped from Barry's trembling hand and shattered on the edge of the bar. Jimmy turned triumphantly to Lorraine. 'See! Whad I tell yer? I told yer we had a spas in. They shouldn't let 'em out!' He roared a sadistic laugh. Lorraine picked her bag from the top of the bar and took a step back. She could see what was coming.

Bobby Chalker's hand struck Jimmy so hard across the back of the head that the boy collapsed to the floor like a brick in a swimming pool. Bobby did not wait for him to get up. He grabbed his son by the hair and dragged the scrambling figure out into the passageway. He heaved him up and pushed him violently against the wall, knocking the wind out of him for the second time. One hand grasped Jimmy's throat, while the other slapped roughly across his face.

'Clever boy, eh?' Bobby slapped him again, even

18

harder. 'Clever little sod!' A third slap and Jimmy's cheek was on fire. 'Now get yer bird and get out.'

'That bast – ' Jimmy protested.

'Don't whine! I hate yer when yer whine. Out! And don't go anywhere I've got money in.'

Jimmy tried to summon up a look of defiance. 'You're gonna die soon,' he said. 'I can hear yer breathing.'

Bobby rocked his son back again, and heard the crack of his head on the wall. 'I know what it is now. I've worked it out. You was born a prat 'cos yer mother never took the fag out of her mouth all the time she was pregnant.' He pushed Jimmy aside, and walked, sweating, back to the bar.

Jimmy pressed his face sulkily against the wall. A look of humiliation was cut short by a small, sharp, self-assertive laugh.

Back in the bar, Mark was saying: 'I'm going to the bog, Bal. You go upstairs and wait in the street. We don't want no more trouble.' Barry nodded and turned to leave. 'Take that thing with yer.' Barry picked the violin case from the floor and walked out of the bar.

Barry looked round sharply when he heard voices coming from the doorway of Chalker's club. Jimmy and Lorraine spilled out onto the dark street.

'But I wanna go up West,' she protested. His reply was to grab her firmly by the wrist and drag her off down the wet pavement. He broke into a run as he passed Barry. Lorraine struggled in his wake, angry and confused. 'You're hurting me, Jimmy.'

Barry clutched the violin to his chest and shivered in the damp night air. For a long, frightened moment he felt abandoned and lost, but his face lit up as he saw Mark step out of the doorway.

Barry thought it was just another game when Mark

reeled away from the wall and staggered down the street like a drunk. He was bent double with laughter. 'Stop it, Mark! Stop it, man,' he cried as he ran after him.

Mark thrust out a hand and caught Barry by the arm. Their hands slid together and Barry swung Mark round. The delight on Barry's face did not diminish when Mark slipped from his grasp, rocked for a few seconds, and then collapsed on the glistening tarmac.

'The jacket!' Barry called down. 'You'll ruin the jacket, man!' He knelt by Mark's side and set down the violin case in the road. 'You are bad, man,' he breathed. 'You kill me. I really love yer, man, yer know?' He bent to plant a playful kiss on Mark's cheek. As he drew back, he saw the smudge of blood, which stained Mark's mouth like an angry sore.

Barry's laughter stopped. His hand trembled out to touch Mark's face, and then pulled back. He heard the far-off howl of demons in the darkness, and knew he was alone.

Cheers Wine Bar stood on Essex Road, near the junction with Cross Street. It was a cairn, an outpost, a mark of where the antique shops ended and the hardware shops and council estates began.

From the outside, the bar was undistinguished. A plain red canopy sheltered the door, and the plate glass windows were draped with bamboo blinds. A sign on the door deceptively read 'Closed'.

Inside, a generous bar stretched along one wall near the entrance. The narrow room led back to a slightly raised area, and beyond that to toilets. The walls held signed photos of pop stars, collages of customers' holiday snaps, an occasional 'arty' poster. The decor seemed quite random, designed to pass unnoticed, and not to fight with the decorativeness of the clientele.

There was a good crowd in that night, as every night. The 'Closed' sign was the signal that Cheers was hotting up. The people there were young: some dressed ostentatiously; most dressed expensively. The overwhelming impression was of a preoccupation with style and social appearance; an awareness of and engagement in decadence.

There were few single people present. The apparent flamboyance and vitality was underpinned by a belief in traditional, conservative, social coupling. The impression of hedonism was tinged with menace: everyone knew their place here.

Carl and Marty pushed their way through the crowd by the door. They greeted acquaintances, refused drinks, caught snippets of news and shunned gossip. Carl moved on to the bar as Marty was side-tracked by a group of friends.

Linda leaned her slim, lithe body back against the bar and smiled when Carl approached. She was twenty-three, and her long pale-blonde hair framed a face that held no imperfection. Her eyes were deep and engaging, even without the mascara. Her complexion was fine and luminous beneath the foundation. It was obvious that her mouth was smooth and attractive despite the bright coating of lipstick. Mario stepped back from her side as 'the man' approached to take possession of his perfect wife.

Carl nodded to Mario and kissed Linda lightly. She glanced down at his shirt. 'You got a button missing,' she said with a grin.

'Shit.'

'Nice buttons too,' she added. 'Don't s'pose yer know where yer lost it?'

'Probably the same shirt yer tried to rip off me last week, when yer was desperate for me body.'

21

Linda looked round, embarrassed. 'Don't be filthy, Carl,' she whispered.

Carl turned to survey the crowd. He spotted Russell a few places along the bar. The tall, half-caste boy was dressed to kill. His hair was bunched up in a dreadlock fan, and a pure white shirt emphasized the gentle curves of his exquisite face. He was deep in conversation with a fine-featured, grey-haired woman in her forties. Carl eased his way along to them.

'Not talking politics again, are yer, Russell,' he said. 'You should get out of Islington, before yer get like all the nice left-wing people.' He looked over to the barman. 'Yes please, David!' he called above the din.

Russell's companion turned to Carl and said: 'Don't you like talking politics?'

'Philippa darlin', I am politics,' he replied, dead pan.

Philippa bent down and picked up her bag. She kissed Russell on the cheek and squeezed his hand. 'I'm going to leave you to your friends.'

'No, please,' he protested.

She began to move off. 'It's late. I'll see you on the market tomorrow.'

Carl watched her go and gave a slight shake of the head. 'Elaine's over the other side. On her own.'

'So?' Russell queried.

'Oh Russ, Russ. You do like these old ladies! Yes please, David!'

On the raised area at the back of the room, Jo Jo had parked himself next to what seemed like the only single woman in the bar. 'Waiting for someone?' he asked, hopefully.

'Yes.'

'Anyone particular?'

She glanced at his swelling, discoloured eye, and judged

that he must have got into a scrap when someone stole his sweeties. 'No,' she replied coolly. 'Any grown-up will do.'

'Mind if I smoke?' Jo Jo said.

'Darling, I don't care if you go up in flames.'

Even Jo Jo realized that this was not going down a storm, and considered it time to bring out his big guns. 'I'm not no one, yer know,' he whispered confidentially.

'No?'

'Naaa. I'm one of the lads down here. Few of us stick together, like. With Carl.'

'Oh, Carl.'

'You know him?'

'Like a sort of gang?'

'Yeah!'

'Not many trees left to climb round Islington.'

Jo Jo looked confused and frustrated. 'No . . . no, not like that . . .'

'Oh look,' the woman said as she heard Carl calling from the bar. 'I think your friend's got you a fizzy drink.'

Jo Jo thought it could do no harm to get straight to the point. Carl had always urged him to use the direct approach. 'So whad'yer reckon to you and me?'

The woman leaned forward. 'I reckon . . .' she said quietly, '. . . don't ask me why . . . but I reckon you're unlucky at cards too.' She rose and left Jo Jo trying to remember the last time he had played cards, and what that had to do with sex anyway.

It was almost two hours after Carl and Marty's arrival that Barry edged, nervous and distraught, into Cheers. The crowd was still densely packed, flaunting the licensing laws.

Carl was entertaining Linda, Freddie, Mario and Marty. He was saying: 'So there he was on a life-support machine. Her poor old uncle Mike. And the doctors wanna turn him off, right? But no one wanted 'em to, 'cos what were they gonna tell the relatives back in Ireland – they'd think it was a sin. So Maureen told 'em to pull the plug, and Linda's mum wrote and told the relatives he'd snuffed it when the hospital had a power cut!' While Carl was bathing in their appreciation, Barry tugged at his sleeve.

Carl swung round to check who was daring to touch his best Comme des Garçons suit. His expression softened when he saw Barry. 'All right Bal? Where's Mark? Gone off and left yer?' he joked.

Barry's lips quivered slightly and he forced out the words. 'He always made me laugh. I just laughed. He's the only one who looks after me. Everyone else just takes the rise. I dunno what happened. Some bloke.' All other sounds in the bar receded and Barry's stuttering, confused speech began to rattle in Carl's head. 'Mile End Road somewhere. And some bloke was having a go at me. And in the street, I laughed at him, 'cos it was funny. I thought it was. And they called me an idiot, and they said I nicked it, but I din't. My brother nicked it, Carl. And they took me down that place and called me things. And see, I thought it was funny when he falled over. But it weren't, 'cos he had . . . all blood coming out of his mouth . . . I seen it on telly, Carl. Dead people have blood coming out of their mouth.'

Carl reached out and wiped a tear from Barry's cheek. He said: 'Don't cry, Barry. Not in here.'

Two

The curtains were drawn in the living-room of Carl and Linda's garden flat in Northchurch Road. The room was stark and tidy. There was an absence of bric-à-brac. The only ostentatious decoration was three brass musical instruments, mounted on the walls. In one corner, an LCD in a bank of gleaming hi-fi equipment blinked that it was 8 a.m.

Carl and Marty were sprawled on the floor, asleep. They were surrounded by comics, magazines on computers and warfare, an open copy of *Face*, the *Sun* and several empty beer cans.

Linda shepherded her two young children down the hall. Even at four, Nicky was the image of Carl: brash, confident, assertive. Karen was a year older, quieter. She clung to her mother. Linda peered in through the open door of the living-room. She 'ssshhed' the children's protests and left the flat.

Marty breathed heavily and adjusted his position when he heard the front door close. He felt his brain screaming *No!* when he forced open his eyes. The blur of consciousness began to clear when he looked over to see Carl's sleeping face resting on a cushion. He glanced up at the clock. 'Oh God,' he murmured.

Only an hour and a half had passed since the boys had drifted into troubled dreams. Marty had waited through the night with the children while Carl and Linda kept vigil at the hospital. When they returned at four, he had held Linda tightly and brushed away her tears; he had held Carl too. They had sat there, reminiscing, drinking, playing the old songs: desperately avoiding the issue. Carl had given Marty the bare facts and nothing more: the surgery was over, the waiting had just begun. The first stab of the knife had pierced the ribs on the right, puncturing a lung. The second blow had done the real damage, hitting low in the midriff and slicing down from the base of the stomach to the intestine. There was no point in staying at the hospital. They could not see him, only sit in the corridor and drink in the atmosphere of sickness.

Carl's eyes flickered with the first ring of the phone. Marty was alert now, on his way out of the room. He called back to his friend: 'Carl? Carl? Get that. Might be yer mum from the hospital, eh?'

Carl wiped his hand across his unwashed face. 'What?' he muttered.

'You want me to get it? I gotta go, Carl.'

'No, no. I'll catch yer. Go on.'

Carl heaved up his aching body as Marty left the flat. He tried to shake himself awake as he picked the phone from a tubular steel shelving unit near the door.

'Hallo?' It was not Bridie from the hospital. It was a wheezing voice he had never heard before. Bobby Chalker identified himself and then a fit of coughing crackled down the line.

'We oughta meet,' Chalker suggested.

'Why?'

'S'about yer brother.' Carl's curiosity grew steadily as Chalker began to recount his son's confession. The panic had set in deep in the night for Jimmy when his father

26

had discovered the blood-spattered clothes in the rubbish bin.

'I sent a bloke down the hospital,' Chalker croaked. 'Saw yer mum, got yer number. Just wanna do what's right. No sense in involving no one else. No witnesses anyway, eh?'

Carl fought to control the flood of rage coursing through him. All thoughts of tiredness had been swept away in the tide of adrenalin. 'Where can we meet, Mr Chalker?' he said softly.

When Carl left the flat, he found London shrouded in a pall of dew-heavy fog. The engine of the Mazda gurgled its disapproval of the weather before it sputtered to life.

He sped out through Shoreditch and Hackney. His gaze was set straight ahead, his knuckles whitened as he gripped the steering wheel.

The blanket of fog lay even heavier on the broad, flat expanse of Hackney Marshes. The buildings of the Homerton estate rose only as grey shadows on the borders of the park. Occasionally, a cry broke through and punctuated the unreal silence: somewhere in the distance, an agitated gym teacher was fighting to control an anarchic schoolboy soccer match.

Carl picked his way across the sodden grass and found Chalker waiting at the meeting-place, near the girder bridge which spanned the canalized section of the River Lea.

They each adopted a pose and the sparring began. Carl listened, severe and cautious, while Chalker launched himself into a warped appraisal of his status and ethics.

'We are honourable men. Born and bred. Know that, son. Oh yes, I know what's right. And when it's not right . . .' The coughing returned to shudder through his body. He spluttered on: '. . . then I know . . . Bobby Chalker

27

knows . . . I know it's wrong.' He clutched at his throat and slapped his chest, trying to beat out the illness.

Carl took a packet from his pocket. 'Wanna cough sweet?' he offered.

Bobby stretched out his hand. He always seemed surprised by acts of generosity. 'Oh, taa.' He took the sweet, but his hand stopped as it reached his lips.

Carl laughed. He saw the suspicion in the old man's eyes. 'Don't think I'd try and poison yer with a menthol and eucalyptus, do yer?' he said incredulously.

Chalker's face broke into a grin, and then was screwed up by another fit of coughing. 'Oh . . . I think we understand each other,' he gasped.

'I understand your boy put my brother in hospital.'

'Silly accident.'

'Silly boy.'

Bobby leaned close to Carl and said intimately: 'Between you and me, and going no farther . . . he's thick as shit. But it's yer mum I really called yer over to have a word about.' He spoke with the beneficence of a tyrant king. ''Cos she's got something coming to her, and I will personally make sure she's all right. Bobby Chalker will. Should the worst come to the worst. Which it won't. Will it?'

Carl stared coldly.

Bobby sought satisfactory approval for his high pronouncement. 'You know what I mean, do yer?'

'I know someone could die in this mess,' Carl replied. 'This weather, Mr Chalker. Someone could die out here and you'd never know.'

'Listen, Carl, and listen good. He made a mistake and I've come down hard on him. All right?' Bobby tried to smile away the threat.

'Is that all yer have to say?'

'Well . . . yeah. Just wanted to let yer know that.'

'Why does everybody disappoint me?' Carl snapped, as he began to back away. 'Bye-bye, Mr Chalker.'

'I'm warning yer, son. You go away and think about yer wife and kids. I know 'bout you.'

'I've upped me insurance, Mr Chalker,' said Carl, his shadow disappearing into the fog.

'You leave the little prat alone!'

Carl's voice came echoing and ghostly. 'It's too late, Mr Chalker. A debt is a debt.'

'I'll deal with you! I can.'

'Old man. Old man. Who are you talking to?'

'Toddy!'

Marty dragged a dusty bag of cement from the open-bed lorry and onto his shoulders. Carl followed him as he carried the bag through a pair of large wooden gates and dumped it in the stockyard next to the builders' merchant on Southgate Road.

Marty drew in a deep breath, shook the strain out of his arms and made his way back to the lorry. 'We're all with you, Carl. We all think the world of Mark, man. You can make those boys do whatever yer like . . . in Islington,' he said as he heaved up the penultimate bag.

Carl removed his suit jacket and tossed it onto the bed of the lorry. He took hold of the last bag and pulled it onto his back. 'You'll get filthy,' Marty warned.

'So I'll chuck it and buy another one.' As they ferried the cement into the yard, Carl pressed home his point. 'There's life outside the Angel. There's life outside pulling in protection and loans, and doing repos on overpriced death-traps.'

Marty let the bag slide to the floor and looked into Carl's eyes. 'I thought we was talking revenge, Carl,' he said.

'Sure,' Carl confirmed.

29

Marty trotted back to the lorry and plucked up Carl's jacket. He dusted it off and handed it to the other boy. 'You're hardly around any more, Marty,' said Carl. 'What yer got to do that's so exciting?'

Marty shrugged and swung shut the gates of the yard. Carl snapped the padlock together and they walked through the open door which led to the flat above the shop.

The flat was an accurate reflection of the shop: neat and well stocked. Two bedrooms, bathroom, kitchen and living-room ran off the narrow, L-shaped hall. As the two boys reached the top of the stairs, Marty's father glanced out from the kitchen to greet them.

Bill was a thick-set, almost cherubic-faced man of fifty. A jack-the-lad in his time, but now the years of manual labour were beginning to take their toll. Marty's mother had walked out in a storm of tears and flying crockery some fifteen years previously, and Bill had found himself fortunate to have a nine-year-old-son who was capable enough to take control of their domestic affairs. The flat had been spotless ever since the day Marie had left. But more and more, the roles were being reversed. As Bill lost his interest in the business, he found himself despatched to do the shopping while Marty heaved cement.

'Watcha, Carl,' Bill called, while unpacking a Sainsbury's carrier.

Carl nodded acknowledgement as he and Marty entered the kitchen. 'When did we ever let anyone cross us with no knockback?' he continued.

Marty turned on the tap and rinsed his hands. 'Mark's not dead, Carl. Anyway, I reckon Chalker still pulls in the East End. I also hear he's got friends.'

'I seen him, Mart. He's a sick old man.'

Bill looked up. 'Who's a sick old man.'

'You are, Dad,' said Marty.

30

'Wos wrong with him?' Carl asked.

Bill reached his hand round to his spine. 'Terrible backache, I got.'

Carl was not impressed. Mark had a lot more than backache. He shot Marty a demanding stare. 'So do I count you out?'

Marty tried to ignore the question. His face lengthened as he sorted through his father's purchases. 'D'yer get flour?'

Bill snapped his fingers and looked pained. 'Aaaah! I forgot.'

'How can I make yer toad-in-the-hole when there's no flour?'

'I'll go, I'll go.' Bill conjured up an expression of over-burdened servility and shuffled off to get his coat.

Carl pressed for a response. 'Marty?'

'You're right, Carl. Things have changed. The Krays ain't been around since we was kids. We all look after ourselves. So Jimmy Chalker plunges Mark, so you cut up Jimmy. So Bobby sends over some maniac to blow you away. So Freddie and me go out East, de dum de dum de dum.'

Carl bowed his head and nodded. He said: 'I reckon yer losing the romance in yer soul, old son.'

'Dad is sick, Carl. He wants to know if yer gonna come in on the shop with me. We been talking 'bout it for months . . .'

'I can't think 'bout it now, Marty,' Carl answered sullenly.

'You don't have to ask me who I'm with,' Marty reassured him. 'We been best mates for twenty years. But I don't wanna bury yer, Carl.'

Carl let Marty make him coffee. He even let him change the subject. But when he drove away from Southgate Road he felt disappointed with his lifelong friend. He had

31

gone there expecting fervour, and commitment, and anger. He had been met with cool, cautious reason. In other circumstances Carl's doubts about Marty might have deepened there and then, but as he sped through Canonbury towards Highbury Corner, his eyes were firmly set in one direction. He was formulating his intent. He had a call to make.

He parked the Mazda in the quadrangle between four medium-rise council blocks. As he trotted up the open stairwell of one of the blocks he heard the low hum of the traffic grinding to a halt on the congested Holloway Road.

Carl banged hard on the scruffy blue door of a top-floor flat. After a few moments the door opened to reveal the face of a woman. She was in her mid-twenties, once pretty but now dishevelled and painfully thin. A baby screamed out from her arms.

'Glenn's not here, Carl,' she said in a timid, weary voice.

Carl brushed past her and into the flat. 'Give over, Vicky,' he sighed.

The short hall to the living-room was cluttered with discarded clothes, old newspapers, and one or two shabby, second-hand stuffed toys. The few sticks of furniture were at least fifth-hand, and no carpet covered the worn linoleum. It was gloomy and unwelcoming. A desperate place.

'He don't need you,' said Vicky, wretchedly defiant. 'He's got a proper job now.'

'I'm so pleased. Where is he?'

The bedroom door slid open and Glenn appeared, bleary, in his underwear. His face was drawn and unshaven, his body gaunt and wasted. Carl walked up to him, entwined one finger in the waistband of his soiled boxer shorts and dragged him back into the bedroom.

32

'Shouldn't you be cleaning something, Vicky?' Carl said as he slammed the door in her face.

Carl pushed Glenn down onto the bed. 'What's yer proper job then?' he asked, uninterested.

Glenn trembled and pulled the untidy bedding round him. 'Night shift down the supermarket. Stacking shelves.'

'Crumbs.' Carl kicked a pair of Levis from his feet and crossed to the window. He said: 'You look fifty-five, not twenty-five, Glenn. If you could see yerself.'

'I can,' Glenn whimpered. 'I dunno why yer here. I don't run with the boys no more. Please leave me alone. I'm tired.'

Carl picked up a ragged towel and used it to dust the seat of a cane chair. He sat and gazed down at the bottleneck of vehicles on the Holloway Road. 'What yer doing in this hole, Glenn?'

'We got a kid, din't we?'

'I got two.'

'Well, we can't all be Mr Wonderful. Looks like all the little scams in Islington are paying off.' Carl confirmed that with a lazy nod. 'But then intimidation's tax-free, ain't it?' Glenn added bitterly.

'Bollocks. You sound like some little prat just out of university. When did you start thinking the world owed yer a living?'

Glenn glanced round the boundaries of his squalor. 'This country ain't done me no favours.'

'You're not doing it any either,' Carl retorted. 'There's nothing wrong with this country, Glenn. You din't buy the smack off this country. You bought if off some little prick in Tottenham.'

'You know what my life was like? I'd had it up to here. You know how much I need it?'

Carl chuckled quietly. 'Should of got a hobby . . . Your

life was just like mine and Marty's. Trouble is, you got like half the bloody people in this country – blame everyone 'cept yerself. Truth of it is, you only get out of bed to complain.'

'So what makes you so much better than me, eh?'

''Cos I get off me arse and look after meself. 'Cos I make meself happy, and if I'm pissed off then I do something 'bout it. You'll die feeling sorry for yerself. But before yer do, y'owe me a favour.'

'Like hell!'

'You owe me. You know that.' The shadow of menace descended once more over Carl's face as he enunciated each word like a hammer striking a nail. 'In fact,' he continued, 'you owe me more than one. But after this, we'll call it quits. I don't wanna see you again. I don't wanna catch what you've got.'

Carl ran down the hospital corridor and clutched his mother in his arms. Tears cut down her sunken cheeks. She screamed and beat at her face with her fists.

Two days after Mark's stabbing, the room in intensive care was vacant again.

Bobby Chalker's Gothic monstrosity of a house in Bethnal Green shook with the roar of heavy metal. Bobby shuffled across the dingy, mosaic-floored hall, and grasped at the heavy oak stair-post for support.

'Shut that bleedin' row up!' he screamed hoarsely. Jimmy slammed shut his bedroom door, but the vibration increased as the music was turned up. Bobby wandered back into his office. 'Blow the bleedin' lot of us up,' he muttered.

The office had once been a drawing-room in the grandest Victorian tradition. Now it held the trophies and records of thirty years of criminality. Every cupboard and drawer seemed about to burst open and spew its over-packed contents onto the floor. Boxes of files were piled high in each corner. A large leather-topped walnut desk fought to maintain a degree of isolation in the centre of the room.

George Klein rested his elbow on the mantel of an imposing marble fireplace and wondered what was causing the damp patch halfway up the wall. Klein was a balding, avuncular-looking man in his late forties. A walrus moustache masked his thin mouth. His waistline betrayed how he had become accustomed to a comfortable life-style.

Klein's musing over the source of the damp was interrupted by a sudden bang. The music died and the room was plunged into darkness.

'Jesus Christ,' cried Bobby. He tottered back to the door and called for assistance. 'Someone fix the bleedin' fuse!' He felt his way back to the desk and fumbled in the top drawer. 'Got a candle here somewhere, George. Sod it!' Bobby pulled a lighter from his pocket and the flickering flame of the candle cast a dim light over the room. With no thought for its antique value, Bobby trickled some hot wax onto the desk. He set the light before him and sat. His face was mask-like in the glow; painted with illness and nostalgia.

Bobby began to sing in a quiet, reedy voice. 'You can cry me a river, cry me a river, 'cos I cried a river over you.' Klein smiled his approval. 'You remember that one, George? They say we never had it so good. I reckon they was right. What a life, eh?'

Klein lifted a glass of vodka from the mantelpiece and took a long swig. 'You could jack it in,' he ventured.

'Man's only as good as his last day's work, George. You know that.'

'How many cock-ups you had recently, Bobby?'

'Give over, George.' Bobby dismissed him with a wave

35

of the hand. 'You know what it's like in business, me old son. This is an empire, George. An empire. Can't keep me finger on every little bit of it.'

'Neither can Toddy. Neither can Motty,' Klein commented gravely.

Bobby sank slightly in his chair. Only the embers were left of the fire which had made him the scourge of the East End. He seemed quietly embarrassed. 'Last couple of years,' he confided, 'seems like it's something new every day. And as if I haven't got enough grief, that little prat upstairs goes and damages some hardnut's brother.'

'What?'

'Oh that'll blow over. S'least of me problems.' Bobby paused and poured himself a hefty vodka. 'S'a bugger, innit? When yer kids grow up and yer realize yer hate 'em. And everywhere I look, I see little gits just like him; s'posed to be working for me. Grabby, grabby, grabby. Don't wanna work; just wanna take. Dogs in the gutter, George. And they'll take yer hand off for a bone these days.' He knocked back the drink in one go, and sucked at his breath as the burning flared up again in his stomach. 'You should of stuck with me, George. 'Stead of setting up with Tony. What we could of done. Songs we could of sung. Tony should of been here too, but oh no. He had to be a big shot on his own. Well, I mean with you, George. Head so far in the clouds he couldn't see his old Uncle Bobby no more.'

Klein moved to the desk and sat on a creaking swivel chair. 'Steady on. He's done yer favours, Bobby.'

'I can do my laundry anywhere. I went to you, 'cos Tony's almost family. I had other friends.'

'I hope yer still have,' said Klein. Bobby looked up, confused. 'We're selling up, old boy. Tony's decided he's had enough of big business life. Wants to go off to that big house in the country he bought for his wife, lock the gates and shut the world out.' A tinge of bitterness crept into Klein's voice. 'And I ain't that happy 'bout it either. Nothing I can do. Tony owns fifty-one per cent of CPC; if he wants to sell, that's it.'

Bobby smiled weakly. 'Lovely.'

'How bad are things, Bobby?'

'Things . . . are fine, George. Don't look at me like that, old son. I ain't on me way out yet. When I go there'll be a big white staircase and a load of angels singing. I can't hear 'em yet. Have another.' Bobby raised the vodka bottle but Klein stayed his hand.

'Tea, Bobby.'

'Huh!' Bobby exclaimed. 'When did we ever drink tea together!'

The boys sat scattered round Carl's living-room. If it had been a few years earlier they would have looked as if they had just come in from a boring day at school. But any schoolboyish banter had long since evaporated from the scene.

Marty stood by the door to the kitchen and looked down at the sombre faces: Mario stretched out on the floor; Freddie and Russell on the sofa; and Carl, grimly silent, staring out of the window to the street. Only Jo Jo displayed any emotion. He sat hunched over the computer console near the television. He was playing 'Wild West'. The terrier face grimaced as his man was shot on the steps of the saloon. A 'dying' scale signalled the end of the game. Jo Jo pressed Y to play again.

The atmosphere of restless grief hung heavily over the room. Freddie fidgeted his way to the edge of the sofa and took his wad of slips from his pocket. He began to lay them out on the floor. He said: 'Who's collecting up the Cope tonight?'

Carl looked round. 'Not tonight,' he said quietly.

Marty crossed the room and took the relevant slip from Freddie.

'Leave it, Marty,' Carl urged.

'I don't mind.'

'Leave it – '

'No, really Carl – '

Carl took two swift steps and snatched the slip from Marty's hand. 'Put the bloody piece of paper down!' He kicked at Freddie's neat display and sent the slips flying.

Russell flinched as Carl sank down onto the sofa. 'We din't do it, Carl,' he said. 'What we gonna do? I'm sorry man, I can't sit here all day, really. I got Philippa looking after me stall.'

'The "antiques" will keep,' Carl mumbled sarcastically.

The tension was broken slightly by the sound of the front door. Nicky came running into the room, tearful and flushed. He sought the comfort of his father's arms. Carl gathered him up and laid him down on the sofa.

Carl looked up to see Linda in the doorway, holding Karen's hand. He said: 'Why's he crying?'

'He pushed Karen over when we was coming out of the nursery,' Linda explained. 'I slapped his legs.' She placed her hands on Karen's shoulders and turned her towards the bathroom. 'Come on, darlin',' she comforted, 'let's go wash yer face.'

Carl leaned over and playfully squeezed Nicky. 'Don't cry, baby. Don't cry.' He tickled him under the arms. Nicky squirmed away and the tears turned to giggles of delight. 'You mustn't hit girls,' Carl cautioned. 'You know that. That's not what little boys do.'

'Not till they're big boys,' Freddie quipped. Carl shot him a stern glance, and Freddie tried to melt back into the leather sofa.

'I beat it! I beat the bastard thing!' Jo Jo cried and

jumped up from his seat. The television screen was a mass of pulsating colour.

'How d'yer do that without a brain?' Freddie said in disbelief.

'Dunno. How did I do that without a brain, Carl?'

Carl was not interested in Jo Jo's achievement; he had beaten the machine a thousand times himself. Instead his head was turned to Marty's questioning gaze.

'What we gonna do, Carl?' Marty asked softly.

'We,' Carl replied, 'are gonna have a party.'

'Do what?'

'Don't worry 'bout it,' Carl added dismissively. 'Go up the Copenhagen.'

Linda was in the bedroom when she heard the boys filing out of the flat. She picked yet another of Carl's shirts from the floor. It was like the five she had already put away: expensive, clean, tried on once and then discarded.

She opened the double doors of Carl's wardrobe and took a hanger from the crowded rack. She ran her hand along the row of immaculate clothes. When she came to a light brown Yamamoto jacket, she noticed a bulge in the pocket. She delved into the pocket, expecting to find a handkerchief for the wash, but the source of the bulge was hard. She drew out a small red and white cardboard box. The lettering on the packet was unfamiliar.

Linda crossed and sat on the edge of the bed. Her fingers gently opened the flap of the box. She lowered it to the bed and a dozen shiny-capped bullets spilled out onto the duvet.

Glenn repaid his favour reluctantly but efficiently. Each night for the next week he was despatched by Carl to perform some act of petty vandalism. The locations varied, but the target remained the same: anywhere owned by Bobby Chalker.

The major damage was inflicted by Carl and the other boys. Jim's Phone Bar on Hackney Road had its front window shattered and the cars of its clientele attacked with sledge-hammers; Chalker's betting-shops in Leyton were firebombed; his lock-ups in Clapton Mews were ripped open and the stock of dresses, hi-fis and pornography cast out into the wet nights of early April; Chalker's prize Mercedes gained the decoration of a scar of paint on one side. And the list continued. Each night, Carl's aggressive, loathing, revengeful grief found new ways to harass Bobby Chalker.

Bobby sat in his office and surveyed the wreckage of his 'empire'.

Motty wearily listed the damage. 'The bookies, Phone Bar, Mary's. And tonight's not over yet.'

'Jesus,' Bobby breathed. There was a clanging noise from the hall. Toddy turned from his position at the door and looked out into the hall. Jimmy sat on the first-floor landing. His legs dangled through the banisters; he looked like an overgrown child in a giant play-pen. He stretched an arm out horizontally and dropped another coin into the enamel cup he had positioned on the hall floor below. He had been confined to the house since the attacks started and his nervy frustration was beginning to boil over.

'There's a lot more stuff that our little friend Carl ain't responsible for,' Motty continued. 'Stuff what was going on well before he come along.'

'Like what?' Bobby barked.

'Webster's – '

'Wos that?' said Bobby. Motty cast a sharp glance at Toddy. Bobby could not even remember the places he had screws on.

'The clothing factory on Commercial Road,' Motty

40

explained. 'Someone padlocked the gates shut when they was all inside.'

'Busby's is Carl's work,' Toddy added. 'Disco in Canning Town. Superglue on the ladies' toilet seat.' Jimmy let out a short, adolescent laugh. 'It might sound funny, but some poor tart glued her arse to it. That's bad for yer customer relations, Bobby.'

Bobby Chalker sank his head in thought for a moment, and then glared up at his right-hand men. 'Well?' he demanded. Their silence jolted Bobby into decisiveness. 'I'm fed up with this. Being pushed round by some little sod just out of his nappies. I'm not happy, and yer know what happens when Bobby ain't happy, oh yeah. We will solve one of our problems right now. You find Mr Carl Galton tonight. I don't care how. And you let him know just how fed up I am. And don't send some bleedin' Mickey Mouse, Toddy. You do it.'

Another of Jimmy's coins struck the heart of the cup, and Bobby launched himself towards the door. He screamed up the stairs: 'I should shoot you and save him the bleedin' trouble!' As he turned back into the office, the pain hit him again: top of the arm, shooting. 'Bloody indigestion,' he muttered. His face screwed up in agony.

Carl and Marty were walking along the tow-path of the Regent's Canal, just above the Danbury Street Bridge. The night was cool and still, a lull between showers. They had seen each other little in the week since Mark's death. Marty had not refused to take part in the attacks on Chalker's property, but he had found a number of reasonable excuses. Carl, driven by obsession, had no time to question his friend's reluctance.

After the bustle of Cheers, they felt calmed by the night air. 'Two quid they gave us,' said Marty.

'You remember that?'

41

Marty nodded. 'Well, I s'pose they knew we had to get rid of it.'

Carl smiled nostalgically. 'Couple of stupid kids with half a ton of lead off the school roof. We must of been mental!'

'Funny though when it started – '

'When it started raining!' They laughed as the prank focused more vividly in their minds. 'And all the time, the motto . . .' Carl prompted.

They shouted in unison. 'We run together!'

Carl stopped and looked sadly at his friend. 'You should of been there this week, Marty.' Marty shook his head, trying to dismiss the comment. He stared over Carl's shoulder, avoiding his gaze. His eyes fixed on the headlights of a car which was parking at the top of the canal bank, in St Peter's Street. 'I din't mean to row yer out or nothing,' said Carl.

'Don't matter. Someone had to keep up the collections round Islington, din't they?' A shiver of foreboding ran through him as he saw a figure get out of the car and begin to walk to the head of the steps down to the tow-path.

Carl's thoughts had drifted back into grief. 'I dunno where he is, Marty. I keep thinking Mark's gonna walk up to me somewhere . . . but he ain't. I dunno.'

The fear was rising in Marty as the figure reached the bottom of the steps. 'We run together, Carl,' he whispered.

Carl mistook his meaning. He slapped Marty on the shoulder and said: 'All right, man! Just like the old times.'

'No, Carl. We run together. Like now, man.' Carl stared at him, uncomprehending. 'Like now, man,' Marty repeated, deadly serious. Carl turned to follow Marty's stare and he saw Toddy approaching briskly. 'Come on,

Carl. We can make the bridge.' Marty began to back away but Carl caught his arm and gripped it firmly.

'Stay put,' Carl ordered.

'What!' Marty looked incredulous. He knew it was trouble coming along that path.

Toddy stopped. He was about thirty feet away now. His hand reached into his jacket.

A shot pierced the dead air and a duck screamed off the canal. The nightmare leaped out of control in Marty's mind. The flapping of the birds' wings were like a deafening hammer. He looked on horrified as Toddy clutched at a glistening crimson stain on his stomach. Carl stood stock-still, his arm outstretched. He was holding a gun. Toddy staggered backwards towards the steps. Carl swayed for a moment and then marched purposefully in pursuit.

Marty stood shocked and numb. 'For chrissake, Carl. Come on. Leave him!'

Carl was deaf to Marty's pleas. Toddy had climbed up to the road now. Carl strode after him, shaking Marty from his arm. 'Leave him, Carl. Please!' Marty shouted again.

Toddy reached his car and slumped down in the front seat. Carl ripped back the door and pressed the gun tight to the henchman's head. From the top of the steps to the tow-path, Marty heard Toddy's hysterical blethering: 'I won't tell no one . . . I won't tell . . . I won't, Carl . . . please . . . please . . .' Carl's finger tightened on the trigger. 'Please!' Toddy shrieked. 'Please God!'

A siren wailed close by. Carl beat the butt of the gun across Toddy's temple and slammed the car door on his sprawling legs. 'You tell 'em what you damn well like!' he raged, and then turned and ran off down Colebrooke Row.

Marty stood for a moment, frozen, disbelieving. The

43

siren moaned louder and stung him into action. He ran for dear life. Down City Road to Old Street. Along Old Street to Kingsland Road. He finally stopped when he reached the railway bridge which marked the head of Shoreditch High Street. He stood beneath the bridge and shivered as he watched the rain fall.

Three

Carl stared down from the bedroom window of his
mother's high-rise maisonette in Highbury. He saw a red
Ford Escort draw up in the car park below. Linda jumped
out of the passenger seat and tugged and tidied at a
tailored black suit before opening the back door for her
mother. Glo still had her daughter's large, warm eyes, but
at forty-five her face had been dragged down by a worn,
long-suffering expression. She bent back into the rear of
the car and began to heave out her husband, Stan. He fell
limply across the seat. From high up, Carl heard Glo's
gentle, persistent coaxing.

Two other people had squeezed out of the car by now.
Linda's Aunt Brenda, and her Uncle Ron. Carl smiled
when he saw Brenda's enormous bust, encased in a cast-
iron bra and jutting out through her fake fox. Ron
dutifully moved to the back of the car, opened the boot
and removed a folding wheelchair. Carl was glad they had
made the trip from Dagenham. He had always hated
funerals.

Brenda sang out in a loud voice as Stan was plopped
down into the wheelchair: 'I know it's a terrible thing to
say, Glo, but sometimes I wish my Ron was on wheels.'

Ron shrugged straight his navy wool overcoat. 'Oh
yeah?'

'Yeah. Make carrying yer home from the pub easier.'

45

As the procession moved to the lifts, Bridie's gentle weeping drifted back into Carl's consciousness. He turned from the window and looked sadly across to his mother. She sat on the edge of the bed in the austere room. The white walls held no decoration except a sculpted crucifix. She looked shrivelled and helpless. Carl had spent his childhood wondering how that slender body had scrubbed and lifted and cleaned perpetually with apparently endless stamina. Now there was no illusion. As she trembled with her tears, he saw nothing but frailty and fear.

He sat down beside her and pulled her to him. 'I've lost him, Carl. I've lost him,' she repeated, in rapid, breathless sobs, almost choking with her grief.

Downstairs, in the cramped little living-room, the funeral party assembled. The coffee-table was already groaning with food and Kathy, Linda's younger, plumper sister, was still busying herself, ferrying plates of sausage rolls and cake into the room. Marty sat in one corner, subdued and thoughtful, avoiding conversation and engagement by trying to replace a broken wheel on one of Nicky's trucks.

Enthroned on the sofa were Connie and Alan: Carl's elder sister and brother-in-law. Alan had fixed his all-purpose smile, but Connie's pinched mouth pulled tighter by the minute as she surveyed the gathering with haughty disapproval.

Brenda filled the room with her voice. 'I was useless. Useless at school. Weren't I, Glo?' Brenda allowed her sister a split second to nod confirmation before she expanded. "Course, I had me mind on other things. Still do, don't I, Ron? Whad'you teach, Alan?'

'Geography.'

Brenda raised the eyebrows which had been plucked to almost nothing for the occasion. 'Oh. I know nothing about it. Do I, Ron?'

'And a little games,' Alan added.

'That's Ron's subject.'

Ron hesitated with his lips closing on a hefty slice of gateau. 'Whad I know 'bout geography?'

'Not a lot. Know a few little games though, don't yer?' Brenda's body rippled with a laugh that cracked into a cackle.

Glo turned to her husband's glazed, unseeing face. 'Wanna drink?' He made no sound or movement. He had not spoken for two years; not walked for three. Glo still talked to him as if he might reply, still phrased questions, asked opinions. In reality, she knew that his next response would be his last. She answered her own question and went to the kitchen to fetch a glass of squash.

'You gonna have a drink, Connie?' said Linda.

'I'm fine, thank you,' was the clipped reply.

'Go on, girl,' Brenda urged. 'Yer old man's having a drink, ain't yer, Alan?' Alan tried to slip his glass down beside his chair, out of Connie's eyeline.

'Actually,' Connie bit back, 'I feel it's rather a solemn occasion.'

Brenda smiled awkwardly round the room. 'Oh . . . yes of course . . . Well, I'll just go and powder me nose.'

Connie watched Brenda manoeuvre her large frame round the furniture and over stretched-out legs. Connie thought fat people were lascivious, and should be compulsorily sterilized.

Brenda passed Kathy coming into the room. She whispered: 'She's a stuck-up bitch,' without breaking her stride to the bathroom.

Kathy bore yet more refreshment. 'Not having any cake, Alan?' she called.

'No thank you, Kathy,' the teacher replied politely. 'I'm not a cakey person.' That drew a look from most of the room. Alan was about as 'cakey' as they come.

47

'Trifle's nice,' said Marty.

'To be honest,' Alan continued, 'I've never been a big pudding fan, have I, Connie?'

Connie felt one of Alan's 'little whoopsies' coming. 'It's a long drive back to Harlow, Alan,' she said out of the corner of her mouth.

Alan felt the need to conclude his pronouncement on puddings with a none-too-guarded reference to his dicky colon. 'I like them, but they don't like me.'

Connie spotted Carl enter the room and pass behind her through to the kitchen. She took her chance to escape. He was struggling to pierce the top of a 'party' can of beer when she joined him.

'I think they've all had enough of that already, Carl.' He reacted in the way he had always reacted to Connie: he did his best to ignore her. 'I'm sure I don't know what they're all doing here anyway.'

Carl belched. 'They're Linda's family. You've met 'em all before.'

'And they think it's their place, do they?'

He cast her a steely glance. 'They loved him. Everybody loved Mark. But you, you couldn't give a toss. I'm surprised the pair of yer bothered. There's no hand-out, Constance.'

She folded her arms across her chest defensively. 'He admired you in some strange sort of way, didn't he?'

'Yes.'

'Then it was inevitable really that something like this would happen.'

'You're too good for us.' He leaned back against the counter-top and sucked the froth from the top of his drink.

'I appreciate our Irish roots, Carl, but we don't all have to behave as if we've just wandered in off the peat bog.'

'Really? I'll try not to be so common.' He belched again. 'Pardon.'

Connie continued to lose the battle. ''Course, none of this would of happened if Dad was still with us. You boys were never dealt with as strictly as me.'

'It was a great loss to us all.' The sarcasm drained from Carl's face. 'You forget, Connie. I was old enough to remember when there was so much puke on the floor that yer couldn't see the empty bottles no more. So be careful where yer lay the blame.'

She moved closer to her brother and manipulated her face into a digusted sneer. It crossed Carl's mind that she looked like a constipated horse. 'I really think it's you who need to be careful,' Connie rasped. 'I mean the pretty little wifey may turn a blind eye, but do you actually think that everyone else isn't aware of the kind of life you lead? One murder in the family is bad enough. I'd find it hard to live down two.'

A flush of anger coloured Carl's cheeks. 'Why don't you and Alan . . . go and make babies.'

Carl strode quickly out of the kitchen, through the living-room and into the hall. Marty rose to follow him. He hesitated for a moment at the top of the stairs and looked down the passageway. Through the open door of Mark's bedroom, he saw Carl staring out over the roofs of Islington. He walked noiselessly into the room. Nothing had been touched since Mark's death. The Arsenal poster still hung on the wall, the wardrobe still groaned with clothes, tapes, records, and magazines still littered the floor.

'I wondered . . .' Carl turned sharply at the sound of Marty's voice.

'What?' asked Carl.

'. . . whether yer wanted to talk about the shop.'

49

Carl looked back towards the window. 'Not now, Marty.'

'Be honest with me, Carl. That means not ever, don't it?' Carl's head lowered and Marty had his answer. 'Least I know where I stand.'

'We're better than that builders' merchant, Marty. And Cheers. And this.' Marty watched silently as Carl's fingers trembled gently across the glass. He wanted to talk about the canal, to confront Carl, to say: 'Enough.' He wanted to drag Carl back from the drunken hysteria of violence he had witnessed that night. But he did not. Perhaps it was the mournful voice persuading him, demanding that he justified his calmness.

'You know what I think of Islington?' Carl asked, hushed. 'I think it was a slum before the posh moved in, and it's worse now. We drink champagne and get respect, but we'll be old soon, and we'll die. I wanna lot more, Marty. And yer know, I'll bet money Chalker is scared of us. We can take Jimmy. We can take the whole damn lot.'

'S'not a film, Carl.'

'I'm sick of doing little things in a big way, Marty.'

Bobby Chalker leaned on his stick for support, and paused to catch his breath in the foyer of Hackney Hospital. He postponed the resumption of his tired progress when he saw Motty approaching from the wards.

'Nice to see someone else is doing their duty,' Bobby called. Motty plodded slowly across the polished tiles. Bobby brandished an unhealthy-looking wad of daffodils. 'You reckon he'll like these? I dunno what Toddy likes. Well, I do. I got a nip inside me jacket. I'll slip it to him when those bleedin' Jamaican women wrestlers ain't looking.'

'He ain't there,' said Motty.

'Where is he then? Up the women's gyny I 'spect. Lord love us; I seen better-looking abattoirs than this place.'

'He's dead, Bobby.'

The muscles in Bobby's face twitched, nervous and agitated. He tried to close out the truth. 'Naaa. I see him last night. He's all right. Ain't he all right? I need him. Ain't he all right?'

'He's in the morgue, Bobby. He had a haemorrhage. This morning.'

'D'yer see him? D'yer put a mirror in front of his mouth? Thas how they tell, ain't it?'

'This is a hospital, Bobby. They know when someone's dead.'

Bobby tottered slightly and then sank back on one of the bench seats which lined the foyer. He gripped hard on the carved handle of his stick. 'Does that make it one all?' he asked quietly.

'I don't reckon Toddy was the right one.'

'I needed Toddy. I needed him. None of the rest of yer've got any idea! Whad am I s'posed to do now? That's bloody typical, that is. Bloody typical!'

The weather had brightened into mild, late spring when Bobby Chalker arrived outside the offices of Commercial Post and Carriage on the second Sunday in May.

The four-storey 1930s block stood in solid, bleached stone on a corner of Tower Bridge Road in Aldgate. Adjacent to the offices was a high, art deco arch, which opened out into a depot quad, bordered on three sides by single-storey despatch rooms, loading bays and work-shops. A fleet of white lorries and vans stood in neat ranks. Each bore a small red logo: CPC.

Bobby left his young driver guarding the Merc from further vandalism and made his way to the plate glass front entrance of CPC. He was sporting his best cream suit, carrying an unused briefcase in one hand and a cigarette in the other. Next to the discreet brass name-plate was a small security intercom. Bobby gripped the cigarette between his lips and pressed the buzzer.

'Hallo?' It was Klein's voice.

'S'Bobby, George.'

'Third floor, Bobby.' There was a whirring from the electronic lock on the door. Bobby tossed down the cigarette and rubbed it out with his foot. He turned to enter the door, but the vibration had stopped. Embarrassed by his incompetence, Bobby pressed the buzzer again.

Bobby learned from his mistake and moved swiftly to the door. He pushed his way into the cool, spacious foyer. On a low marble plinth in the centre of the area stood a 1959 Vauxhall Cresta PA. The unblemished chrome glinted brightly. The 'Haven Blue' paintwork was immaculate. Bobby bent to read a small rectangular sign which rested against the front bumper of the car. 'From little acorns . . .' He shook his head and crossed to the lifts, wondering why George and Tony would want that heap of old junk in their nice clean offices.

Bobby's face was cramped and confused as he stepped breathlessly out onto the third floor. Before him, he saw an array of open-plan units, each impeccably tidy, bordered by plants and partitions. He wandered, bewildered, through the office. When he reached the far end, he stopped to consider whether or not he was completely lost. He spotted a narrow corridor leading from the office area and made towards it. On the right of the corridor was a promising-looking door. When he opened it he discovered a well-stocked cupboard of cleaning material.

'Bobby?' He was saved from further frustration by Klein's voice.

52

'Bloody maze, innit?' Bobby laughed as he turned to greet his old friend.

'You get used to it,' said Klein, and led him back through the open-plan units to a door at the opposite end. They entered an airy, expensively furnished office. Bobby's feet sank into the plush carpet as he moved to a tall, middle-aged figure near the window.

'Tony! S'been a long time.' Bobby held out his hand, expecting a firm, friendly shake.

Tony Slater turned slowly from the window, deflating Bobby's hopeful cheeriness with one look from his piercing blue eyes. He said: 'I hope you're not going to ruin my Sunday, Uncle Bobby.'

Jimmy jumped up from his seat when Bobby Chalker slammed the door of his drinking club in Mile End. He rushed to the bottom of the stairs and called up at his father. 'Well?'

'Well,' Bobby echoed dourly as he made his way unsteadily down to the basement. He was breathless and sweating again when he reached Jimmy's side. He took a small ticket folder from his inside pocket and tossed it at his son.

'Wos this s'posed to be then?' Jimmy barked.

'Wos it look like?' his father snapped back, groping for a chair. 'We'll get no help from Slater and Klein.'

'But I don't want to go to poxy Spain,' Jimmy protested.

'I don't care what yer want. You've landed me right in the shit and now you'll do as yer bleedin' told. Weren't easy getting that today.'

'I can handle him!'

'You can't handle yerself with a hard-on,' Bobby spat.

'What am I s'posed to do in Dagoland then?'

'Same as yer do here: sod all.' Bobby reached into his pocket again and took out a dog-eared manilla envelope.

'Anyone would think I'm a bloody moron,' moaned Jimmy as the envelope flew at him.

'In there's the keys to Joan's place and two grand.'

Jimmy looked incredulous. 'How long's that meant to last?' he demanded.

Bobby raised his eyes in a tired, resigned look. 'Quite some time,' he said. 'So don't go and spunk it up a bleedin' wall.' His face contorted as the pain struck again. He had eaten nothing all day. He could not blame it on indigestion this time. 'Jesus you've cost me,' he breathed.

Later that night, Bobby lay slumped across the desk in his office. Before him lay an empty vodka bottle, a handful of pills which had spilled from their bottle and a sheet of paper on which he had been trying to write. Motty stood just inside the door and stared anxiously at 'the boss'. There was no movement. He could not hear Chalker breathing.

Motty crossed noiselessly to the desk and peered intently into Bobby's face. He jumped back with a start when Bobby opened one eye. A defiant glare met 'the accountant'.

'Leave the vodka alone, Bobby. You're sick,' said Motty.

Bobby brushed away the empty bottle. 'Crawl off with the rest of 'em,' he spluttered.

'I can pack yer a few bits. You can get out now.'

'Pack what!' What was meant as a roar came out as a cracked whisper. 'I got an empire out there. Man's only as good as his last day's work.'

'Empire's gone, Bobby,' said Motty sadly. 'Fallen apart. We've all got old, fella. We all got knives in our backs.'

'You make me sick,' Chalker coughed. 'Go on. Clear

54

out then. And make sure someone's on that front door . . . and the back.'

'There's no one here, Bobby. They've all gone.'

Bobby's eyes fell shut. 'Find me someone,' he muttered.

Motty returned to the door and looked back at the dying old man. 'I'm going now. . . . Go to bed, Bobby.' He left the room and gently eased shut the door behind him.

Bobby's fingers twitched slightly. He mumbled in the silence: 'Tell that little sod . . . to shut . . . that row up.'

'Why can't I come?' Linda questioned from the steps of the flat.

Carl stopped by the side of the Mazda and looked back at her. 'You said you was picking up the kids from yer mum's, darlin'.'

'I can call her. They can stay there.'

He sighed and tried to reason with her. 'I'm only going for a drink with Marty. Be fair. Boys' night out.'

She was unconvinced. As she trotted down the steps and approached the car, the feeling of distress and mistrust hardened inside her. She gazed into Carl's smiling, persuasive face, pointed to the boot of the car and said: 'Open this, Carl.'

He feigned complete surprise that anyone should want to inspect the boot. 'What? Why, darlin'?'

'Open it please,' she insisted.

'If you'll just tell me – '

'Open the bloody thing!' she screamed. Carl angrily ripped open the car door and released the boot catch. The boot lid floated up gently and silently.

Linda began to sort feverishly through the tools and accessories which littered the boot compartment. Finally she came to a plumber's tool-bag which was nestling beneath a pile of AA literature. She rolled open the grease-stained cloth and saw the soft metallic glimmer of the Smith and Wesson barrel. A feeling of angry disgust filled her as her hand wrapped round the butt and brandished the weapon in her husband's face.

'Got any more of these hidden in the house?' she said acidly. 'Well, I hope they're well hidden, 'cos yer know how yer gotta keep dangerous things outa the reach of children!' Her voice rose to an embittered scream. He snatched the gun from her hand and tossed it back into the boot which he slammed shut.

'You said, you promised, you swore by the bloody Virgin Mary this would never happen!' she shrieked. 'What kind of an idiot d'yer think I am!'

'Shut up,' he ordered.

'You think I'm a fool?'

'Shut up!' He grasped her hard by the arm and dragged her back towards the flat.

'You said never,' she moaned.

'Shut up!' He pulled her up the steps and pushed her against the door-frame. He clamped his hand over her mouth; not brutally, but firmly enough to silence her. 'Now shut up, Linda!'

Suddenly, exhaustion seemed to overtake her. As he removed his hand from her mouth she sagged back. He collected her up and clutched her close to him. She began to shake convulsively with silent sobbing.

'Why d'yer do this, eh?' he demanded. 'Why d'yer make me raise me voice to yer? You know I don't like to do that. D'yer know why yer do it?' She wanted to speak but he hushed her quiet and held her tighter. 'Yer don't know, do yer?'

'S'because – '

'Ssshh.'

'Bec – '

56

'Ssshh. Yer don't know why, darlin'. Yer know I only do the best for yer.'

Her head fell limply on his shoulder. 'Mmmm,' she murmured, surrendering to his dominance and strength.

''Course yer do. Now I'm gonna take yer inside, make yer a nice cup of tea and yer going to pull yerself together. 'Cos I don't like to see yer like this. I like to see yer pretty. Eh? . . . Then I'm going for a drink with Marty.'

Her tear-filled eyes gazed up at him. 'I'm sorry. I love you.'

He smiled. 'I love you too, babe. Be good to me, and we'll be good together.'

She let him walk her into the flat and make her tea. When he left, she sat quietly confirming her own weakness.

Carl drove past the builders' merchant in Southgate Road, cursing the delay. When he arrived at Chalker's house in Bethnal Green he found no one on the door, front or back. He entered quietly and stepped into the gloom of the hall. He stepped back into the shadows when he heard a clatter from Bobby's bedroom. He studied the old man's contorted figure as he staggered out onto the landing.

'Motty?' Bobby's voice tremored thin and weak. 'Where are yer gone?'

'There's no one here, Mr Chalker.'

Bobby flinched with dread at the sound of that calm, stony voice. Carl stepped out into the light. 'We're all alone. Isn't that cosy. Just you and me.' He crossed the floor to the foot of the stairs, composed, poised and determined. 'Ever see a Cagney film, Mr Chalker? Well, 'course yer did. This is what it always comes down to in the end.'

Bobby's whole body jerked in anguish and he fell against the banister rail. 'Help me!' he cried.

'Oh I'm going to. Yer shouldn't have sent yer son away, Mr Chalker. I know yer have. I been watching you. Someone's got to pay, old man.'

'Help me, son,' Bobby gasped again.

'I've got a gun, Mr Chalker. Are yer frightened?' Carl stretched out his arm and took careful aim at Chalker's heart. 'A debt is a debt, Mr Chalker.'

But before Carl's finger could close the last deadly millimetre on the hair-trigger, Chalker's arms shot up in agony. He slumped along the rail and tumbled flailing down the stairs to Carl's feet.

The gun fell from Carl's grip as he bent down and shook Bobby furiously. The lips parted, dry and cracked: 'Hear no singing.'

'Don't die like this,' Carl begged, angry and cheated.

Bobby's eyes flickered. 'No singing,' he breathed, as life left him.

'Don't die like this,' Carl repeated. His voice rose in a howling scream: 'You mustn't die like this!'

Four

Carl stood with Marty on the Bow flyover and surveyed the wide, untidy stretch of the East End. Ambition and frustration pestered him like an itchy gland.

'There has to be more than this,' he said, as much to himself as to Marty. The other boy glanced up sullenly. Marty was thinking of a delivery of stock brick and the hired power sander, which had not been returned to the builders' merchant. He stood there simply out of loyalty. He was tired of this game; besides, it was getting dangerously out of hand.

In the week following Chalker's death, five of his closer associates had followed him. That morning's newspaper report of Motty's asphyxiation was printed graphically and indelibly in a prominent place in Marty's brain. The other murders had been just as gruesome. He knew Carl was not responsible, but the continually close proximity of death meant fear held him tight in its grip.

Carl's anxiety was centred elsewhere. He had cleaned out as much as possible from the office that night when Bobby's tired heart sent him plummeting to death. There were half a dozen leases to lock-ups and garages, a file of contacts for pornography mailings, and a jumbled collection of papers indicating twenty or so establishments which regularly paid protection. Those lists had proved unreliable, to say the least. Mario and Russell had discovered that Fraser Tool Hire was now the new centre for the Jobstart scheme; Jo Jo reported that Shampers Disco Pub had been mysteriously transmuted into a Dockland superstore; and Freddie . . . poor old Freddie. Carl had to smile slightly to himself as he thought about it: eight large black boys in a Hackney pool-room did not take too kindly to intimidation from one white boy, however large he was. Freddie had limped back to Fiorelli's that night, bedraggled and battered. Even Jo Jo backed away and kept his mouth firmly shut when he saw that look of pained thunder.

Some of the addresses had proved genuine and accommodating to a change in the 'management': the boys had upped their income considerably. But it was just more of the same to Carl, and not an expansion he particularly welcomed. Carl believed the air was dirtier in postal districts which were prefaced with the letter E.

Carl beat his hand on the guard rail of the flyover. 'He said he had a bloody empire. There has to be more than this. There has to be something bigger.'

'He was a sick old man,' said Marty. 'That's what yer told me. Well, p'raps things had fallen apart completely.'

Carl shook his head. 'I wanna go back to his place.'

As they parked the car and walked up to the now boarded-up house in Bethnal Green, Marty was reminded of the Bates Motel in *Psycho*. 'This place gives me the shits,' he said quietly.

'There ain't no one there,' Carl replied as they picked their way through the piles of garbage and abandoned furniture which littered the garden. They walked round to the rear of the house and looked for a point of entry. Carl tugged at one of the planks which masked the kitchen window and was surprised when it fell easily away from the frame. Inside the room, a tribe of mice scattered in all directions. Carl shielded his eyes and smashed the glass with the plank. He reached inside gingerly and lifted the latch.

Marty gazed round the echoing, dark hall. 'Who the hell could live in this dump?'

'An old prat like Chalker. I wonder where the cellar is?'

After a short search, they discovered the creaking door which led down a flight of rotting steps to a dank, skeletal shell beneath the house. The cellar was packed with old newspapers and boxes of 'lines' which Chalker had not been able to 'shift'. Marty discovered a carton containing a hundred sets of Clackers. He could not resist playing with them, smacked himself painfully in the face and remembered why his mother would not let him have any. Carl prised open a grime-encrusted wardrobe and jumped back sharply when a half-inflated rubber 'sex doll' floated noiselessly to the floor. 'Needs a good blow, don't she?' said Marty, smiling.

The two boys' laughter was cut short by a small explosion and the accompanying sound of breaking glass from the hall upstairs. They exchanged an anxious look. 'Shall we check?' Carl suggested quietly.

When they edged round the door at the top of the steps they saw a meagre, waspish little man in the centre of the mosaic floor. He wore a shirt and tie beneath a 1960s tight-fitting black suit which emphasized the angularity of his short frame. At his feet was a pool of shattered, opalescent glass, and the pronged brass fitting of a light bulb.

'Now who are you?' asked Carl curiously. The man jumped back and clutched his hand nervously to his chest. The boys saw his face properly for the first time. A pair of small, round, sunken eyes occupied very little space between his cropped black hair and lantern jaw. 'Who are yer?' Carl repeated as the boys emerged into the hall.

61

'Nobody. I'm nobody.' It was a soft, lilting Kerry accent. Marty had judged him to be forty, but his voice placed him closer to twenty-five.

'And what are yer doing here, Mr Nobody?' said Carl.

'The bulb's gone in my kitchen. I came for a light bulb.'

'A thief!' exclaimed Carl.

'A poor man,' the stranger corrected. 'Why add to my poverty with unnecessary expense. The old man's dead. Nobody else wants his bulbs.'

Marty stared closely at that twisting mask of a face. 'How d'yer know he's dead?'

'Why, I worked for him.'

Carl's interest leaped. 'Wos yer name?'

'Patrick Connor.'

'Well, Paddy – '

'I dislike being called Paddy, Pat, Mick, or Irish.' Carl was surprised at the defiance of such a flimsy figure. 'You can call me Con.'

'Well, Con, I think you might be what we was looking for.'

They moved into the office and Con began to outline the details of his association with Chalker and how his father had worked for the old man before him. He spent a good ten minutes explaining how he himself was an educated human being, employed below his potential; how his mother had regretted the liaison with the criminal fraternity and had hoped for a career in politics or medicine for her son. However much he wandered, he always returned to his loathing for Chalker's vulgarity.

'I wrote letters for him,' Con wittered on. 'You could say I was his secretary. Not a very demanding post. Bobby Chalker preferred the shouted word to the written word. He preferred his fists to both. Towards the end he couldn't even sign his own name properly. I had to do that for him. Sick old fool.'

62

'You talk a lot to strangers,' Carl commented accurately.

'Strangers? Well, perhaps. But I think I know you. You killed him.'

'He had a heart attack,' said Marty quickly.

'Whatever. He's gone and I'm unemployed. Chance has thrown us together and I thank it. Our liaison could be of mutual benefit. I noticed you cleaned out the files.'

'Bits and pieces of protection. Peanuts,' Carl said dismissively.

Con sighed and nodded sagely. 'Half of them out of date. I know.'

Carl stared hard at the Irishman. 'Where's the rest? The old fool said he had an empire.'

Con shook his head slightly and adopted a disapproving expression. 'Chalker embodied all the clichés you would expect of someone who knew the Krays. Lust, degradation, corruption, squalor, and a rather unimaginative little line in torture and extortion. Surprising how a congenital idiot could inherit so much . . . But the twenty years since dear old Ronnie and Reggie went down . . . well, they come as no surprise: spend, spend, spend. He was not the kind of fellow who invested for his old age.'

Carl looked askance. He said: 'You trying to tell me I've dirtied me hands for nothing?'

'No, I'm not. Not quite. He trusted very few people, you see. There's no record of most of his wealth. Follow the leprechaun.'

'Where's Jimmy?' said Marty, interrupting the exit.

'Oh yes,' Con replied, 'you'll be wanting to know that. A starkly beautiful place called Mojacar. It hangs off the side of a mountain and looks rather like Jerusalem.'

In the next two days, Con took them on a tour of Chalker's unrecorded world. Lock-ups and stores, back rooms and warehouses. All the locations were in the heart

63

of the East End, and they each told a similar story: they were all empty.

'That was very impressive, Con,' Carl quipped sarcastically as the Irishman took the relevant key from a large ring and locked the rear door of an expansive warehouse in the Isle of Dogs.

'Least it's a nice piece of property,' Marty said, looking on the only bright side.

Con said quickly: 'You won't get it. Bobby died intestate. It goes to the Crown. Like the bookies and the clubs, and most of the lock-ups.'

'Even the Queen owns a bit of Bobby now,' said Carl. 'Wonder if she knows.'

'It was stripped four days ago. Right after Chalker's death. Pity, 'cos there was some good stuff here – '

Carl decided he had heard enough of this blarny. He grabbed Con by the shirt and pushed him roughly against the wall. He said: 'What did yer do with it?'

Con spluttered, feeling his starched collar biting into his neck. 'I don't know . . . what you – '

'Now s'pose yer cut out the bull,' Carl warned, 'you posy little liar. I'm not interested in all this crap 'bout yer being an educated man and Dublin University. You come looking for me, waving some tatty little treasure map in yer paw. . . .' Carl wrenched Con forward and then pushed him back hard to the wall. Con's head cracked against the brick and he let out a yelp of pain.

'There's been some misunderstanding, really – '

Marty turned away, weary of his friend's escalating violence. 'Leave it, Carl, it's not worth it.'

'All Chalker's lock-ups,' Carl said, 'thousands of quids' worth of gear. How'd I know yer din't clean 'em out? Like yer did the bank account. See, I got his chequebook, mate.'

'There was only a few pounds in that,' Con exclaimed.

'He owed me that. I didn't have time to take the rest. Honestly, I didn't know they were all empty. I didn't.'

Carl released his grip on the shirt and Con sank back, rubbing at his injured throat. 'Where's it all gone, Mr Nobody?' Carl demanded.

'Stalky must have been here,' Con said, coughing away his discomfort.

'Now who the hell is Stalky?' asked Marty.

Con's eyes seemed to sink even deeper, and a look of glazed terror came into them. 'Stalky's an animal. He was a henchman who freelanced for Bobby. All the people who've died. They all knew about these places I've shown you. Stalky massacred them to get the information. I'm the only one left. I didn't know they were all empty. I thought he'd kill me for a fiver to stop me interfering. I thought you were my best bet.'

Carl looked deep into those dark, fearful eyes. 'Is this the last?'

'No. There's one more. If it's full he might still be after me. He didn't know where they all were, you see. The others told him.'

Carl said: 'Is Stalky trying to take over Chalker's patch?'

Con let out a short, disgruntled laugh. He was beginning to regain his composure now. 'There's a hundred little vultures in the East End, all picking on Chalker's carcass. Stalky's just the biggest grabber. People know about you, Carl. They think you might be different. They're waiting. Get rid of Stalky and you'll get respect.'

The glint of ambition began to burn again in Carl's eyes. Con recognized his hunger for power and fed it further. 'I can help you, Carl. I know Stalky. I can lead you to him. I can give you a lot more than hi-fis and soft porn.'

Con did lead them to the last location. It was a narrow,

three-storey building off Leyton High Road. The bank of rusting industrial sewing-machines which lined the entrance lobby gave evidence of its former use as a manufacturing sweatshop.

Carl looked sceptically at Marty on the ascent to the second floor. Con hurried ahead, scampering in and out of rooms like a bloodhound on the scent of the fox. A look of warm satisfaction finally crept over his face when he pushed open the last door to the back room on the top floor.

About a third of the way down the high-ceilinged room, a make-shift partition had been constructed by leaning a sheet of plasterboard against a woodworm-infested upright piano. Jutting out from behind that partition was the edge of a stack of a hundred large cardboard boxes. They all bore the marks 'Zanussi', 'Philips' and 'Sony'. They were all unopened.

Con lifted the lid of the piano and gently depressed one of the keys. He noticed how the central two octaves had been wiped clean of the dust which had invaded the instrument. He said: 'Stalky plays the piano in pubs.' Then, with a note of quiet triumph and relief, he added: 'He's been here.'

'I know,' said Carl. He had found the previous day's paper on the grimy floor.

Con shot a glance to Carl. 'He hasn't finished. He'll be back.'

Above them, the discoloured, yellow fluorescent tube flickered, coming to the end of its life.

Nicky beat a stick on the slatted wooden fence which ran along the central footpath of Highbury Fields.

'Stop it,' ordered Linda. But he took no notice. Linda took Karen's hand and began to walk away from her son.

'No,' he called aggressively when he saw them abandoning him. He ran after them.

'Well do as yer told,' Linda chided him. Instead he turned his attention to attacking each bench and rubbish-bin they passed.

Behind them, children and parents were continuing to flow out of the small nursery school on the edge of the park. A man of about thirty, with long wavy hair the colour of hot sand, eased gently through the crowd by the school gates and began to jog after Linda and the children. His jeans had been ruined years ago by some over-enthusiastic finger-painting. His sweatshirt bore the more recent scars of misdirected potato prints. A sheet of daubed-on paper flapped in his hand.

He arrived breathless at Linda's side. 'Forgot your picture, Karen,' he said. The little girl did not smile up in appreciation as he had anticipated. She did not want the picture: Nicky had wiped his hand across it and ruined it for her. 'OK, I'll keep it. I like it,' the man said. Ten years in the south had shortened his Mancunian vowels.

'Chris's brought it for yer. Take it, Karen,' said Linda. Karen reluctantly obeyed. Linda and Chris exchanged a smile.

Nicky had found the clatter of the stick on the metal rubbish-bin an irresistible attraction. 'Don't do that, Nicky,' Chris urged. 'Look. I bet you can't run to that tree over there before I count to twenty.'

'I can,' shrieked Nicky, and hurtled off.

'He can only count to ten,' said Chris, as they walked on.

Linda looked anxiously after her son. 'I wish he'd calm down a bit.'

'He's attention seeking.' Chris's soft, engaging face broke into a grin. 'It's common in boys. Of all ages,

Linda.' The flirting had begun again. 'We crave affection,' Chris added.

'Stop it,' she said, but there was no harshness in her voice. She had actually begun to enjoy this daily routine of offers and rejections. Especially recently. Carl's intensity may have remained constant, but any light-heartedness seemed to have dissipated since Mark's death. The little game of make-believe with Chris took her out of herself.

'Stop what?' he queried, with a look of abashed innocence.

'You know what. I'm married.'

'Is that the best place to find affection?'

'And you live with someone, Chris.'

He lowered his voice and said dramatically: 'Someone I don't love any more, my dear. Someone who never really knew how to love me.'

Nicky interrupted the conversational ping-pong. 'See! I did it! I did!'

'Yes, you did,' Chris conceded generously. 'And I thought you couldn't.' Nicky ran off again to the edge of the park. 'Mind that road.'

They walked on for another twenty yards and stopped when they came to the pavement. Chris looked across to his flat in a purpose-built, 1950s block and said: 'You know I'm off Tuesdays. When are you coming up for that coffee?'

'Six months ago it was dinner,' Linda replied. 'Least it's getting easier.'

He made a hound-dog face. 'I think it's getting very, very, very much harder . . . You could even bring the kids, Mrs Galton.'

'Maybe sometime.'

'Maybe never. Hey? Didn't your husband say it was a

funny job for a man? Didn't he tell you to find out more about me?'

'I don't think that was what he had in mind, Chris.'

'Oh well. Bye-bye, married lady.' He watched her lead the children off down the road that circled the park.

'Got a chance with that piece,' he said under his breath, and then castigated himself for being sexist.

When Linda walked into the living-room at Northchurch Road she was met by the gleam from a hundred candles which Carl had placed round the room. The instruments on the wall were illuminated and abstracted by the flickering light; their shadows danced blackly.

Carl sat in the leather armchair by the stereo. He was surrounded by vases of pure white tulips, which gently inclined their heads. Nina Simone sang 'My Baby Just Cares For Me' and Carl mouthed the words as his eyes met Linda's.

'How was yer dad?' he asked softly.

Her gaze wandered slowly through the eddying light of the room. 'The same. You don't even know if he sees yer any more.'

'Have I neglected yer?' She shook her head uncertainly. He held out a hand to her. She took it, knelt before him and turned her face up to his. 'So beautiful,' he whispered.

She turned away. 'Stop it. I ain't got no make-up on.'

'You are.'

'I wanna talk to you,' she said.

'What about?'

The confusion that had been festering and growing within her finally re-surfaced. 'I'm sure if we try really hard we can think of something.'

'You need anything?'

'Yes . . . I want to move.'

69

He wondered why she had such a troubled expression. 'We can move now. We'll start looking tomorrow. There's some beautiful property up round Highgate. . .'

'I wanna go further than that, Carl.'

'We can go a bit further.'

'A lot further.' She bit at her lip and rocked with agitation. 'I wanna go to the country. I want our kids to grow up there and I want us to be in the country and together.'

'Don't be stupid.' He tried to laugh the suggestion off.

'I'm not.' A gnawing desperation was seeping into her voice. 'You've always been everything to me, and I understand 'bout Mark, but now it's like I've only got half of yer – '

'You wanna be married to a nobody?' he snapped. 'You wanna say "Have a nice day at the office, dear" every day? You want our kids to grow up like I did? You want them to see their old man like I did? Drunk out of his brain and crying on the floor 'cos he's so bloody bored? That what yer want?'

'I don't wanna open the paper every day and see people cut up and murdered and wonder if it's you!' They stared hard and long at each other. 'Yer wife don't want that!'

She flung out an arm and wiped one of the vases from the table beside Carl. She screamed: 'And take that bloody record off!' He swung round, grabbed at the arm of the record player, snatched off the disc and snapped it in two. Her response was to overturn the coffee-table, spilling twenty candles and their spattering of hot wax onto the carpet.

Carl rose from his chair and before either of them realized exactly what they were doing, they began to smash every breakable item in the room. They watched each act of destruction and then turned, flushed and hungry for another. They tore the room to pieces. The

70

senseless, violent destruction rushed to their brains like heroin.

They only stopped when Linda hauled their wedding picture from the wall. She was about to mangle the frame on the upturned leg of the coffee-table when she saw Carl's face. They stood frozen for a moment. Their chests were heaving, their breath was short and desperate. The smoke from the extinguished candles floated round them and stained the air.

She said quietly: 'I don't wanna lose yer,' and the picture slipped from her hand.

'Yer never will,' he replied.

They moved together in the wreckage. She clung to him like an infant clings to the comfort of a tiny, flickering night-light in the dark.

'Let's get Kathy over to look after the kids,' she whispered. 'Let's go out. Let's go up West.'

'Let me make a phone call and we'll go.'

'Let's be in love, Carl.'

Kathy came. He made the phone call. And they went up West. In love.

At eleven o'clock, Linda's fantasy evaporated as she sat opposite Carl in Wren's restaurant. She looked up from her champagne, saw Jo Jo's face and knew why Carl had made the phone call earlier. She wondered how many other people knew where they were. Carl left her with no explanation and no apology. He paid the doorman to make sure she got a cab home, and left the restaurant.

Marty looked at his watch when he parked his van opposite the three-storey building off Leyton High Road. One o'clock. The phone call had come at eleven thirty: Jo Jo's voice had been tense and excited. Marty had grappled with his rollercoaster conscience for almost an hour and a quarter before grabbing his coat and going in search of the other boys.

He looked round. The side-street was deserted. No light shone from inside Chalker's building. Marty was about to leave, convinced that whatever Carl had planned must have already happened, when another thought struck him: what if it had gone wrong? How many of his friends might be lying in that building, injured, or even . . .

Marty reached forward and took a torch from the glove compartment. He got down from the van and crossed slowly to the building. His hand pushed at the door, expecting to find it locked. It swung open at his touch. He stepped cautiously into the entrance hall. He placed his feet down as if he were placing cut glass on steel, terrified that the least little jerking movement would send an echoing clamour through the building.

After half a dozen steps he stopped and listened in the dark. The blackness swirled round him but he did not dare turn on the torch. What was that? He strained to hear. He held his breath to try to stop the interference of his pounding heartbeat. It came again. A slight moaning, and a scraping sound from above. 'Carl?' he called softly. The scraping sound again.

Marty began to climb the stairs. Each creaking step vibrated fear through his body. A thousand nightmares rattled in his head as he ascended to the second floor. He stood at the head of the corridor. He could make out only shadows in the dim light which filtered in from the street, but the moaning continued. Closer now. And a dragging sound. Another sound, as Marty approached the door at the end of the corridor, almost like choking. 'Carl?' he whispered as he stood in the doorway of the store-room. It touched him! His trembling hand flicked on the torch and his eyes shot down. It was clawing at his leg! Oh God!

A hand, with mangled, flapping fingers. A hand the colour of blood! He kicked it away and the burning rose in his throat. His hands beat frantically along the wall, groping for the door. He struck the panel of light switches and the faulty fluorescent tube shuddered to half-life and began to pulse like a strobe.

Marty stood frozen against the wall as he watched the long-limbed creature crawl towards him. Its face was a crimson, glistening mask. The gashed mouth spewed a fountain of blood as it heaved itself up and staggered closer. Its arms danced like a puppet's for a moment and then it reeled sideways and crashed into the piano. The mutilated hand left a wet, red trail as it slid along the ivory keyboard. The deafening scale cut into Marty's numbed brain. He raced for the door as the vomit convulsed into his mouth.

Five

Marty woke to find his room filled with hard, morning sunlight. The dull throb started again between his eyes. He sank his head down in the pillow, to hide from the day. He was aware of a hundred tiny sounds. It was as if he were inside an airless, white box, with walls made of fine membrane. He could hear his fingers scratching to escape.

Bill appeared in the doorway. 'You making tea?' he asked.

Marty did not stir from the pillow. 'I s'pect so,' he murmured.

'Well, Carl's here, and he wants some too.'

Marty expected the storm to break. Where were the thunderous clouds scudding across the sun? Why couldn't he just walk out of that room and say 'no' to Carl? Just once in his life?

They took their tea quietly. Carl occupied himself in conversation with Bill. Marty's silence was accepted as the consequence of semi-consciousness.

Marty allowed Carl to help him dress. He let himself be escorted to Carl's car. They drove north. At Hendon, Carl turned onto the M1. Nothing was said about the creature in the dark. Marty stared at Carl's invigorated face. The boy who had always told him everything had said nothing about that.

'Where are we going, Carl?'

'Doncaster.'

'For chrissake why?' said Marty.

'Mario goes up there all the time. He says the birds are fabulous. And easy. They're all out of work. You come up from London with a few bob and they think yer a film star.'

'Or a villain.'

'What's the difference, Marty? Besides, you need a day out.'

Was that it? Was that his response to the nightmare Marty had suffered? No more than 'You need a day out'? Marty gazed out at the faceless Hertfordshire landscape. He said: 'You've forgotten 'bout Jimmy Chalker, ain't yer Carl?'

Carl did not avert his eyes from the road. 'I'll never forget Jimmy Chalker. Con's flying out to Mojacar in a couple of days. He was almost on his knees. Begging me to let him do it. You don't trust him?' Marty shrugged. 'Freddie went over his place,' Carl continued. 'Filthy little bedsit 'bout half a mile from Chalker's. Only thing he found was a bank statement what said he had thirty-four quid to his name. I don't trust him either, but if he takes out Jimmy I might.'

'Sure, Carl.'

'Anyway,' Carl added, 'I went on holiday to Spain last year.'

Marty's thoughts began to race again. Was that the only consideration in whether or not Carl murdered someone? That he was bored with the scenery?

Carl began to fumble through the plastic rack of cassettes. He said: 'Someone called Tony Slater called me real early this morning. He invited me to the Derby. Said he knew Bobby Chalker. You reckon I oughta go?'

*
75

Carl had already taken the children to school when Linda got up that morning. She was woken by a bell.

Linda opened the front door of the flat, still in her nightdress. Jo Jo's face beamed up at her.

'Jo Jo.'

'All right, Linda?' He sank his hands deep in his pockets and danced from one foot to the other.

She hesitated for a moment and then made the decision to expose the boy to her private torment. 'Come in . . . yes, come in.'

He followed her into the living-room. The door stuck half open, jammed by shards of broken china. She went and sat on the wax-spattered sofa and ignored his expression of disbelief. 'Sit down, Jo Jo.' He nodded uncertainly and picked his way through the debris. She took a packet of ten Silk Cut and a disposable lighter from a small pocket of her nightdress. She lit one of the cigarettes and sucked the smoke deep into her lungs.

'Din't know yer smoked,' said Jo Jo, grappling to overcome the awkwardness of the situation.

'Carl don't like me to,' was her explanation. She wanted to add that Carl wasn't there, so she would do exactly as she bloody liked for once. But she settled for the satisfaction of witnessing Jo Jo's discomfort.

'Just thought I'd pop round and see if yer was OK, like,' he stumbled.

'That's very thoughtful of yer, Jo Jo.' She wondered for a moment whether sarcasm might be wasted on him.

'Actually . . . errr . . . Carl phoned and asked me to check on yer.'

'Isn't that just like him? Well, as yer can see, I'm fine. Just fine.'

His nodding and fidgeting was increasing all the time. He chewed furiously at a wad of tasteless gum. 'Good, good.'

'How's yer job, Jo Jo? Qualified down that printers yet?'

'Naaa. I chucked it.'

'That's a pity. What yer doing now?'

'Oh I'm . . .' He stopped himself. 'This and that.'

'Isn't that fascinating.' She was beginning to understand a lot more about 'this and that'. 'Oh, excuse me, Jo Jo, can I get yer a coffee?'

He jumped up off the sofa. 'No, ta. No. I just sorta come to see if yer was all right, that's all. Can't stop, like.'

'I'm fine.'

'Better be going then.'

'Yes you had. And Jo Jo? Give my love to Carl. If yer see him before me.'

She drew hard on the cigarette and kicked at the shattered fragments of a vase when she heard the front door close. She sat for a moment and then stubbed the cigarette out on the carpet.

She went into the bedroom and dressed quickly. She turned to check her appearance in the dressing-table mirror. She had not wiped away the message Carl had scrawled in her favourite lipstick. It criss-crossed her blank reflection: 'Lover. Gone up north on business. Miss you. The place is a mess.'

She left the house and hailed a cab on Essex Road. The taxi motored up to the junction with the Balls Pond Road and stopped at the traffic lights, in the slip lane to turn left, next to the Aladura church. Linda glanced over her shoulder and then leaned forward to the driver. She said: 'Can yer just hang on a minute here. I'll leave my bag on the seat.' The driver gave a reluctant nod and Linda got out of the cab.

She walked back along the file of waiting traffic until she reached Freddie's regency-red Daimler Sovereign. Jo Jo was at the wheel. He stared out through the wind-

77

screen, pretending not to notice her. She slapped her hand on the bonnet. He gave a little jump and conjured up an expression of pleasant surprise. She motioned him to roll down the window and he obeyed.

'Hallo, Linda. All right?'

'I'm still fine, Jo Jo.' She reached into the car and switched off the engine. He watched, dumb and bewildered, as she extracted the keys from the ignition. She jangled them in front of Jo Jo's face and then stepped back and hurled them into the overgrown churchyard. 'Next time, borrow somebody else's car. Humphrey bloody Bogart!'

She walked calmly back and got in the cab. The lights changed to green and the line of cars behind Jo Jo began to hoot their horns.

Linda pressed the bell of Chris's flat for the third time. There was still no response. She determined that the fourth attempt would be the last. Her finger snatched back from the button when she heard his voice. 'I'm not in.'

Linda turned and saw Chris standing on the edge of the road holding a cardboard box which was overflowing with shopping. His expression was one of uncontrolled and unashamed pleasure. 'Nice day,' he said.

They spent the rest of the morning innocently chatting and enjoying the weather. She mentioned that she and Carl were looking for a new house, and the afternoon disappeared in a flurry of estate agents' details and disappointing viewings. In the hour she had left, before the children had to be collected and washed and watered, they decided to try one last address.

Linda took an instant dislike to the large semi in Crouch End. It sat on the corner of a side-road off Cranley Gardens. The square-walled garden was mostly laid to lawn. The narrow flower-beds held a desultory selection of plants: only an hypericum and a bay tree appeared likely to see out another winter.

Inside, the house was expansive and bare. Echoing. Edwardian with a gloss of varnished boards and Habitat. French windows filled almost all of one wall in the living-room. Inset in the centre of the windows were two stained-glass fleurs-de-lys. Linda thought they made the room look like a mausoleum.

They sat on the stairs in the hall and denounced other people's tastes. They dismissed the house in five short minutes. As had happened in all the others, the house was just the backdrop to their conversation: it rarely dominated it. Chris tried to keep to abstract subjects and a mood of flirtation, but Linda always found herself returning to the same theme.

'We grew up on the same estate,' she said. 'Everyone knew Carl and Marty. Everyone said, some day I'd marry one of 'em. Like a film. It was just what people expected. But they never talked to me . . . Until one night in Cheers. Well, it weren't Cheers then. Just a café where people all went, and no one minded if yer took beer in a carrier. They were all there that night. And Carl just walked over and stood there in front of me. Din't say a word. Just smiled. Marty went to the toilet. I think it was 'cos he was so embarrassed.' She laughed quietly and then continued. 'I was sixteen. And it was like I'd been waiting for that moment all me life. He was only eighteen, but he already acted like he owned that place. I could feel everybody watching. And then he bent down next to me and he said really quietly . . . really quiet . . . he said, "I love you. Do you know how to love me?" And then he just walked away. And Marty come back from the toilet. And they went somewhere. And we got married.'

Chris was beginning to feel like a marriage guidance

counsellor. This outpouring was not what he had planned for the day when he had smiled at her on the steps of the flat. 'I wish all the things I expected had happened that easily.'

'It weren't easy, Chris. It's never been that. Yer see, he's always been the most exciting thing in my life.'

Chris sank back into the self-pity that underpinned even his cheeriest moods. 'I don't think I've ever been that to anyone,' he said.

'You've done lots of interesting things. You've told me,' she responded.

'And I've got the badges to prove it, yes. But never anything important. It's like I always just missed everything. A bit late. I arrive at parties when the booze has run out and the political argument has just begun. And that's not much comfort in the circles I mix in, 'cos I wasn't in Brixton for the riots, I didn't go on a miners' picket, and I certainly wasn't in Paris in '68.'

Linda started to walk upstairs to check the bedrooms. 'Why?' she said. 'What happened there?'

Marty was fighting through the haze of booze. He was glad to be out in the cool night air, and he was glad to have the teenage girl on his arm, for support.

She led him down the street of terraced boxes on the outskirts of Doncaster. He applied all his concentration to placing one foot functionally and solidly in front of the other.

They stopped at a door like all the others in the street: the flaking scarlet paint was scarred with racist graffiti. Marty leaned back against the wall as she fiddled for a key in her glittery sequined bag. Marty tried to focus on her petite features. She was an attractive girl; like all the girls Carl tried to pair him off with.

'You going to come in, Marty?'

'You live alone?'

'With me mum and dad.' He nodded, thinking that would be reason enough to excuse himself. But she was taken with the boy from London, whose eyes flickered from devilment to sadness. 'They don't mind,' she insisted. 'I have blokes back.'

He searched his scrambled head for other escapes. 'I've drunk too much, Carmen.'

'Oh come on,' she cajoled.

'No. I'll see yer.'

'You're a funny one. Coming up again?'

'Maybe.'

'Look us up. Colette and me are always down Cinderella's on a Tuesday. You meet nice-looking fellas up from London sometimes.' He smiled at the compliment and she moved her face close to his. 'Oh come on,' she whispered. 'I want to kiss you.'

He started to back away. 'I need some fresh air,' he said weakly.

'Don't go too far, or your friend'll never find you.'

'He always finds me. I'll have a walk round that park we come past.'

'OK. Pity though . . . Mind your back.'

His eyes flashed back at her. 'What?'

'In that park. Mind your back.'

'Oh yeah. Yeah . . . You're a nice girl, Carmen. I'll see yer.'

He traced a serpentine path down the street. She watched for a moment and then entered the house. The light came on in an upstairs bedroom and the sounds of an argument filtered out into the night.

On the opposite side of the city, Colette stared out at the lights of the Doncaster bypass.

'What a shit-hole,' she sighed and lit another cigarette.

Carl stretched out his naked body on the wide, 1930s

81

bed and gazed at the grey cloud which spiralled round the girl's chaotic hair. 'You shouldn't smoke so much,' he said.

'I like smoking,' she replied enthusiastically. 'I have to get up really early to cram forty into a day.' She gave a short, high-pitched giggle and then her face returned to its blank despair. 'Besides. What else is there for me to bloody do up here?'

'Me.'

She adjusted the shiny, pink nylon nightdress to make it sit straight across her full breasts. 'Well,' she said, 'You're something else. And I've already done you.'

Carl looked round the room. It depressed him. In his mind, high-rise council equalled hell and this was a particularly bad example. The furniture was all heavy and second-hand. The piece of tatty, antique lace could not disguise the Tesco's lamp beneath it. A few items struggled to brighten the atmosphere – a heart-shaped candle, a stuffed panda, a sprinkling of pop posters – but everywhere there was a feeling of resignation and sadness. Frustrated romance had committed suicide in that room.

Carl glanced at his watch and decided it was time to leave this hole in the sky. Colette looked round as she heard the bed-springs creak. 'What do you do in London?'

'This and that.' He crossed to a chair by the grim Victorian wardrobe and began to put on his neatly folded clothes.

'I want to go to London. Or Liverpool. I'm going to be an actress. There's a lot of actresses in Liverpool, I've heard. Must be 'cos of that film about Brezhnev. You don't think I'm serious. But I am. Blokes never think I'm serious.'

'Wonder why.'

'I'm at drama school, you know.'

82

'No yer not,' he said coldly as he struggled with his shirt buttons.

'Well, no, I'm not. But I do acting lessons. There's this daytime course for the unemployed. We do one play a month. Not with costumes, 'cos we haven't got any money, and not all of it, just the good bits, 'cos we wouldn't be able to learn it all and I don't suppose people would want to watch it if it was too long and boring. Last month we did *Macbeth*.' She was becoming more voluble by the second. She saw him leaving and did not want to be left alone in that miserable place. 'You read it?'

He straightened his collar. 'I know the story,' he said, uninterested.

'After *Macbeth* I started reading some of the others.' She plucked a library copy of the complete works of Shakespeare from the windowsill. 'There's some good stuff in here. *Hamlet*'s really good. Well, the beginning's good. There was a bit in the middle I didn't understand so I gave up on the rest. There's this great bit at the start, well, just before the start actually. Well, you know. This bloke kills his brother by tipping poison in his ear while he's having a kip. Isn't that amazing?'

'No.'

'I think it is. Funny though, 'cos Hamlet's really famous, and millions of people must of seen the film, and you'd think it would put ideas into people's heads. You'd think there'd be more people tipping poison in each other's ears.'

She waited for some response. He did not avert his attention from his own reflection. 'You do prattle on, when yer get going,' he said.

She stepped across the cramped little room and flopped on the bed. She said: 'You're not like most fellas up here, you know.'

'This is no cheap meat, honey,' he said as he slipped on his jacket.

'You don't talk about yourself all the time.'

'I think about meself instead, darlin'.'

'Do you?' she breathed. 'I do too! I try to make myself a better person. Tell me to shut up if you want to, but every Sunday I take a piece of paper and I make a list of three things I like about myself and three things I don't like. And then in the week I give myself one point for every time I do one of the good things and I take off a point every time I do one of the bad things and if I've got ten points on a Saturday then I treat myself to a Mars bar.'

'You'll never get fat,' he laughed.

'You can help me make the list for next week!'

Sensing some amusement was to be had at the girl's expense, Carl postponed his exit and sat on the edge of the bed.

'Right,' Colette announced. 'Tell me three things you like about me.'

'You've got nice legs.'

'Give over.'

'You've got a great arse.'

'No, that's no good.'

'And you've got really beautiful tits.'

She threw herself back on the pillows, exasperated by him. 'Now how can I write any of those things down?'

'Don't yer wanna know any of the bad things?' he said.

She grinned. 'Go on then. I'm game for a laugh.'

His face smoothed into a hard, cold stare. 'I don't like girls who wear skirts up round their crotches and look like slags. I don't like girls who use four-letter words and ask me to screw them. And I don't like girls who talk too much.'

'You're cruel,' she said quietly.

84

'Maybe. You'd like me to come back though, wouldn't yer?'

Her head bowed and the grim sadness filled her eyes again. 'I'd like you to take me away from this shit-hole. I'd like you to take me to London. But you won't do that.'

'No.'

'I hate this bloody place.'

He brushed his fingers lightly against her cheek. He said: 'You're an actress, darlin'. Pretend.'

'Will you come back?'

'Maybe.' He leaned forward and kissed her and then got up from the bed.

'Just stay five more minutes,' she pleaded.

'Darlin', I've got a wife and kids to get back to. Din't I tell yer?'

Carl saw the back of Marty's hunched figure on a bench in the park. He trotted over noiselessly to his friend. When he was about ten yards away he called out: 'Hallo, sailor!'

Marty jumped up in surprise. 'Jesus Christ, Carl!' he snapped. 'Come on, let's go. This place is full of queers.' He started to stride off down the dimly lit path, but Carl grabbed at his crutch.

'Go on then, Mart, gis a feel! You are a big boy, yum yum!'

Marty wriggled angrily out of his grasp. 'Get off, Carl!'

They walked on a few paces before Carl casually said: 'You give her one?'

''Course I did.'

'Good. I love yer, man,' said Carl and draped his arm across Marty's shoulder.

'Where's the car?'

'I gave it to a girlie,' said Carl. 'It was a pile of crap. I din't want it no more.'

'You are mental, man!' said Marty, incredulous.

Carl smiled and shrugged, unconcerned. 'Boys will be boys. Or girls. Or nothing. I dunno.'

They caught the night train back to London. Marty drifted back into restless sleep. Carl stayed awake all night. He was thinking about Hamlet; about poison in people's ears. He was trying to remember something Bobby Chalker said on the night he died.

Six

On the first Wednesday in June, Epsom Downs swarmed with people. At midday, cars streamed along the approach road from Ewell and Banstead to fill the already densely ranked parking areas. The expected crop of Rolls-Royces, Daimlers and BMWs were punctuated by a liberal sprinkling of Escorts, Metros and Capris. The affluent bourgeoisie were wandering among costumed status.

Linda and Carl argued hotly as they walked towards the grandstand, rising stark and grey against the bright sky.

'Don't think I won't walk home, 'cos I bloody will,' she warned.

'How much more of this shit do yer expect me to put up with, Linda?'

'As much as I do!' she screamed.

A car park picnic party looked up from their champagne and smoked salmon. Carl lowered his voice. 'Yer embarrassing me,' he hissed.

'So where were yer that night, Carl? Where are yer all the bloody time?'

'Screwing old slags left right and centre!' he rapped back.

'I'm sure.'

'And if yer believe that yer really are thick as shit.'

87

'You call me stupid a lot, don't yer, Carl?' The argument had festered and inflamed for a week. Now that the wound was open she was determined to cleanse it.

'Whad'yer expect?' he demanded, bad-tempered now.

'Then why don't yer divorce me?'

He stopped and looked patronizing and superior. He said: 'Because, my dear, it would make you unhappy. 'Cos yer'd never get my kids and yer'd never have another man. You can leave me right now, darlin'. Go on. Totter off across the fields in yer pretty little high heels. But you just remember, I din't marry yer to make a fool of me.'

'Why did yer marry me then?' He cursed his decision to bring her and marched off towards the course.

Slater's box was set high up in the grandstand and commanded a prime view of the seething mass of humanity which teemed across the Downs. Linda leaned over the edge of the box and gazed mournfully down at the throng. She envied the smiling, carefree faces bathing in the warm sun.

A handsome, willowy-figured woman of forty came and stood next to Linda. She shook the mane of red hair from her smooth, bare shoulders and smiled. She took a compact from her patent-leather clutch bag and dabbed at her fine nose. In a deep, confidential voice she said: 'I can't think of anywhere I'd less like to have lunch. Do you like horses?'

Linda shrugged. 'They're all right.'

'George took me to France once. I believe we ate part of one. We weren't properly introduced, were we? Boys are like that.' She stretched out a manicured hand. 'I'm Pat Klein.'

'I'm Linda. Carl's wife.'

'I wasn't sure if you were married. Used to be so many young people didn't. Become quite the done thing again.

Oh and by the way,' she nodded over to the men, 'you'll soon stop trying to overhear. You only get half the story and it makes it twice as bad.'

Dinner was over. Slater, Klein and Carl still sat round the white-clothed table and swilled brandy.

Carl was saying: 'The only other time I come here I was over in the middle with the gypos and the funfair.'

'It's a rags to riches story,' gurgled Klein. Too much champagne had left him biliously uncomfortable.

'I wasn't in rags, Mr Klein.' Carl shot him a steely look and Klein wondered yet again why they were entertaining the little bastard.

Slater knew. The bustling little detective from CID had been forcefully persuasive. Bobby Chalker was dead and so were five of his colleagues, taking with them the flimsy façade of order in the already dissipated East End underworld. Of course Klein was the obvious person to approach, Slater knew that. Good old reliable George could never completely drag himself away from the gutter he grew up in. Those regular binges on vodka and nostalgia; they were common knowledge. Slater had sat next to that little detective at enough charity dinners to understand his shorthand: he knew what 'have a word' meant. They were having that 'word' here because that was Slater's style. He refused to do business in back rooms any more.

Slater brushed a crumb from his immaculate morning suit and set an expression of calm determination on his lean, urbane face. He said: 'A lot has happened since Bobby Chalker fell down the stairs, Carl. I hope you realize your responsibilities.'

'And yer friends,' Klein interjected.

'That might be too strong a word, George,' Slater cautioned.

Carl noted the tension between the two associates with

quiet amusement, but felt the conversation had slipped into an unnecessary semaphore. He pushed aside his brandy and said: 'Mr Slater, Mr Klein. Your manners, as I heard David Niven say in a film once, are impeccable. They're not my manners, but they are impeccable. That's the right word, isn't it? In fact, they're so nice, that you've managed to talk to me for two hours and not say a thing. Let me tell yer where I stand. That way, at least two of us won't be confused.'

Slater fidgeted slightly in his chair. The boy's brashness was beginning to irritate him almost as much as it did Klein.

'I'm not a poor East End boy,' Carl continued. 'I grew up in full view of an awful lot of wealth. I din't have it, but I did learn that money means more than a flashy broom-broom. I weren't born in a gutter, Mr Klein. And I'm not gonna crawl into the one Bobby Chalker has just vacated.'

'So what do you want?' Slater said, direct and hard.

'A profit. Not some cruddy empire that only existed inside the head of a sick old fool. Just a profit. Ain't that what we're all after?'

Klein was getting angrier. He had had an affection for that 'old fool'. Carl's smug, confident face was gnawing at his already diminished composure.

Slater jumped in as he saw Klein about to speak. 'You must understand, Carl, our connection with Bobby Chalker was never more than slight. He wasn't really my uncle. He was just a . . . friend . . . of my mother. We are wholly legitimate businessmen, Carl. I appreciate that questions need to be asked, but we have an important deal going through – '

'And a bloody workforce what's up in arms!' Klein exclaimed.

'What George means, Carl, is that people often jump

to the wrong conclusions. Although we're not implicated in any way in anything Bobby did, we certainly do not want to be haunted by him. You're the man on the street: we'd like to see you exercise some . . . self-control.'

Carl chuckled to himself and said: 'That whad'yer meant, George?'

'Why ruin what yer got?' Klein answered sourly.

'Oh I won't. I'm taking what I want. Not what I can.' He reached out for the brandy glass and raised it to the two men. 'Cheers. Very nice of you and yer wife to invite me, Tony.'

Slater stared coldly. 'My wife's dead, Carl.'

'She's my wife,' Klein hissed.

'Ain't that funny?' said Carl with a grand naïvety. 'Now why did I think that? Whad'you fancy, Tony? In the first?'

The afternoon lurched on into pleasantries. The good-byes were clipped. Linda and Carl's journey home in their hired Rolls-Royce was silent.

They got back to Northchurch Road at half past seven. He made a thirty-second phone call, changed his clothes, and then drove the Roller into the East End.

Con's cramped bedsit squatted damp and overflowing with books and papers on the top of a run-down terrace in Bethnal Green. But Carl was more interested in the Polaroid in his hand than in the squalid surroundings.

Jimmy Chalker's face was swollen into a pale death mask.

Con offered Carl a passport. Another likeness of Jimmy. This time corpse-like in his pose for officialdom.

'*Y viva España*,' Carl breathed.

Con locked his bony fingers together and cracked his joints. 'Henceforth, June the second will be the anniversary of his death.'

'Did he suffer like my brother?'

'Perhaps more.' Con slithered his shrunken frame down

into a coffee-stained armchair. 'You haven't trusted me much, Carl. Oh I know you had someone go over this room. I don't blame you. But I have helped you, and there comes a time when you must know enough to stop being suspicious.'

'You have helped, yeah,' Carl conceded. 'We picked up a few bits of protection, few naff hi-fis, you got rid of Jimmy. That's a big help.'

'There'll be more,' said Con greedily. 'There will. Believe me. Word will be getting round about Stalky and soon people will realize that you are the man in control. The man to come to.'

'I hope it don't take too long, Con. I'm a very impatient man.'

'Trust me. They'll come. Bowing and scraping. I'm useful. Use me. I've rotted long enough in Chalker's stagnant pool. You're a new age. I want to be around you. You're exciting, Carl.'

Carl cast a sceptical smile towards those small, watery eyes. He said: 'There's just one more thing I been thinking 'bout . . . Before Chalker took his tumble. I thought he said "Motty? Where are yer gone." But now, I reckon he said "Where are yer, Con?" You were in the house that night, weren't yer?'

'Heavens no. There was carnage in the wind. I kept well away.'

Carl nodded. A shadow of disbelief passed over his face.

Linda sat clinging to the very edge of the bed in Chris's room. She surveyed the poster-clad walls: Solidarity, Troops Out, Free Abortion On Demand. The wood-chip wallpaper had been masked with protest.

She heard the flush of the toilet and then Chris wandered back into the room. He sat close to her on the bed, awkward, unsure how to touch her. She curled herself up a fraction more, sharing his feeling of clumsy embarrassment.

'I'm sorry there's nothing to drink,' he said. 'There's never anything to drink,' he added ruefully. She shook her head slightly in an all-purpose gesture of indifference and tried to smile.

He reached over to the bedside table and took a tissue from a box of Kleenex. 'Look at me.' She obeyed and he gently dabbed at her over-made-up eyes. 'That's better,' he decided. She felt it was worse. She felt exposed and vulnerable. The feeling strengthened as he reached out and tentatively took her hand. 'I never thought you'd come like this, Linda,' he said.

She floundered. 'Well, we known each other quite a long time, and there's nothing wrong with . . .' Her voice trailed off.

'Please don't feel guilty?'

'What about?' She fought to shift the exchange away from her weakness. She said softly: 'You are lonely, aren't yer?'

'I know people.'

'Yer girlfriend.'

'Now she makes me feel lonely,' he said bitterly.

'Is she with someone else?'

'Several. They're all out of the same mould. Mainly vegetarian, mainly nylon socks, Labour Party socials, shop in Habitat, drink too much real ale, and know roughly where Nicaragua is.' Linda laughed at his party-piece.

'You're not like that, are yer, Chris?'

'Oh no, and that, my dear, is why we didn't last. I saw the look on her face the first time I sank my teeth into a dead chicken's leg . . . I just wish she hadn't made such an issue of everything. On top of that she was constantly unfaithful.'

Chris felt the shiver run through Linda's body and realized his mistake. 'Oh God,' he said, 'I'm sorry.'

'S'all right.'

He took up her hand and rubbed his cheek against it submissively. 'No, it's not. I'm sorry.' Her head dropped and he began gently to kiss her neck.

She tried to ease out of his grip. 'Look, I've got to go, Chris.' His grip tightened slightly as he held her back. She felt the panic rise inside.

'No really,' she protested. 'I've got to go.'

He stared at her frightened face. 'What's wrong?'

'Nothing. It's all my fault. I'm sorry.'

'Linda, we haven't done anything!' he exclaimed.

She moved quickly from the bed and collected her coat from the back of a chair.

'You can't catch AIDS from fancying someone, Linda!' His expression was hurt and rejected. A pouting little boy. Linda made no judgement of him, however. She was caught up in a floodtide of agitation and self-disgust.

'I've got to pick up the kids from me mum's,' she explained unconvincingly.

Chris stared, cold and accusing. 'Didn't he tell you he was going off the other day? What did you do, Linda? Wake up and find a note? "Darling, lover, woman, wench. I'm off for a bit. Have a horrible day. Cry for a bit. Feel rejected. Fall back on the sanctity of marriage." How many times has he done that? That why you're here now? Gone again, has he? How many horrible days have you had before this one came, Linda?'

She hurried to the door. 'Yer too clever for me,' she muttered.

He raised himself from the bed and launched himself into another attack. 'You didn't come for me, or you.

You came for him. You'll walk away from here so full of guilt that you'll be able to put up with all his bullshit for another seven years.'

She turned, incensed. Perhaps because he was so close to the truth. 'Shut up, Chris!'

'Tell me one thing. Did you intend to go to bed with me?'

'Yes!' she cried. The rage in his face softened and he reached out to her with a look of pained disappointment. 'Yes, I did,' she repeated tenderly.

Outside the flat, Marty leaned against a tree on the edge of Highbury Fields. His eyes were tired and empty. He was trying to forget a hundred things, and each one of them was sinking its claws ever deeper into his consciousness.

Of the other boys, Marty judged Russell's disquiet to be closest to his own. On Friday morning they sat opposite each other in Fiorelli's. The spaghetti house was empty except for them. A faint, tinny sound of a straining soprano came from the flat upstairs: Mrs Fiorelli was topping up her holy water to 'Ave Maria'.

Marty gazed down into his tepid, grey coffee. 'I had yer marked down different from that, Russ. Why you sticking with all this?'

Russell stared out of the window and smiled as he saw Philippa make a sale from his stall in the Camden Passage Market. 'Dear me . . .' He sucked hard at his breath. 'I stick with it 'cos she says I'm beautiful. 'Cos she opens very nice bottles of wine. And 'cos there's always just a little bit of smoked salmon in the fridge when her husband's away buying paintings. That's why.'

Marty rolled his eyes impatiently. 'I weren't talking 'bout Philippa.'

'No, I know yer weren't.' A cynical smile illuminated

the half-caste boy's face. "Course Carl would want the whole bloody fish in the fridge. So he could be sick on it. That's what yer talking 'bout, ain't it?'

'Tell me why – '

'Don't push it, Marty.' Mario pushed his way through the saloon doors and walked behind the counter. Russell glanced up at him and then continued. 'We ain't ever been best mates, Marty. I was always one step behind you and Carl, weren't I? I was the one with the O level, remember? Pair of yer laughed about that for two years. P'raps that's why I see straight through yer, Marty.'

Marty's expression of surprise was cut short by a sharp cry of laughter from Jo Jo, when the boy threw open the front door and ran into the restaurant. He rushed down to the far end of the room, holding a half-eaten meat pie in his hand.

Freddie loomed large and menacing in the doorway of Fiorelli's.

'Here we go again,' said Russell.

Freddie's angry voice boomed out. 'Gimme back that pie, runt.'

'You'll end up down the outsize shop,' Jo Jo taunted. 'You'll be wearing tents, fatty!' But his face began to lose its colour as Freddie strode slowly towards him. 'No, now look, no don't. I din't mean it . . .'

Freddie snatched the pie from his hand. 'Gimme that!' He grabbed Jo Jo roughly by the hair and began to grind the pie into the smaller boy's face. Jo Jo squirmed and spluttered and coughed. Freddie walked back to the front table, leaving a disgruntled Jo Jo muttering and checking if all his teeth were still there. The other boys paid little attention to his complaints. They had all witnessed this ritual many times before.

Carl walked through the door and casually said: 'Whad'you do that for, Freddie?'

"'Cos he's friggin' mental,' Jo Jo cried fiercely.

Freddie looked unusually harassed. He stared hard at Carl and said: 'I did it 'cos I'm bloody overworked. D'you know how many pick-ups I have to make now? D'you know how early I gotta get – '

'Where's Con?' Carl said.

Mario looked over from the counter. 'Gone to the doctor, he says.'

Carl slapped his fist down on the table. 'I'm royally sick of this.'

'You are?' said Marty.

Carl shot him a withering look. 'Oh, it speaks. P'raps you know where all these people are. The ones Con said were just waiting for us to make a mark before they come running.'

Jo Jo wandered up to the others, still wiping the grease from his jaw. 'We got the screws on dozens more gaffs now, ain't we?'

'And I gotta get up at six in the morning to collect,' Freddie exclaimed. 'I'm overworked.'

Carl stared down at the table, as if he might find an answer in grimy, knotted pine. 'There must be more than this. What kind of bull has Mr Nobody fed me?'

'How much more do you want?' asked Russell.

Jo Jo had not quite clued into the debate. He pointed to his new jacket and made a hopeful contribution. 'Look at this. Three hundred cool notes!'

'And look at Marty's face,' said Carl. 'He knows it should be better than this. There's a whole bloody lot missing somewhere.'

Marty said: 'You were right about the fish, Russ.' Then he got up and walked out of the restaurant. The other boys fell silent as they watched him go. Carl jumped up and ran after him.

97

'You should see your face,' Carl called after Marty. 'When did yer last laugh?'

Marty stopped and turned back to Carl. 'Let me see.' He sounded harsh and uncompromising now. 'I laughed when we nicked the lead off the school roof. I laughed when we lifted Christmas presents for our mums. I even laughed when you beat the shit out of some poor prat 'cos he called yer toffee-nosed sister a slag. I dunno when I stopped laughing, Carl, but it's just not funny any more. Were yer always this greedy? When's it gonna stop?'

'When we get what we deserve.'

Marty shook his head with astonishment. 'They got money coming out of their ying yangs! A few people died and Jo Jo got a jacket! Look at yer, Carl. You're designer violence, mate. Yer time is now. Don't waste time with me. You've got a whole bunch of morons in there to call yer "hero".'

'What's wrong with you?' Carl said.

Marty stepped close to Carl and stared him straight in the face. Quietly and deliberately he said: 'Something grabbed me in the dark. Someone you'd beaten the brains out of. And yer know, for the first time in my life I started thinking 'bout the future. And I decided I wanted to live a long time – but I felt like I was dying.'

Carl began to recite the Act of Contrition, but it was with a contemptuous sarcasm. Marty turned and strode away.

Carl's obsessive ambition quickly blotted out the vision of Marty walking away towards the Angel. That afternoon, his mind was focused only on his suspicions of Con.

At two o'clock Carl took a cab to the Isle of Dogs. At three he had an appointment with a solicitor. After that he sat silently in his living-room and ran the tangled scenario through his head a thousand and one times. He was waiting for two further things: for Freddie to return

98

from Aldgate, and for Jo Jo to return from St Catherine's House.

By ten o'clock that night, both those things had happened and the riddle began to unravel.

At eleven o'clock, Con turned the key in the door of his bedsit, only to find it was unlocked. Carl's voice called out to him, 'Come on in, Con.'

Con covered his fluttering nerves. 'What a surprise. A shock even. Can I make you tea?'

Carl sat back in the armchair and dismissed the idea with a wave of the hand. He said: 'Where were yer this morning, Con?'

'Didn't Mario tell you? I left a message. A little present from a Spanish whore.'

'Don't believe yer.'

'Oh, but it's true. I was – '

'Now where were yer from the first till the third of June, Con?' Carl was enjoying this part of the interrrogation. At this point he still knew all the answers.

'I was in Mojacar.'

'Nope. Try again.'

'I was killing Jimmy Chalker for you!' The agitation was creeping into Con's voice. He could feel the sharp point of the pin and feared he was wriggling back onto it. He stared at Carl's disbelieving face. 'I was. Really I was. The picture – '

'Oh please, please, please, Con. No.' Carl pushed himself up out of the chair and took Con by the arm. 'Don't take that smelly old coat off, Con. 'Cos we are going for a ride.'

Con continued to protest his innocence of deception for the whole of the taxi journey. Carl's only comments were directions to the driver. In fifteen minutes they arrived outside the empty warehouse on the Isle of Dogs which Con had shown Carl ten days before.

Carl paid the driver and dismissed him. Then he ushered Con to the door of the warehouse. 'Got yer keys, ain't yer?' he said. Con nodded and tried to appear curious and confused together. 'Open it then,' Carl urged.

Con fiddled with the ring of keys and finally selected one that appeared shiny, recently cut. He inserted it in the lock, saying: 'I told you. It's Crown property now.' The key obligingly failed to turn the lock. Con appeared vindicated for a second, but then Carl ripped the key-ring from his grasp and began to rifle through it. He selected a second recently cut key and placed it in the lock. He turned it and the cogs of the device clicked into alignment. Carl smiled and saw the nervous agitation invade Con.

'Shall we enter, Mr Connor?' said Carl.

Inside, the large, empty interior was lit by a forest of shafts of light, allowed access from the street by two rows of high-set windows. Con stood pensive and stiff in the shadows, while Carl wandered between the illuminated pools.

Carl said: 'Jimmy Chalker was dead the day I met yer, Con. And you knew it.'

'No I didn't.' The soft lilt had gone now. His voice was thin and unconvincing.

'You stood outside this place with me and Marty and . . . now what did yer say? Bobby died intestate. It goes to the Crown.'

'That's the procedure. It is – '

Carl was angered by the interruption to his deductions. 'I know what the bloody procedure is Con! I checked. When you ain't made a proper will, then everything you own goes to yer nearest relative. If you've got one. Well, Bobby did. His own son, dammit. And they don't like naughty boys like Jimmy in Spain. He had to have his death registered here. I got the certificate, and he definitely din't die on the second of June.'

'But I didn't – '

'When were yer in Mojacar, Con? Day before yer met me? You hated Jimmy. You said so, spitting feathers. It must of been a rare moment when you pulled the gun on him and told him to sign this place over to yer, or you'd blow his brains out. A rare moment. 'Course, then yer killed him anyway.'

Con smiled broadly, while trying to judge how likely it was that he could reach the door before the powerful boy could lay those large hands on his slender neck and snap it like a twig. He had seen Carl's violence first-hand, and did not doubt that he would resort to it at the slightest provocation. He said: 'Your imagination rivals mine, Carl.'

'Shut up!' Carl ordered. 'Look at this place, Con. No tyre marks, no fag ends, no old papers. It's been empty for months . . . maybe years. There's another one just like it down the road. Almost identical. "To be developed: forty residential units." However thick he was, Bobby Chalker knew this place was worth a fortune. So did you. P'raps that's why you was in the house, the night he died; lifting all the papers on it.' Carl reached into his pocket and removed the sleek Smith and Wesson.

Con started to back away as Carl approached with the gun held firmly out before him. Carl said: 'Are you afraid of me, Con?' Con's throat tightened and he shook his head. 'You should be,' Carl breathed.

'Please don't point that thing at me. Please!'

Carl prodded the gun in Con's ribs and the Irishman stumbled against the wall. 'Open yer mouth,' said Carl. 'It'll make less noise.'

'It wasn't for me. It was for Klein!' Con blurted.

Carl laughed deeply in his moment of victory. 'Yeah. I reckoned it was one of 'em. Freddie saw yer there. How long yer been working for him?'

'Five years,' Con said breathlessly. 'He liked Bobby. He knew things were going downhill and he wanted to keep an eye on him.'

'And when the end come, he grabbed the best thing he had. That's a real mate.'

'Yes . . . not very friendly really.'

'One thing I'm curious 'bout, Con. Why d'yer ever show me this place?'

'Stalky was after me. I thought another empty warehouse might anger you enough to see him off for me.'

Once more, Carl's face darkened with menace. 'You've been pouring poison in my ear, Con. See, I've read *Hamlet*. There ain't no one gonna come bowing and scraping. There ain't no empire. Just a few bits of tatty protection and a couple of lock-ups. This place was all there really was and Klein's stolen it from me. You think I'm gonna let that go?'

'I'd say it would be out of character.'

'You been Klein's ears and eyes over here long enough. But now, you are definitely gonna work for me.'

'He'd kill me.'

'So would I. He need never know. You can carry on reporting back. But you'll tell him exactly what I want him to hear.' Carl turned away and Con's body sagged with relief. 'Mr Klein's a nervous man, Con. I want to know why.' Carl called back. 'That bastard stole this from me. I ain't gonna let that go.'

Carl's pledge echoed round the walls of the warehouse. Con watched him walk away, dragging up the fine dust from the floor.

A smirk tugged at the Irishman's mouth.

Seven

In Slater's office at Commercial Post and Carriage, the striking, young hispanic woman continued in a low, mellifluous voice. The ease with which the Los Angeles lawyer's razor-sharp mind breezed through the baffling sheaf of legal documents stimulated a gentle nod of admiration from Tony Slater. George Klein was in no mood to offer the slightest sign of approval. He slouched down in his chair, detached and thoughtful. To him, Dot Fleming was simply the tool which would swell his bank balance and dull his mind with inactivity. CPC was founded on Slater's brain and Klein's graft. Slater could take the money and run: he could exercise his mind anywhere, apply himself to any amount of 'Teach Yourself Philosophy' books. But Klein . . . Klein was already in mourning for the company, and the labour he lived for. George Klein definitely did not want to sell.

The bulldog-faced accountant, Jamieson, set aside his calculator and copious notes and listened intently as Dot began to sum up. She said: 'My clients will maintain and expand the International Courier Service, of course. Also the Intercity business here. In all other areas we would like to see a de-escalation. That means the London Couriers, the bikes as well as the car services, and naturally that includes the executive cars.'

'They're very profitable,' Slater noted.

'They're too diverse. And so are the van- and truck-hire areas.'

'They could be leased out,' said Slater.

In the months she had been negotiating the purchase of CPC, Dot Fleming had learned to differentiate between Slater's genuine protests and the superficial utterings which were designed to placate George Klein's unease. She ignored this suggestion and continued to dissect and discard various areas of the company. From the depot yard below, there came a dull booming sound. Slater's face twitched slightly as he heard the testing of a PA system. He cast an anxious glance at Klein. He had hoped to have this meeting closed and Dot whisked away to an expensive lunch before the union got into its stride.

Klein was out of touch when it came to the practice of subtle diplomacy. He tried to make rising from his chair and sloping to the window look casual and unaffected. He gently eased open the window and the chatter of four hundred company workers drifted up into the office.

Dot had pushed aside her documents and notes of reference. She settled back a few inches in her seat and carefully crossed her slender, lightly tanned legs. She glanced at Klein, and then turned her attention to Slater. Fifty-one per cent of CPC smiled back at her.

'We have discussed this before,' she said. 'As a matter of course, my clients will want to bring in some of their own office personnel. Confidentiality is of prime importance in obvious areas. So jobs will go there.' She shook her head slightly and wondered how forty-nine per cent of CPC had ever made it out of the machine shop. 'They were gathering when I came in, George. What do you want me to hear? A vote of confidence in the management over promises of no redundancies?'

Klein tried to laugh off his heavy-handedness. Slater's laughing face barely concealed the rebuke in his voice.

'Something like that, eh, George?' Klein smiled weakly and pulled shut the window. Slater asked: 'How many is it altogether?'

Jamieson glanced down at his figures. 'Redundancies are estimated to total in the region of . . . about two hundred.'

'Good God,' breathed Klein.

Dot paid no attention to his grief. 'Your financial reports have gone through our offices in New York. All we are waiting for is the Panel in Takeovers and Mergers. In the present climate in this country, I'm assured that will be a formality. But I do have one further question . . .' Her voice rose expectantly. There was a waver from the cool efficient tone. 'The same question, Tony.'

'And the same answer,' Slater replied. 'When all the papers are signed and rubber-stamped, when this company is registered in whatever name your clients care to choose, then you can do what you like. While my name is still on it, trial runs are not part of the deal.'

Dot sighed and looked resigned. She began to gather together her papers and said: 'Well, if I can't persuade you over lunch, then I'll have to go elsewhere. For the trial run, that is.'

'I think we've compromised enough,' Slater reasoned. 'We don't want to take unnecessary risks.' With that he rose and accompanied Jamieson out into the open-plan office.

Dot walked slowly to Klein's shoulder and glanced down into the depot. The union meeting was about to begin. 'My, you are the quiet one, George,' she said.

He looked for some sympathy in her expression, but thought he noticed a faint glimmer of contempt. He said: 'Good cop, bad cop.'

'How quaintly old-fashioned England can be.'

He saw her turn to leave. He sensed his world slipping

away. 'Miss Fleming?' She stopped and cast an impatient look. 'Tony's gonna cut and run when the deal goes through – '

'And you're not?' she queried.

'I din't wanna sell,' he said bitterly. 'Just tell me. When your people take over, do I get rowed out?'

She moved a step closer and read the rites on George Klein's career. 'I'm not absolutely acquainted with how it works over here, George, but in the States, I could find a thousand twenty-five-year-olds who could do your day's work before breakfast. They'd all have coronaries by the time they're forty, but they'd make me a handsome profit and they'd have something nice to leave their kids. You don't work any more.'

'This bloody company was built on my sweat!' he blustered.

'No, no. You misunderstand me. The way you work, doesn't work any more. Anyway, don't look too sad, George. Sweat and tears have one thing in common: they both dry up. Don't hang onto something that's gone. You are out of place at this party.'

'You wouldn't of said that to Tony.'

'Tony's a different animal. He may not like a situation, but that doesn't cloud his judgement.'

'Oh no,' Klein agreed. 'He's a very clever man. Good, up here in the office, in the boardroom.' He cast a meaningful glance down to the gathering crowd in the depot. 'Not so hot down there. And 'course, he couldn't tell yer where half our fleet was, day or night. That's my end of the operation. Perhaps we should talk about my end of the operation. Maybe you could get yer trial run. At the right price.'

Klein sensed Dot postponing his funeral. She said: 'What is the right price?'

106

'A lease-back of all the CPC operations that your clients want to phase out.'

'You'd be going back twenty years, George.'

'Tony's the one who wants to live like a monk in the country. I don't wanna run away.'

Dot glanced behind her and realized the suspicion this conversation might arouse if it continued much longer. 'I don't like doing business in back alleys, bedrooms or public places,' she said. 'I'm realistic enough to know that you should think about this very carefully. Come back to me when you have.'

As she walked out into the open-plan office Dot noticed Slater's hand move sharply from the shoulder of the well-dressed woman seated beside him. He turned to Dot and gave a small clap. 'Shall we go?' he said. Dot nodded and he accompanied her towards the lifts.

Pat Klein looked up and saw her husband in the doorway of Slater's office. She said quietly: 'She's a stunner.'

'Not my type. Where's the car?'

'Out front.' Klein walked over to the windowsill and picked up an internal phone.

Pat smiled as she watched the lift doors close on Dot's statuesque figure. 'Does that mean you didn't meet her in the Cat's Whiskers, and she wasn't drinking a pint of Guinness?'

'You were quite a challenge,' said Klein as he dialled.

'I'm easier now.'

'By all accounts, yes.'

Pat pulled her dress down over her knee and wriggled into a more comfortable position. 'I blame it on that lorry-load of Beaujolais Nouveau you and Tony got your hands on that time. It's an altogether nicer pint.'

Klein spoke into the phone. 'Dave? Can yer send

someone round to have a look at me wife's car? Yep . . .
She thinks the track rods need checking. Ta.'

Pat's expression clouded as she watched George put
down the phone. 'You don't have to say it as if I don't
know what a track rod is. Anyway, I want to take your
car. I'm going away at the weekend. I need to buy some
clothes.'

'I half promised my mother,' Klein protested weakly.

She emphasized every word when she said: 'I totally
promised myself.' He reached into his trouser pocket. Pat
got up from her chair and kissed him lightly on the cheek
as she took the keys. 'You don't mind,' she said in a
pouting voice.

Klein attempted to push back any disquiet he harboured. He said: 'You look very nice today, yer know.'

'That must be a compliment,' she laughed, 'but coming
from you it probably means I look like a shop girl from
Balham.'

'I still loved yer when yer were a shop girl from
Balham,' he said, trying to stimulate affection.

'And you don't now?' She dredged up an insincere
smile and turned away from him. 'You old romantic,' she
murmured as she walked away. Klein stood for a moment
and wondered what it took to communicate with his wife
these days. In reality, the situation had changed little
from the day they had met: George and Pat had spent
twenty years, each quoting from a book that the other
had not read.

The sharp squeal of interference on the microphone
below snapped Klein out of his regretful reverie. He
stared down to the depot and was met with a sight he had
not expected. Broderick, the hollow-cheeked, crew-
cutted despatch manager, stood at the microphone. The
transport supervisor, Tom Simmonds, had his hand
clamped over the top of the mike and was whispering in

Broderick's ear. 'What the hell's Broderick speaking for?' Klein muttered to himself, with growing unease.

Broderick's voice rang out unamplified. 'Take yer hand off, Tom!' The crowd erupted with jeering and booing. Simmonds removed his hand and stepped back with a grim-faced reluctance. Broderick turned his glare from Simmonds and resumed his address to the meeting. 'I'm going to continue, whether you like it or not, Tom Simmonds. Because there's questions to be answered, and these blokes, our colleagues, deserve to know the facts. And if you don't think that, Tom, then you shouldn't be holding union office.' A great roar of approval rose from the crowd. 'There's people here, I see you, I know you, who've given over twenty years' loyal service to this company, and who want to give another twenty. Not take a couple of grand redundancy and spend the rest of their lives gardening. And I'm one of 'em. You may not be, Tom. These men, and women, have a right to hear both sides of the argument. Free speech is not something Mr Slater and Mr Klein do a lot of!' His voice rattled into a passionate shout. 'Yes, they speak. But they don't say a lot. Not the last time I heard 'em. Well, I say to Mr Slater and Mr Klein to put their mouths where their money is, and to come down here now, to this platform, and give us the assurances we seek that there will be no redundancies!' The clenched fists of the crowd shot into the air in militant consensus. 'And I also say that after they've done that, then they should sit down with the branch committee and draw up a written document to the same effect. And if they won't then I shall be tabling a motion at tomorrow's general meeting, and comrades, it will have one subject: industrial action to protect our right to work.'

Klein screwed up his eyes in disbelief. *Comrade?* When had Broderick ever said *Comrade?*

'They shot Jimmy Hoffa,' Dot called to Klein as she

marched back into Slater's office. Klein turned and saw Slater's cold stare from the other end of the floor.

'Open a window, George,' Slater scowled. The two men moved back into the office, and the door closed on an afternoon of harsh words.

Broderick usually spent his lunch at the junior mechanics card school in the workshop canteen. Today, he went home. He had an appointment to keep. When he arrived at the tower block behind Bow Road tube, Carl and Freddie were waiting for him on the gravel forecourt.

The two boys accompanied Broderick into the decaying foyer as he recounted the events of the morning at CPC. They reached the lifts and Broderick pressed the call button. The lift started its pedestrian descent from the twenty-third floor.

Carl said: 'Which way's it gonna swing tomorrow, Mr Broderick?'

Broderick shrugged. 'It'll be close.'

'I hope yer'll be on top form, old boy,' said Carl.

'I can't push it much further – '

"Course yer can.'

The middle-aged man looked anxiously round the foyer, fearful of being observed. 'They cornered me after the meeting. Simmonds and Klein.' A shiver ran through his thin, gangly limbs. 'I've done what you wanted. Just gimme the money.'

Carl made a show of considering carefully for a moment, then he turned to Freddie and pronounced: 'Give the gentleman . . . ten per cent.'

'That weren't the deal!' exclaimed Broderick, as Freddie offered him a small wad of folded ten-pound notes.

'The deal's changed,' said Carl.

Broderick bristled with defiance. 'Why are you so sure I won't go and tell 'em what you're up to?'

Carl raised a smile. 'Because I bought you. Because

you are a little lame pig, and I am a great big hungry lion. You were very easy to find, Mr B. You don't have the money or the class to lose in casinos. You'd have to work till yer dropped to pay off what you owe. If they lay you off, well, the redundancy might just clear yer debts. Then yer can spend the second half of yer life building 'em back up again. If yer find another job, that is, at your age. This is the best offer yer'll have. Now you just be a good little pig.'

The lift arrived and the doors opened in a tired shudder. Broderick stared into the urine-stained little box. 'I'm a union official,' he said quietly. 'I'm s'posed to be incorruptible.' The two boys laughed their contempt and Broderick stepped into the lift. 'Why you so interested in screwing up Slater and Klein?' he asked.

'One of 'em stole something from me,' said Carl. 'And they annoyed me. In fact, everything 'bout 'em annoys me. And because . . . because I want to.'

Broderick stared at the boys' self-satisfied faces as the lift doors began to close. Freddie quickly poked out his foot and when the doors jammed against it, they sprang open again. Freddie said: 'Yer know why they make these lifts this shape, don't yer, Mr Broderick? It's so they can fit coffins in 'em.' The doors closed again.

As Broderick ascended to his flat, the two boys walked back out to Carl's new crimson Porsche 944.

Carl may have bemoaned the paucity of his inheritance, but in the past six weeks, the 'bits and pieces of insurance' which he had picked up from Chalker's 'empire' had certainly paid some dividend. Freddie had left his new Cadillac at home.

Linda slammed the door of Carl's second recent addition to his status: the house in Cranley Gardens. They had been there less than twenty-four hours and her loathing for the place had only grown. Things had worsened considerably when Kathy told her that the murderer Denis Nielson had promenaded his wretched victims along that very street.

Carl had abandoned her early that morning. She had sat, half-heartedly unpacking their life from the ranks of tea-chests, and the depression had settled on her again. It came accompanied by anger and resentment. If she had been at Northchurch Road, then she might have strolled out into the garden, sunk down on the grass and sought comfort from the one perfect, peach-coloured rose which had opened in the last week. Instead, she found herself dialling a number which she thought she had forgotten. The children were at the nursery. It was Tuesday.

She walked along the edge of Queen's Wood and took the tube from Highgate to Chalk Farm. When she arrived at the tarmacked viewing area on top of Primrose Hill, he was there, sitting on the wooden bench.

'I'm late,' she called breathlessly. 'I'm sorry.'

Chris turned his eyes from their survey of the London skyline and smiled.

'You been here long?'

He shook his head. 'Nope. Five minutes.'

She walked up to him and settled down on the bench. 'I was going to come in a cab, but then I thought . . . well, maybe someone . . . so I got the tube. Anyway . . .'

'Haven't seen you for weeks,' he said. 'Got to know your mum quite well though.'

She had hoped it would be easy, a release, an escape from the tense silence that had descended between her and Carl. But she picked up the note of bitterness in Chris's voice. 'He wouldn't – ' she began, but he cut her off.

'You came to that nursery three times a week for six months. Then the last six weeks . . . nothing. This morning, you call me to say how upset you are 'cos you moved yesterday, and you wanted me to have your new number. What for, Linda? I'm not sure how we got from that to both of us being sat here on top of a bloody hill, with neither of us knowing what to say. I don't know why I'm here, Linda. Do you?'

'I'm sorry – '

He threw his head back in exasperation. 'And since I've known you, you've apologized to me ten thousand times! Why? 'Cos I like you? 'Cos a couple of times I happened to show that I more than liked you? You sorry 'bout that?'

'No – '

'Was I too crude? Too vulgar? Tell me if I was. It's good for me to be humiliated; it's part of my essential rehabilitation as a dominant male!'

It was Linda who felt humiliated and inferior. He could batter her with his vocabulary. She apologized because she believed the over-dramatized portrait he painted of his own suffering. He may not have 'cracked' her as easily as he had expected, but he had learned where most of the pressure points were.

Linda gazed out at the outline of the city, which shimmered in the heat haze. 'It all looks so clean and simple from up here,' she breathed.

'What does, Linda?' She bowed her head. 'You wanna leave?' he said.

'No. Yes. I have to. I'm sorry . . . I shouldn't have called yer, but it was so sad to leave that flat, and me mum was upset, 'cos me dad . . . well . . . that's all. I just wanted to see someone.' She paused and breathed deeply. 'No. That's not it . . . it's this . . . oh I can't. I have to go. I can't do this, Chris! I can't. I have a husband and a family. I dunno what was in me head. It's just . . . this isn't such a good idea.'

113

'No. It's stupid. Look at us.' They stared at each other and the words dried up.

'So,' she said, finally cutting into the silence.

'So,' he echoed. 'So have a nice life, Linda. Let me have your new address. I could even send you a Christmas card. Even though I never send them.' He saw the panic beneath her awkward smile. Slowly, he moved his face close to hers and raised his hand to brush her cheek. 'You wanna go?' he whispered.

'Where?'

'Friend of mine lives on the edge of the park down there. He's on holiday. I've got the keys.'

She thought of the cold tomb waiting in Cranley Gardens and she went with him.

She tried to make love to him in that anonymous, elegant flat. They kissed on a bed which was surrounded by three walls of *trompe-l'oeil*. Beyond her desperate embrace stretched an orangery, a maze, a benign rural landscape, a cricket match, and a sky which would never lose its soft cobalt warmth.

She sat frozen with disappointment and shame. She said quietly: 'You'd call him a criminal. Not someone you'd meet at a demonstration or a dance. I never told yer, did I? He hurts people for a living now. And he's everywhere I go. Everyone's face. You must go away. He will find out. You don't deserve to be hurt like the rest of us.'

The third-floor office on the corner of St John's Street and Pentonville Road was not Centrepoint, but it was better than the front room, or Fiorelli's. The spacious conference room and neat reception were Carl's third major acquisition. The other boys were supposed to be equal partners, but now there was no confusion about who prowled those floors as 'leader of the pack'.

Carl sat at the head of a large, rectangular mahogany table which stood, glossy and imposing, in the centre of the conference room. To his right side sat Con. Behind them, the door to reception was open. Margie, the dumpy, thirty-five-year-old secretary, was at her desk. She was Carl's fourth purchase.

'I hate bloody unions,' rasped Carl. 'They should all be shot. But I don't care if they're only out for one day. 'Long as it screws up Klein and Slater. Long as it makes 'em chew another inch off their fat little fingers. Get me?'

Con got him very well. The Irishman had continued to meet Klein and report on the state of affairs in the wake of Bobby's death. Klein harboured a grudge against Carl for precipitating Chalker's demise and had expressed his wish to Con that the 'upstart bastard' should suffer in his turn. But Klein had other worries which had interrupted any plan he had for vengeance. Carl, on the other hand, had developed tunnel-vision.

'P'raps we should put the squeeze on Simmonds, too,' he suggested.

'You can't bribe a man who keeps pigeons,' Con replied. He was enjoying this game. 'No. This is a matter of delicacy, Carl. The manipulation of mass emotion can be very easy, but you have to wait for the circumstances to be right.'

Carl said: 'You wouldn't be putting me off, would yer?'

'Be patient. Wait for the results of the general meeting,' Con advised.

Russell laughed from the doorway to reception. He was clutching a file in his hand. Con shot a stern look in his direction and said: 'You find that amusing?'

'I bet you do,' Russell answered. 'I'd rather sell junk off a trestle-table than bother 'bout Slater and Klein.'

'Then p'raps yer'd better do that,' Carl said. 'I been meaning to have a word with yer. We can't keep holding

115

up meetings, waiting for you to flog an old teapot to a vegetarian.'

Russell sauntered over to the table. 'Why don't yer give it a rest on the two old boys, eh?' he said to Carl.

'Cos I don't want to. What else d'yer suggest? 'Part from spending money?'

Russell tossed the file down in front of Carl. 'I'd suggest you looked at that. S'a record of all the trouble we've had in the last month. While you're plotting and scheming how to put the boot in on Slater and Klein, there's fifty evil little bastards in the East End doing the same to us. I'd "suggest" the situation's getting out of hand. But then I s'pose it depends which way yer looking, Carl.'

Russell did not get a response to his objections. Just as Carl was about to condemn the boy's nagging caution, they were interrrupted by Mario, running breathlessly into reception. He stood for a second, flushed, taking great gulps of air, then looked to Carl's questioning face and said: 'You should see it down at CPC, man.'

'They out of the meeting?' Carl demanded.

'They're out all right. Stone me! There's a riot going on!'

Slater and Klein stood shocked and numb in the centre of the depot yard. Klein tried to count the police and gave up at two hundred.

Outside the arch, on Tower Bridge Road, the swirling core of thirty pickets clashed violently with the uniformed cordon. The faces were contorted and grotesque in confrontation. Some were cut and bloodied, some spattered with the blood they had drawn.

In the centre of the mêlée, inching forward – battered, pounded on, jolted, spat at and kicked – was a car. In the rear seat, Dot Fleming covered her flinching, terrified face.

Eight

Marty sat perched uncomfortably on the edge of the black leather armchair in the living-room at Cranley Gardens. As the late-evening sun struck the stained-glass fleurs-de-lys in the French windows, the room was filled with abstract patterns of pastel light.

'Carl'll kill me when he sees I've not sorted all this out. . . .'

Linda's voice trailed off as she continued to search through the row of tea-chests which hugged the wall by the fireplace. Marty glanced over at her. She tried to be cheery: she gave a slight laugh as she unearthed toiletries and Paracetamol, children's toys and Mills & Boon romances. She tossed the soft blonde hair from her face and it settled in a wave on her shoulder. One hand reached behind her and tugged at the T-shirt which had eased free of her jeans and exposed the smooth, golden skin of the small of her back, while the other hand still sorted furiously through the contents of the chest. An addict in search of a syringe.

Suddenly, she stopped, half turned to Marty and stared at the varnished floor-boards, her face bathed in warm orange light.

'You know, I've forgotten what I was looking for.'

'A pen,' he replied.

117

She laughed and threw back her head. 'I found one of those ages ago.'

She rose quickly and returned to a small pile of newspaper-wrapped articles she had removed from the first chest she had searched. She unearthed a biro from the pile and offered it to Marty, together with a page torn from a diary she had never kept. He began to write an address and telephone number. She turned from him and wandered to the French windows, dragging her feet across the floor like a bored child.

'This is the only time of day there's any light in this room. Carl wants to put up Venetian blinds. Don't you think that would make it worse?' In her agitation she gave him no time to answer. 'What time's your train?'

'Ten past ten. Where is he, Linda?'

'At his mum's, I think. Yes, he must be.'

Why had he asked? He knew where Carl was. He had made the taxi driver pass the office at the Angel and he had seen Carl's car. The last thing he had wanted when he arrived at Cranley Gardens was to be greeted by Carl on the doorstep. Perhaps he just needed one more confirmation that Carl was a liar.

Linda crossed and took the paper from him. 'I'll only ring if it's an emergency. Don't you worry 'bout your dad. I'll get Kathy to look in on him any time I can't.'

'He ain't gonna die of shingles.'

'I don't think so. Now let me make yer some coffee.'

Marty's hands gripped the edge of the seat and he cast a glance up to the clock on the mantelpiece. 'Well – '

'Oh, how daft of me.' She clapped a hand to her mouth. 'You gotta run.'

Slowly, he eased himself out of the chair, desperately groping for a line with which to escape. 'You take care now, Linda.'

118

'Oh I don't need to, Marty. What could happen to me? Carl has people following me most of the time.'

'Yeah. I know.'

He bowed his head and prodded at the corner of the rug with the toe of his shoe. When, after a short moment, he raised his head again, he saw that her smile had gone. Her expression was ice, and seven years of friendship hung by the smallest thread. The few feet between them had become miles. The anger in her eyes burned into him; he half expected the word 'Traitor' to be branded on his forehead the next time he looked in a mirror.

He tried to repair the damage: 'I was a lot better at it than Jo Jo.'

'Well, isn't that nice.' Her lips barely parted as she spat the words at him.

'Linda,' he almost shouted, 'I didn't tell him.'

As she continued to stare at him, the anger seeped away. A tender silence settled on them, and slowly, they moved together. They held each other, rocking gently. His hand stroked her hair and her cheek pressed against the soft fabric of his jacket.

'Does he talk to you 'bout me, Marty?'

He lied. 'No.'

She raised her face from his shoulder and said: 'What am I gonna do?'

How could he answer her, when he had the same question rattling in his head? So he did not answer. He said: 'He'll find out, Linda. You know he will.'

Riding down Cranley Gardens in a black cab, Marty wiped away the perspiration which had gathered on his forehead. The driver had taken what seemed like an eternity to arrive after Linda had put through the call, but now he had broken free. He forced down the window of the cab as far as it would go, leaned back in the seat and waited for the rush of cool evening air to sweep away the pounding tension in his head.

119

The relief never came for Marty on that journey. The image of Linda's face, so thin now and distressed, did fade as he stared into the blood-red sun which was settling behind the well-ordered semis of Cranley Gardens; it only left him to make room for a new paranoia. He began to think about Nielson; another murderer who had lived in this street. He studied each house as he passed, wondering if that were the one. He imagined children playing on a broad expanse of pristine carpet. He saw them rolling and laughing, scooting toys across the floor, spilling drinks and food. One day that carpet would wear out and need to be changed. Would the owners dare change it? When they prised it up and peeled back the felt, would the boards be spattered with the dried blood which had dripped from the butcher's knife? Then, would they suspect? And if they did, could they sleep that night in the house which had been a coffin to so many dismembered souls? What dreams would come to them that night? A hand smashes through those boards. Just a hand, severed and bloody, twitching like a nerve, flapping across the floor, the yellow nails tapping on the wood, bucking and kicking like some deranged mechanical toy. Then it stops. The fingers tremble in a little wave, and then one digit rises slowly, like a sensor. That hand is thinking. Deciding. And now it's moving again, deliberately, purposefully, directly back to the splintered hole it rent in the floor-board. It's going – the fingers claw their way back into the bowels of the house. But it stops! The ragged skin twitches round the shattered, hacked-off, wrist-bone, and the putrifying, exposed flesh swells and seeps deep-brown liquid as the fingers tighten to a fist and ease back out of the hole. It pulses back across the floor, gripping, pulling something out of the hole. A rope. No, not that. A cord, of gristle, and mucous, and stretched-white tendon. The floor heaves and then, with a deafening

120

crack, a severed arm bursts out into the air. The cord of gristle coils round the hand like a whip and snaps it back onto the forearm. All over the room now, limbs are bursting through the stained wood, cementing together torn flesh, moving to one central position, and combining, moulding, fusing, until, slowly, it begins to rise. It has a face now. An almost unrecognizable mask of dusty red jelly. But the gash that is the mouth widens as the reassembled corpse shivers forward through the shadows, and a weak voice sings: 'Stalky's coming for you . . .'

'Six pound eighty, mate.'

Marty gave a slight start as he opened his eyes and nervously surveyed a dark, underground place, which he did not recognize. The taxi driver was craning his head back over his seat and glowering at him.

'Where's this?' breathed Marty.

'Where you asked for. Six pound eighty, and I'm not sitting here for the good of me health.'

Marty pulled himself upright, twisted in his seat and glanced out through the rear window of the cab. The nightmare began to recede as he saw other taxis descend the steep slip road and pull up adjacent to a large sign, which demanded: 'Put down here. All passengers for Euston Station.'

He took a ten-pound note from his pocket. The driver accepted it sulkily and made a half-hearted attempt to fumble in a small-change bag. He need not have bothered. Marty, with no desire to linger in this place, grabbed his bag, alighted from the taxi and moved quickly to the lifts.

It was with relief that he emerged into the well-lit main hall of the station. The bustle of rush hour was long past. He seemed calmed by the cool emptiness of the hall and the low boom of an incoherent public address. He wandered towards the Departures board, occasionally focusing on the faces of hardship which were drawn to this

121

night-time sanctuary: vagrants and drunks, the young homeless, the lost; punctuating the broad sweep of the hall like rocks in a Japanese garden.

Marty stopped and let the bag drop to the floor beside him. His eyes wandered across a hundred potential destinations before they finally fixed on '22.10. Grantham. Platform 12.' Why there? Because 'Mum' was there.

Marty's conscience held an armful of objections, and now it began to toss them at him like missiles. Someone you've seen five times in twenty-five years isn't a 'mum'. Someone who ran off with a brush salesman and abandoned you to a father who couldn't pick his nose without help isn't a 'mum'. Someone who sent you a card of a boy on a BMX for your twenty-fourth birthday isn't a 'mum'. Someone who always looks so bloody guilty in your presence isn't a 'mum'.

The missiles stopped; repelled by the perfect shield. She was so 'guilty'. He was running away to a place where the odds were all in his favour. She would fuss and worry, and demand nothing of him. No obligation, no responsibility, no involvement. She was guilty. It was a game he could not lose. That was why he was going.

He dragged himself back to the moment, and reached down for his bag. It was gone. The sweat broke out in an instant. Damn! How could he be that stupid? Anxiously, he surveyed the four corners of the hall. Damn! But the swell of panic subsided and his heart sank when he heard a familiar voice.

'Can't get away from me that easily.'

Carl smiled broadly and eased himself off the low wall which guarded the escalators to the Underground. In his hand was Marty's green plaid overnight bag. Marty stood, still and angry, as Carl sauntered up to him and playfully planted a kiss on his cheek.

122

'You were miles away, man. Come on. I wanna talk to you.'

'Sod off, Carl.' Marty glared at him, demanding the return of the bag. Carl hesitated for a moment and then danced away a few steps. 'Come on,' he repeated, 'I wanna talk to you.'

'I've got a train to catch!'

'There'll be another one. There'll be a hundred bloody trains. Christ, before you know it it'll be tomorrow, Marty.'

Carl backed away, dangling the bag like bait on a hook. When he reached the glass swing-doors, he smiled once more, clicked his tongue, and then turned and pushed his way out into the night.

Marty glanced round at the Departures board. He stared hard at the information on the Grantham train. For a brief moment he thought of his mother, and of the game he could not lose. Then he swapped it for one he could not win, and ran after Carl.

By the time he caught up with him Carl was already at his car, which was causing an obstruction in the bus bays in front of the station.

Carl tossed the bag to Marty across the roof of the red Porsche, and then stood waiting expectantly. Marty made one last show of resistance. He said offhandedly: 'Lately, when you say you wanna talk to me, usually means you wanna tell me. Well I don't wanna listen any more, Carl.'

'I love yer, man. Otherwise I wouldn't be here.'

'How many times you said that, "I love yer, man"?'

'I dunno. Thousands.'

'Sounds good. Say it again.'

Carl turned his head slightly and looked out to the steady stream of traffic on Euston Road. After a moment he returned his gaze to Marty and said, almost mockingly: 'I love yer, man.'

'OK, Mr Smartarse, Mr Know-it-all, Mr Cool. What does that mean?' He pressed on, his voice growing louder. 'You say it enough. Come on. What does it mean?'

'Means you're my best mate.'

'Yep.'

'Means it was always you and me.'

'What a pair we were.'

'We got around.' Carl tried to sound casual, but all the time he was fighting the twitch of the muscles in his face.

Marty shook his head. 'We turned each other into bloody heroes!'

'No one else was going to,' Carl snapped back.

Marty's head dropped slightly. He looked hard at his watch, waiting for the quartz movement to click round one more precise minute. After a few seconds, the slim mechanism obliged. 22.11. The train was gone.

'You can't kill people just 'cos you're disappointed, Carl,' he said distantly.

They set off into the night, and into the West End, as they had done a thousand times before. They stopped in wine bars and pubs, for one drink, for half a drink. Carl reminisced and tried to buoy up Marty's flagging spirits. Marty just kept taking the drinks and checking his watch, to see how long it was before day would come and illuminate this charade for what it was.

By the time he found himself in the Video Café, Marty's head was spinning. The garish colour and blaring pop music from the screens all round him disorientated him further.

He moved uncertainly through this world of the affluent young bourgeoisie. The video screens would pulse out a single image and then splinter into twenty different images. Flamingos, Jumbo jets, tanks and oceans, soaring views, all assaulted Marty's brain.

Carl moved easily and assuredly beside him. And in

this place where reality was shattering all round them, he tried to drag Marty back into a memory, and into a time where he thought they had shared the same ambition.

'What you gonna do, eh? What's gonna turn up? Eh? Shifting cement down your old man's? Making him a nice cup of tea? What kind of man are you, eh?'

Marty turned unsteadily to Carl.

Carl pressed on; determined to ram his point home as he felt Marty's defences rising.

'I thought we stuck two fingers up to the world and said "Screw you, the choice ain't good enough." Decided we were the only people worth believing. We din't feel sorry for ourselves, or ask favours. I never been down the dole in my life! We made something happen and got respect.'

'You and me, and daft Jo Jo, and Mario, who calls his mum a whore, and Freddie, who thought mouldy cheese would cure his clap. And Russell. Quiet old Russ, who's the biggest bloody taker of the lot. One day you won't see him for dust.'

'We're bloody successful,' said Carl calmly.

'Bloody stupid!'

'There's people – '

'No, shut up!' Marty cut him off, and forced his disordered thoughts into slurred words. 'You know, you've . . . you've . . . just convinced yerself that . . . that . . . nothing's important 'cept you. You're like some little kid, you know. Playing hide-and-seek, and you park yerself under a table with yer legs sticking out. And . . . and 'cos you can't see no one, you think no one can see you. And you get pissed off when someone finds yer, so you wanna change the rules, and you do . . . and I bloody loved you!'

'You know why we had a good time?' responded Carl coolly.

''Cos we had nothing to worry 'bout, I s'pose.'

'We din't go to friggin' Eton, Marty. We got on 'cos we was hard. Harder than the next little prat. You whine on 'bout Slater and Klein . . . well, they pissed me off, but I'm harder than them, so I'll show 'em. And after them I'll show someone else.'

'So where does it end, Carl?'

'It don't. Welcome to the real world. Wanna drink?'

Marty turned his eyes onto the crowd in the bar. It was becoming busier by the minute. The feeling of unsteadiness had sunk into his stomach and become nausea. 'Someone should drop a bomb on this lot,' he said.

He drained the last inch of beer from his glass and then set it down heavily on the counter behind them. He saw that, once more, Carl's face had broken into a smile. He was together enough to know why.

'Oh I remember what you said, Carl: "If they ever drop the bomb, and the world's blown to bits, and we've got five minutes left, I'll find you in the flames".' He paused, and then said: 'Read it off a record cover, din't yer?'

Carl shifted uncomfortably and averted his gaze from Marty. Marty did not wait for any further response. He turned on his heel and made his way, as directly as he could, for the exit.

Surrounded by the noisy, neon suggestiveness of Soho, they sat in the car in silence for some time. Carl drummed his fingers on the steering wheel; Marty picked his bag from the floor and clutched it to him, like some faceless teddy bear.

Marty knew full well that this little journey of reconciliation had failed. He had never expected it to succeed. In truth, it was just another act of self-flagellation. Carl, too, knew failure when he saw it; but he was too used to avoiding responsibility to admit his share of the blame. 'Where to?' he asked.

Marty replied quietly: 'The station.'

'Jeez, you can be a real old woman.'

With a weary sigh, Carl turned the key in the ignition. The Porsche roared to life and Carl screwed himself round in the seat to check if it was clear to back out of the space. His head came close to Marty's. He expected him to ease back, to turn his face away, to fix his stare on the flashing signs selling imitation sex at knock-down prices. But Marty did not. He did the opposite. He looked directly into Carl's eyes. And he began to laugh.

'What?'

Marty made no reply. The laugh grew louder.

'What?' repeated Carl.

'Russ told me once that he could see straight through me.' The laughter began to peter out. 'Dunno why, but I thought you would too.'

Carl settled back in his seat and turned off the engine. 'What you on about, Marty?'

A voice in Marty's head told him to shut his mouth. It reminded him that all he had to do was get out of that car, hail a cab, and within half an hour he could be out of this town. He was standing on the edge of a precipice, and below him was blackness. The drop could be ten feet, or a hundred. He could tumble safely onto a grassy bank, or be dashed to pieces on jagged rocks.

He jumped.

'You remember one night – just after you and Linda got married,' he began softly. 'Her mum was sick, so she had to go round and look after her dad. And I come round that night. We got drunk. You had a dirty movie, remember?'

Carl nodded almost imperceptibly.

'You threw me in the spare room, and went to bed. In your room. Next door. And 'bout an hour later . . .'

The words came harder now, but Marty drove himself on, and down.

''Bout an hour later, I started to cry. But you din't hear. So I cried louder, and louder, 'til you come in the room. And you sat on the bed and you asked me what was wrong.'

'You was upset 'bout that bird you just split up with. Wos her name? Janet? Jeanette?'

'I din't say that. You did,' Marty continued. 'Then you put yer arms round me and you held me 'til I went to sleep.'

He paused, and his eyes filled with tears. 'I was crying, 'cos that was the only way that I could think of to make you do that, Carl.'

He was shaking now. He could not help himself. He pawed at his cheek, wiping away the tears which would not stop. For a few moments, Carl did not look at him, did not touch him, said nothing. When he finally spoke, the words were cold, superior, and uninviting: 'You wanna go somewhere and talk?'

'No,' said Marty, collecting himself, 'I don't wanna talk.' He paused. 'I wanna go somewhere. I wanna show you something, Carl. But I don't wanna talk, 'cos I reckon you don't wanna listen.'

The spotless, red Porsche reached the top of Tottenham Court Road in less than five minutes. Carl drove smoothly and quickly; but not so quickly that Marty could accuse him of being reckless, or angry, or even digusted.

'Turn right.'

Carl did, and accelerated on, expecting further directions from Marty. Marty did not speak. They continued in a straight line. Along Euston Road, past the glare and bustle of King's Cross, up Pentonville Road and across the Angel, down City Road.

Marty finally spoke again as they reached the borders of the East End, where Old Street narrowed into the junction with Shoreditch High Street. 'Stop here.'

128

Carl obeyed. Marty jumped out of the Porsche and slammed the door behind him. He wandered towards a great monolith of a building, which squatted heavily on the side of the road, flanked by dilapidated Victorian sweatshops.

The dark grey façade was bare and unwelcoming; the windows blacked out; the doors closed. But then, the London Apprentice had no wish to advertise itself to the general public.

Marty pushed the buzzer on an intercom which lurked discreetly near the front door. The door swung open immediately. A blast of dance music and the buzz of a crowd signified that this was a portal to a hidden world.

Inside the pub, Carl stood marooned in the crowd of gay men. His eyes searched for something to focus on. He had been here before, but now the place was almost unrecognizable to him. The high ceiling of the barn-like room had been lowered with festoons of netting and camouflage material; the posters advertising saunas and bars in Amsterdam, Berlin, and San Francisco had been replaced by Second World War relics. Tin hats and gas masks hung from the wooden pillars which supported the canopy of the central bar. A sign draped across the lintel of the entrance announced that this was Combat Night.

A mass of uniformed homosexuality swirled round Carl, brushed against him, eased past him. He thought back to the night of his previous visit to the London Apprentice. They had gone there 'for a laugh'. A wet Monday in January. A handful of customers who had not fancied what was on the box was no threat then. He had strutted through that bar; announced his superiority with loudness; made Jo Jo piss down his own leg by sneaking up on him in the urinal.

He gave a slight start as he felt a purposeful nudge in

his back. He turned sharply and saw Marty holding two bottles of Pils.

Marty handed him the drink and then made to turn away. Carl clutched at his friend's sleeve. 'Remember when we come here last, Mart? Day before me and Linda's anniversary. Remember how she said she was getting worried 'bout me?'

'Yeah. Had a good laugh, din't we?' Marty replied, deadly. 'Funny how you never got worried 'bout me, Carl.'

Before Carl could make any response, Marty slipped off into the crowd. Carl hesitated for a moment and then hurried after him.

They squeezed into a small space, in a neon-lit area on the far side of the bar. A few feet from them, a temporary stage had been erected. A sweating, rotund, arch-camp roadie flailed a microphone stand before him like a scythe in an attempt to cut through the throng to the structure.

Marty searched for a patch of the bar not swimming in spilled beer, and rested his arm back onto it. His gaze was inconstant; his eyes darted from man to man. Unlike Carl's.

A dark-haired survivor of Passchendaele gripped Marty's forearm as he passed. The full moustache which masked his mouth twitched as he made a comment Carl did not catch.

Marty nodded an acknowledgement.

'Who's that?' Carl asked.

'Just someone.'

'Marty, it don't – '

'I've been here quite a lot, Carl.' Marty was almost shouting over the sound system. 'I hated it at first. Well, I pretended to hate it with you and the lads. But on me own . . . well, I din't pretend. I knew why I was here.' He paused to take a swig from the bottle. 'The worst thing was . . . they din't all fancy me. Some nights, no one did. It was bloody awful. I thought they would, see.'

'It don't make no difference, Marty.'

'To you! Not to you!'

'I still love yer, man.'

'My friend the faggot.' Marty smiled as the roadie squealed his disapproval at a six-foot Marine who was blocking his path. 'So if I find Prince Charming he can join the "Gang" can he? Long as he can shoot straight, and don't spit on Jo Jo and give him AIDS?'

The roadie's clamouring protests turned to mock ecstasy as the obliging Marine reached down and lifted him onto the stage. The dance music cut out and the lights lowered.

Carl glanced across the long stretch of the bar. He considered the tortuous path to the exit. Seeing the crowd milling even thicker towards the area by the stage, he decided that escape was impossible.

A spotlight snapped on and an unco-ordinated cheer went up from the audience as a young woman stepped gingerly onto the stage in six-inch stilettos. A catsuit of shiny, black rubber gripped every contour of her body. Studded leather gauntlets covered the hands that waved in welcome, and chains clinked from her shoulders and waist. Her hair was a peacock fan of colours.

The high priestess of bondage screamed her arrival in the temple of the male. 'Good evening!'

The response was inadequate and prompted the growling of a threat: 'I can't hear you, and you know what happens to naughty boys when I can't hear them. Good evening!'

Several hundred sweating, upturned faced obeyed the order. The roar was deafening.

Carl tried to drag Marty away from the ritual.

'I still think the world of you, Marty. I'd still do anything for yer.'

'Would yer?'

'Yes, goddammit!'

The priestess screamed again: 'Welcome back from the front!'

Marty stared hard at Carl. 'Kiss me then,' he said eventually. The pause seemed to last a shuddering eternity; the banter of the priestess receded to a faint, distant blur, before Marty continued: 'You kissed me in the middle of Euston Station. You kiss me all the time.' He had Carl on a hook and he was not going to let him off. He felt the barb biting deeper. 'Kiss me now that I'm asking you to.'

Carl felt as if every face in the bar was observing him and demanding a response. Within seconds, they were.

'Heavens!' the priestess's voice shot towards Marty and Carl. 'We've got a couple of sweet little soldier boys in civvies down here. Can we get a spot on you?'

The turmoil in Carl's head turned to glowering anger and embarrassment as the spotlight illuminated his face. He wanted nothing more than to force his way to that stage, drag down the bitch, strike her hard across the face, teach her not to make a fool of him. He glanced at Marty, expecting to see a reflection of his own discomfort. But the light was not exposing Marty: he was beaming, bathing in it, enjoying it.

'Bet you two have tramped across a few minefields together,' joked the priestess. 'I'm gonna dedicate this first song just to you.'

The introduction of a taped backing track began.

'Let's go soon, eh?' said Carl.

The floodlit façade of the Russell Hotel pierced the phalanx of trees which guarded the east side of Russell Square.

Marty lay on a bench in the centre of this precious piece of Bloomsbury turf. His eyes darted as he observed the shadowy figures which skirted the perimeter of the square. A few feet away, Carl was sprawled on the grass, staring at the mist of pollen and pollution in the shaft of light from a street-lamp.

They each clutched a bottle of vodka: souvenirs of the London Apprentice for which they had paid well over the odds.

'They don't do it here?' Carl questioned, disbelieving.

Marty replied in a loud whisper: 'You don't think all these blokes come out for fresh air, do yer?'

'Not here! They ain't at it out in the open, Marty, are they?'

''Course.'

'You are well pissed, man.'

Marty was well pissed. The buzz of the London Apprentice had sobered him up for a while. The confrontation with Carl had sharpened him. The elation he felt at being able to make Carl squirm had steadied him. But now that was behind. The protection of the crowd had been blown away. Three a.m., and he felt the alcohol beginning to seep back into his brain as he clambered up and stood, precariously perched, on the bench.

'It's true, ladies and gentlemen,' he announced to slumbering inhabitants of WC1. 'Before your very eyes in fashionable, down-town Bloomsbury. One hundred times nightly, I present to you soliciting . . .' The shadows on the edge of the square began to move rapidly towards the exits as Marty continued his performance. '. . . prostitution, and open-air copulation!'

Carl rolled over, convulsed.

'Thrill to the sight of these adult, red-blooded males. Marvel at their speed. Wonder at their technique.' He fought to hold his balance as he pressed on. 'This isn't

133

pretty. This isn't love. This, ladies and gentlemen, is raw sex, and not for those of a nervous disposition. And the price, ladies and gents, I can hear you ask. The price is not one hundred pounds. Not fifty pounds. The price to you good people – for one night only – is only . . .'

Marty's legs buckled beneath him and he toppled off the bench. Carl beat his fist on the grass, beside himself with laughter. Marty lay still and silent for a moment. Then he said quietly: 'The price is only . . . one dead dog.'

Carl raised himself onto his elbows and looked over to Marty. 'Mart?'

'What?'

'You ain't done all that stuff here, have you?'

'No.'

Carl's head sank back down onto the grass and he closed his eyes. He opened them again when Marty began to speak, softly, but deliberately.

'There was an old man. I was seventeen, and I din't know why people come here then . . . well, I did, but I didn't.' He paused and ran his tongue across his dry lips. 'It was late. He was walking his dog. I knew what he was.' Wearily, he climbed to his feet and looked towards the refreshment hut in the north-east corner of the park. 'I was walking along the path over there when he come up to me.' Carl followed Marty's stare to the small wooden shed surrounded by rhododendron bushes. 'He asked me what the time was. I told him. He said "Thank you." Then he said, "I live just round the corner in Marchmont Street. I don't get much company these days. I don't s'pose you'd be interested in coming back for a drink, would you?"'

Marty paused briefly, and then he said: 'I wanted to, Carl . . . so I hit him. He dropped down on his knees,

134

and I kicked him. He let go the dog. It was like him – old and frightened. It ran off through the gate over there . . . a paper van hit it. And when the old man heard it scream . . . he screamed too.' Marty's voice lowered to a whisper: '"My little baby."'

'S'just a dog, Marty.'

Marty turned on him. 'You're wrong. You ever know when you're wrong, Carl?'

'Yep. When me luck runs out.'

Marty began to walk away. He put a hand to his forehead and felt the vein pulsing in his temple. Carl sat up and called after him: 'Where you going?'

'I wanna see the river.'

On the Embankment, just below Albert Bridge, Marty and Carl stopped and leaned over the low, grey wall to look down at the Thames. The shell of night had begun to crack, and the smoky glow of South London was fading into the dawn light. No wind ruffled the oily surface of the river. Only the muffled bellow of a barge upstream broke the stillness.

Marty looked up at the lights which stretched like strings of jewels between the suspension columns of the bridge. He laughed to himself. 'You know why there's so many of them bulbs missing, don't yer?'

'Nope.' Carl did not raise his eyes from the river.

'S'cos people come here to jump off and kill 'emselves, but when they look down at the river and see it's so full of shit, they change their minds, whip a bulb out, and stick their fingers in the socket instead.'

Carl shrugged slightly and said: 'S'beautiful, man.'

'S'only a dirty old river,' Marty replied.

Carl shrugged again. 'There's three million unemployed moaning for sommit to do: let 'em clean it.'

Marty swigged the dregs of vodka from the bottle and then hurled it out into the river. Carl glared at him. 'Well,

135

one more won't make no difference,' said Marty in his own defence. He pushed himself away from the wall, staggered for a few paces, and then felt his legs buckle again.

Carl's earlier reverence was quickly translated into a fit of laughter when he saw Marty lying helpless at the side of the road.

'Shut up, you sod.' Marty tried to sound disapproving: the gutter was still wet from the efforts of the road-cleansing lorry, and a feeling of damp discomfort was beginning to dispel his drunkenness. But eventually he too gave in to an uncontrollable bout of laughter. All the tension and the tiredness of the night seemed to erupt in that laughter. And still gripped by an almost hysterical mood, Marty said: 'You should of put your coat down, Carl.'

'What!' Carl approached him and reached out a hand. Marty grabbed it.

'That's what noble gentlemen do for queens, Carl!'

Carl gripped hard on Marty's hand. The expression of amusement slipped from his face, and he said coolly: 'Don't be camp, Marty.'

A great guffaw exploded in Marty as he echoed Carl's words. 'Don't be camp!' Carl's hand closed even tighter and he looked deadly serious.

'Don't be camp, Marty. Just . . . don't be that.'

Marty snatched his hand away from Carl's and struggled to his feet, unaided. He walked slowly back to the Embankment wall before he rounded angrily on his companion. 'Just what would you like me to be, sir? What's best for you? What's not gonna be embarrassing? What can you handle, Carl?'

Carl looked back intently. 'What you gonna do?' he questioned. 'Jump?'

'No, no. It's day-time now, Carl. No one kills 'emselves

in day-time.' He forced himself to take the three steps needed to approach Carl. 'I'm gonna go to me mum's. Then in a couple of weeks, I'm gonna come back and make me dad a nice tea, and I'm gonna wait for you to die.' He gave a small, derisive sigh and glanced up at the lightening sky before continuing. 'You really think you're it, don't yer, Carl? Big man who's gonna make this country great again by pissing on everybody. You should of gone to the Falklands, Carl. You wanted to, din't yer? You should of died there. Then we'd all remember yer as a hero. Now go home to yer wife. Be a hero, Carl.'

Marty returned to the wall. He felt his body sag wearily against the stone. The sick feeling of exhaustion had joined the nausea from the drink. His eyes stared out sadly over the placid river.

'Remember, Marty,' Carl's voice floated past in a steady, sober tone, 'it won't be me who calls you queer boy, or faggot, or filthy little bender, or pervert, or shirt-lifter, or poof, or cocksucker, or shit stirrer, or the one who touches up his mates for a cheap thrill.' The voice was getting fainter. 'Others will, old son. But not me. Remember that, pretty boy.'

'I don't hear you, Carl,' breathed Marty. 'You're not real. I made you up.'

When, finally, he did turn, Marty saw only the empty street. Carl had disappeared into the shadows.

Marty wandered slowly to where Carl had parked his car. It was gone. On the pavement sat the green plaid bag. He picked it up and winced as he felt a sharp pain from his left hip. He stared up at the now-pale sky, and he knew that the comfort of retreat into the night was no longer a possibility.

He began to walk towards Euston.

*

Carl fixed his stare straight ahead on the drive back to Cranley Gardens. As he wearily manoeuvred the Porsche through the back streets of Holloway, the pale sun rising over the grey roofs of the East End began to hurt his eyes.

He meandered through impressions of Slater and Klein; of wealth divorced from ambition. His mind noted down a lengthy shopping list of electronic gadgets. He wondered how much it would cost to buy a case of the best champagne. He admitted to himself that he did not know what the best champagne was, and reminded himself to find out. He invented a device to stop hijacks on planes, and came to the conclusion that he needed to get Linda pregnant again. As soon as possible.

He rounded Archway without even noticing the straggling tribe of party-goers: displaced persons like him, angry to find their day had ended when everyone else's had just begun. As he accelerated up the hill to Highgate, he considered the necessity for a larger second car, tried to think of the name of five public schools, and decided to buy Linda a bunch of flowers. No. Five bunches.

He drew up outside his house, turned off the engine and congratulated himself. He had set himself a task at the beginning of that short journey: that he would put Marty O'Reilly completely out of his mind. As usual, he had not found it difficult to pass his own tests.

Carl eased shut the front door of the house and hesitated for a moment, deliberating whether or not to make a cup of tea. He decided against it, and began to mount the stairs.

If he had walked into that kitchen, the panic might have struck him sooner. He might have seen the empty wine bottle, the half-empty brandy bottle. He might have seen the screwed-up package of Paracetamol, which earlier had contained at least a dozen pills. On his way down the hall, he might have glanced into the living-room and noticed the glass, which had fallen from Linda's hand. He might have seen the stain of make-up which had smeared the arm of the sofa when her head lolled against it. He might have found the stylus of the record deck stuck and clicking on the last groove of 'My Baby Just Cares For Me'. But he did not.

Carl walked softly along the upstairs landing. He glanced in through the open doors of the children's bedrooms to find them sleeping. He moved on to his own room. The bedside lamp was still on, but giving way to the thin light of early morning. Linda lay on the bed. Her eyes were closed and she made no sound.

She did not stir as Carl moved to the side of the bed and crouched down on the floor. He reached out and took her hand. It drooped limply in his grip. He rubbed it gently. She remained deeply unconscious.

'You're cold,' he whispered. 'Wake up and hold me, darlin'.'

It took a few seconds; but then it came. A cold, quivering paranoia shot through his entire body. He began to rub harder on her hand, and then squeezed it as firmly as he could. Still, she remained motionless. He jumped up onto the bed and took her by the shoulders and shook her. The trembling inside him grew and he started to slap her face.

He screamed: 'Linda!'

His anguished cry was cut short by another sound. The sharp crack, as a bullet left a gun and the explosive shattering of the bedroom window seemed to come simultaneously. Carl's brain ran in fearful, exaggerated circles, and he was frozen for a split second. He saw the glass, which had showered down onto the bed; he felt it in his hair and on his clothes. He saw the fragments glisten

139

on Linda's lifeless body. He screamed again, inside this time, and forced his numbed limbs into action.

When he moved, he moved quickly. He slipped down beside the bed and pulled her on top of him. As he held her in his arms, he reached out his right hand and ripped the cord of the lamp from the socket. He pleaded again, with hushed dread: 'Linda! Wake up! Don't bloody well die!'

'Mummy?' Karen stood bleary and dishevelled in the doorway.

'Go back to bed!'

The tears were immediate, and the harshness in Carl's voice sent her running.

Carl moved like a hunted animal now. He set Linda down gently on the floor beside the bed and began to crawl towards the landing. He reached out a hand to the banister rail and pulled himself up. He peered down into the hall, and then quickly ran downstairs. His hand flicked off the hall light. He pressed himself against the wall and breathed deeply for a moment. He craned his head forward to observe the kitchen. Who was out there? And what were they waiting for, goddammit! It was at least a minute since the shot. Perhaps this was just a warning. Perhaps they had gone now. Perhaps he should just stay where he was.

The thought of Linda, corpse-like on the bedroom floor, dragged his mind away from speculation. He had to go out. If they were gone, he had to know. He had to get help for Linda for God's sake. Move Carl. Do something quick.

He slipped noiselessly down the hall, hugging the wall for security. His hand moved to the inside pocket of his jacket and his fingers closed round the butt of his automatic pistol as he cautiously drew the lock on the back door. There was no sound from the garden.

He turned the handle silently and then pushed open the door.

Nothing.

He took half a step into the doorway and began to scan the garden. He was trembling: if the second shot was going to come, surely it would come now.

There was no shot; just a plaintive little voice, calling through the dew-filled air. 'Carl? . . . Carl?'

The fury in Carl was boiling as he ran to where Jo Jo was lying at the foot of the rockery. The younger boy was clutching at his left ankle and looking thoroughly sorry for himself. He attempted a half-hearted smile. 'Hallo, Carl,' he offered.

Carl bent down and wrenched him up by the shirt. 'What the hell's going on?' he demanded.

Jo Jo felt a stabbing pain in his ankle and tried to hop onto his right foot. 'You told me to keep an eye on the place, din't yer?' he blurted. 'I must of dropped off in the car. And I woke up when I heard the front door. And I din't know it was you, and I come round the back to have a butchers, and I had to climb over the soddin' wall, din't I? And I had it in me hand when I went arse over.' He motioned towards a gun that lay in the embrace of a geranium. 'Just went off,' he pleaded. 'I narf hurt me leg. I'm sorry.'

Carl pushed him off roughly, and said: 'Get out of here before the street's crawling with pigs.' He gestured to the gun. 'And take that thing with yer.'

Jo Jo watched disconsolately as Carl ran back into the house, and turned and cursed the wall.

In the house, the lights came on one by one.

Nine

Linda let the light gauze of net curtaining fall back into place at the bedroom window and turned to make her point.

'I was drinking,' she stated wearily, 'and I don't drink, do I?'

The question was not really begging an answer, and Kathy did not give one. Instead, she simply offered a small, all-purpose sort of nod, wriggled even deeper into the pillows behind her on the bed, and continued to flick distractedly through a copy of *Cosmopolitan*.

Linda continued: 'I was just trying to get rid of a headache, that's all.'

Kathy shot a furtive glance towards her sister. 'Sure,' she murmured, as she dipped her hand into the box of Terry's All Gold beside her. She prodded expertly for something with a nut in: her fingers read the piped patterns on top of each chocolate like brail. The high-calorie package flashed to her mouth unobserved when Linda returned her mesmeric stare to the window.

'Just trying to get rid of a headache . . .' Linda's voice trailed off. The headache had sliced through her like a knife when she had regained consciousness in the Accident and Emergency Unit; her senses had ebbed and flowed in a great brittle tide when she had felt Carl's hand

142

clasping hers; her entire body had felt bruised and distended by the dreadful pain trying to beat its way out.

She gazed out at the shimmering, liquid heat in the sunbaked garden. Even now, three days after 'that night', the dull throb inside still nagged at her to justify herself. 'Carl thinks I'm sick. He thinks I'm . . . sick. He says I must be having some kind of breakdown . . . otherwise, why would I try and kill meself.' A note of bitterness began to creep into her voice. 'So he thinks I should go to the quack once a week and get some pills to stop me taking pills.' She paused as a breath of wind made the mottled shadow of the pear tree dance on the lawn. Her lips clamped tightly together, and the thought crossed her mind that the weather had no right to be so cheerful.

'Of course,' she went on, 'it was all luvvy duvvy and "I thought I'd lost yer, darlin' "', till he started thinking I might of done it on purpose.' She turned sharply to see Kathy's incisors on the verge of victory over a caramel; the brail had failed her when she had been distracted by 'The Six Steps to Orgasm'. She flicked on quickly to hide her guilt. Lighting on a subject that seemed a lot closer to home she announced: 'Women's legs age slower than the rest of their bodies.' She peered down at the limbs which formed a bulky bridge between her feet and her pelvis. 'And I was looking forward to a change in that department,' she said mournfully.

Linda walked over and parked herself listlessly on the edge of the bed. Kathy let the magazine fall into her lap and gazed glumly at her. 'Why can't you just get on with things, Linda?'

'He's taken the kids today.'

'You need a rest – '

'He said he's gonna get a woman in to clean the house.' She tried to say it in a throwaway manner, but her voice

143

faltered, her head dropped, and a veil of hair tumbled across her cheek to hide the disquiet in her expression.

'You're bloody lucky, Linda.'

'Why?'

''Cos you can't even kill yerself proper!'

'Properly,' Linda corrected. 'Carl says I've gotta talk better.'

'You think I don't get fed up?' Kathy exclaimed. 'Stuck at home all day with Mum and Dad. Wiping his nose, doing all the chores, hearing her crying in the middle of the night. I feel bloody middle-aged, and no one gives me second-hand chewing gum – let 'lone all this.' She tossed the magazine aside and swept her eyes round the expensively furnished room. 'No one said it was gonna be perfect, Linda.'

Linda raised her head and said coldly: 'That's the trouble, Kathy. They did.'

'You're not gonna see Chris again are yer?'

'No.' Linda tossed the hair back from her face and forced out a smile. 'No, I'm not.' She reached for the box of chocolates.

Kathy quickly took up the magazine and buried her nose in it as Linda lifted the lid of the box and surveyed the ransacked selection.

'Kathy!'

The flying box struck the Cosmo Girl between the eyes. Kathy lowered the magazine and pronounced gravely: 'S'nerves. I'm suffering for yer, see.'

Linda laughed for the first time in three days and flopped down on the bed. She stared up at the ceiling, as her sister put an arm around her and pulled her close. For a fleeting moment, they retreated ten years.

'It wasn't like a film, Kathy. Not like we were made for each other, me and Chris,' said Linda softly. 'He uses words I don't understand, and he's always feeling sorry for himself . . . It's not that it was so right . . .' She closed her eyes, nestled against her sister's shoulder, and tried to shut out reality. But it didn't work.

'It's not that it was so right,' she repeated. 'It's just . . . that it's made everything else seem so wrong.'

Con stopped for a moment and considered the problem: four melting ice-creams in his two bony hands. The necklaces of droplets which were gathering round the lip of each cone looked dangerously close to dribbling down between his fingers. The prospect was offensive enough to sting him into action, and the tongue that launched a thousand metaphors snaked out to rescue his fastidiousness. The creamy liquid in his throat disgusted him. God, how he hated ice-cream.

He walked on, picking his way gingerly through the minefield of cooking bodies which littered the Lido area round Highbury Swimming Pool. He had removed his jacket, in deference to the flaming, mid-afternoon sun, but the starched, white shirt was still buttoned to the neck, and the pristine black trousers still seemed glued to his painfully thin legs.

Con rounded the corner of the shallow end of the pool and walked over to where Freddie lay sprawled on the worn grass. He stood for a moment and considered Freddie's bulky frame. He tut-tutted at the noticeable inflammation beneath the slick of tanning oil, and thought the overstretched cotton shorts a rather distasteful display of sexuality.

'Where are the little darlings now?' he asked in his best 'Camille'.

Freddie's eyes flickered open behind his Raybans. On cue, Nicky and Karen began to squeal with delight on the far side of the pool. Con looked round to see them tugging at their father's arms as he heaved himself out of the sparkling water.

Carl took the children by the hand and led them over to Con and Freddie. He nodded a silent acknowledgement and picked up a towel to dry himself.

'There you are, little boy. Little girl.' Karen happily accepted Con's offering, but Nicky stared up at him with a shadow of distrust.

'You licked it,' he accused correctly.

'Well, yes, I'm afraid I did.'

'Don't want it.'

Carl smiled as Nicky wandered off to join Karen, then he too looked down at Freddie and said: 'Swimming would take some of the air out of that spare tyre.'

Freddie glanced at the valley in his midriff, where the waistband of the shorts was cutting into his belly. He shrugged and changed the subject. 'Ain't you ever coming down the office again, Carl?'

'I'm looking after my kids.'

'Someone needs to shut Russell's whingeing up,' said Freddie. 'Two more of our places got done over last night.' He looked expectantly up at Carl.

'I ain't interested in that. You seen Broderick?'

Con decided that no one was going to relieve him of the remaining ice-creams, so he tossed them onto the paved surround of the pool – hoping some small child might slip on them and sustain a compound fracture at the very least. He settled down on the grass with Carl and Freddie.

'I spoke to him on the telephone,' said Con. 'Slater and Klein have made the union an offer they can't refuse. There was a ballot at lunch-time. They go back tomorrow.'

'Damn.'

'Why "damn", Carl?' Con's mouth stretched into his

quirky little smile. 'You should be happy. You've cost them thousands, and embarrassed them to boot. Isn't that what this little game is all about?'

'Where were you all weekend, Con?' Carl's voice was sharp. Con looked slightly flustered. It was not a question he had expected: he did not think his absence had been noticed.

'Oh . . . a sojourn in the country.' He paused for a moment, but found no reassurance in Carl's face. 'I am,' he continued, 'the servant of two masters.'

Freddie's head rose and he shot a look at Carl. 'Are yer?'

'Just for appearance sake,' Con countered. He saw the scepticism in his companions and decided it would be politic to expand. He reached back to a brown manilla envelope which lay on the grass behind Freddie. He offered the envelope to Carl. 'Klein had a little task for me.'

Carl gave a chuckle and a nod as he studied the five 8 x 10 photos the envelope contained. 'Oh deary me,' he sighed, and was about to pass the prints to Freddie when he spotted Nicky dangerously close to the edge of the pool.

'Nicky, come here,' he yelled.

Nicky turned, his face beaming. 'But Daddy,' he protested, 'it's Chris.'

Carl's eyes followed Nicky's outstretched arm to see Chris's head and shoulders bob under the water at the deep end.

Carl pushed himself up off the grass. He looked down at his lithe, tanned body, adjusted his swimming trunks, ran a hand through his hair, and then strode purposefully along the edge of the pool.

Chris surfaced at the pool wall. He gave a splutter and a cough as he reached out for support. He wiped a hand across his face and looked up. Carl stood above him; erect and self-consciously poised.

'Hi,' Carl said cheerily. 'You teach my kids, don't you?'

Chris looked round to see Nicky waving at the opposite end of the pool. 'Yes . . . yes, I do.'

'I just wanted to check,' said Carl, smiling intently.

Chris half expected a hand to reach out and assist his exit from the pool. Instead, Carl ended the exchange with an overblown politeness: 'Thank you very much.'

He walked back to Freddie and Con.

Con's curiosity for intrigue was uncontainable. 'What, may I ask, was all that about?'

'It was about nothing,' snarled Carl. 'It was private.'

'I'm sorry. I didn't mean to pry.'

'Like hell you didn't,' said Freddie.

Con judged himself unwelcome and got to his feet. 'I must be off to make my delivery.' He clutched the envelope to his chest.

'You don't have to run away so fast, Con,' said Carl as he lay back and closed his eyes against the glare. 'Take yer shirt off. Get some sun, man.'

'Good heavens no!' Con shrieked with affected horror. 'The sun is the reward of the working class. I don't wish to be exposed to it.'

The two boys paid Con no further attention as he backed away. They did not see him take the monogrammed handkerchief from his pocket to dab his perspiring forehead.

They did not see the sneer on his face.

Carl stayed at the pool until Chris left. Then he quickly gathered up the children and returned to Cranley Gardens. As he entered the house he heard the sound of the TV drifting down from the main bedroom. He assumed the same air of collected superiority he had used on Chris, and went upstairs.

148

Linda's concentration on the Australian soap opera did not waver when Carl strode into the bedroom. In his turn he, too, made no concession to her presence. He undressed slowly, near the window. He was sure that it was within her peripheral vision. He stood for a moment, naked. He raised his arms and stretched, and then walked into the shower.

When Carl returned to the room, Linda was still frozen in the same position on the bed, but the clothes he had discarded on his return had been picked up and placed, neatly folded, on a chair.

He dressed: white cotton trousers and a royal-blue polo shirt. He checked his appearance in the dressing-table mirror, and went over to the clothes, folded on the chair. He tugged the jeans he had been wearing earlier from the base of the pile, and the items on top tumbled onto the floor. He took some change from the jeans pocket, and then dropped them beside the chair.

He said nothing. She said nothing. He left.

He arrived at Broderick's flat in Bow at half past four. Broderick arrived at five. It was not the lunch-time strike ballot that had delayed him at the depot; that had been quick and painless. The seven-card-stud school in the mechanics canteen had proved less predictable. Lady Luck had been a full-blown bitch this time.

Broderick slouched along the graffiti-decorated corridor and reached in his pocket for his front-door key. It was not hard to find; there was nothing else in there.

The key was unnecessary. The door was ajar. Broderick's pulse quickened as he stepped nervously into the flat.

He sucked in his breath and surveyed the hall with pained disbelief. The lovingly nurtured plants had been torn from their pots and strewn across the floor, the

149

pictures ripped from the walls; shattered crockery and glass spilled out from the kitchen.

'I'm through here, Mr B.,' Carl's voice sang.

Broderick wrenched his numbed body across the hall and slid open the door to the living-room. The destruction was complete. Anything which could have been ripped up, torn down, smashed or overturned had been.

Carl sat with his feet up on the sofa; an immaculately groomed island of calm in the ruins.

'What are you looking for?' Broderick whispered, defeated.

'Something you haven't given me yet, Mr B.' Carl swung his legs off the sofa and stood. 'Oh, I know it's not here. I knew that before I come in . . . this is just a free sample.'

'I don't want any more,' pleaded Broderick.

'You're not getting any more, Mr B. The game's just changed. You work for nothing now.'

'What?'

'Well, you wouldn't want me to tell Slater and Klein what you done . . . I could . . . I got nothing to lose. Unlike you.'

The last vestige of self-respect drained from Broderick and he sank to his knees. His body lurched forward as he clamped his hands over his face and began to sob.

Carl picked his way through the debris and stood over the pathetic, trembling figure. 'You walked right into it. Don't cry, Mr B.'

'I don't s'pose you've got kids,' Broderick howled.

Carl squatted down beside him. 'I don't care what you "suppose",' he said, swollen with victory and full of charm. 'You said it yerself, Mr B.: you were meant to be incorruptible. But you got corrupted. I think that's disgusting.' He paused to pick a splinter of china from his sock.

150

'But don't you fret too much,' he continued. 'I'm not gonna ask you to do nothing too difficult. In fact, you could do it with yer eyes closed . . . in fact, there you go . . . do it with yer eyes closed . . . if it makes you feel any beter.'

After a few seconds' silence, Broderick croaked out in a timid voice: 'What do you want me to do?'

Five minutes later, Carl left Broderick fumbling through the wreckage of his life.

Carl drove impatiently through the heavy rush-hour traffic of Holloway Road, and arrived home uncomfortably hot.

As he marched down the hall to the kitchen, he noticed Linda, curled up on the sofa in the living-room. The kids were playing on the floor in front of her; she was still in her nightdress.

Carl opened the fridge and took out a Budweiser. He rolled the frosted metal can over his cheeks and forehead, smiled at the reviving *hiss* as he pulled the ring, and drank down a long, icy mouthful of the beer.

He glanced at his watch, tightened his grasp on the can, and called out: 'Why ain't you ready, Linda?'

Her voice wavered along the hall. 'Carl . . . Carl, I think Nicky's got another summer cold coming on – '

'He's been fine all day.'

'No . . . I think he must . . . look, why don't you go, and I'll stay here . . .'

She faltered, and the unease in her voice was reflected on her face when she saw Carl in the doorway of the living-room. She had seen the shadow of menace over his eyes before.

'Please, Carl . . .' said Linda shakily.

'I . . . am . . . royally . . . sick . . . of . . . this.' He hammered each word home as he crossed to the sofa and grabbed her wrist.

151

'No, please – ' she moaned, as he wrenched her from the sofa. Nicky and Karen remained motionless on the floor. The tears began to well up in their eyes.

Carl dragged Linda roughly out to the hall and up the stairs. Her free arm flapped against the banister and she let out a cry of pain. He ignored it, and pulled her on to the bedroom. He shoved her down onto the bed, moved to the bank of wardrobes and threw open the doors.

Linda tried to sit up. She shook her head wretchedly and closed her arms tightly across her breasts. A vast, mute tremor shook her body. Carl yanked a dress from a hanger and tossed it unceremoniously at her. 'You put that on.'

A second dress flew at her.

'Or that.'

A third.

'Or that.'

He slammed shut the wardrobes, turned, and stared at her. 'For the first time in my life,' he fumed, 'I don't give a shit what you look like. But you are my wife, and you are gonna be there.'

The dinner at Bridie's was meandering tortuously towards its conclusion. Karen and Nicky sat obedient and quiet at one end of the table. Linda sat obedient and quiet, sandwiched between them and Carl. While Connie and Alan poked their way through bowls of fruit salad, Bridie looked down from the head of the table with the same benign, glazed expression she had worn for two hours.

Carl gazed at his mother and wondered whether her face was beginning to ache. Connie felt compelled to break the awkward silence. 'This really is very tasty, Mother,' she said with all the surprised generosity of someone who had expected it to taste like manure.

'Very nice,' chirped Alan. 'And I'm not a sweet freak.'

152

Carl just managed to suppress a giggle. Everyone knew Alan was not a 'sweet freak', and during the course of this meal they had also discovered that he was 'suspicious of soups' and 'just a teensy bit picky when it comes to pork'.

'Have you ever tried making it with fresh fruit, Mother?' Connie was not one to give an unqualified compliment. 'We find it just that touch more refreshing, don't we, Alan?'

Bridie shook her head, seemingly unconcerned that her dessert would not pass muster in the more mock-Georgian parts of Harlow. Alan could not say anything except 'Whoops', as a trickle of syrup escaped from his over-packed mouth, slid down his chin, and was smeared on the back of his hand. Considering that he was 'not really a big pudding fan', the Del Monte and evaporated milk seemed to be going down rather well.

Alan's lapse in 'New Town' etiquette did not go unpunished. Connie's head jerked round a few degrees and her lips snapped shut like a handbag. The effect this had on her face had already been described by Carl earlier in the meal: 'More pinched than a waitress's arse.'

Alan felt the dagger. His sticky hand slid off the table slowly, and rested on his thigh. Connie's concern did not stretch to her husband's trousers: they were an 'easy wash poly-cotton mix', and had been bought for him to eat in.

Carl picked up a bottle of red wine and reached across to Alan. 'Alan?'

Alan's hand re-surfaced, cleaner, and eased his glass towards the bottle.

'Alan. Driving,' cautioned Connie. Alan quickly withdrew the glass, as Carl began to pour. The wine splashed onto the white linen cloth in an untidy wound. Connie's hand flew to the salt.

'Many a slip,' said Bridie calmly.

153

But Connie was not amused. Thank God it hadn't happened in front of other members of staff! 'What did I tell you, Alan?'

'Let the man have a drink, Connie,' said Bridie.

Connie tossed her head disapprovingly at this sanctioning of excess. Alan hesitated for a moment and then pushed his glass back across the table. Carl filled it.

'We will drink to the family,' announced Bridie.

'What there is left of it,' Connie muttered.

'Linda?' Bridie's voice dragged Linda out of her daze.

'Huh?' Linda looked up from her dessert. 'I'm sorry, Bridie. The family.' They raised their glasses and drank.

'Not quite with us tonight, Linda?' said Connie.

'Don't worry 'bout it, Connie.'

Connie was determined to worry about it. 'Must have a lot on your mind, poor thing.'

The words 'po-faced cow' were on Linda's mind. She thought better of it and turned her attention to the children. 'Eat it, Nicky; don't play with it.' Carl took up the attack on her behalf.

'You still trying for kids, or is it too late, Alan?'

Connie spat back before the question mark had dried: 'Yes we are, and no it's not.'

'Some top medical men have gone into it,' Alan offered.

'But Alan,' said Carl, fighting back the laughter, 'you're the one who's s'posed to go into it.'

Connie's spoon crashed down into her fruit salad. Alan was confused. 'No, no,' he elaborated, 'you see, they've discovered that Connie is allergic to my sperm.'

'Alan!' Connie's lips pursed together so tightly that it looked as if she was trying to suck her own nose down her throat.

Linda diplomatically despatched the children to the kitchen.

'I was only telling them, Connie,' whispered Alan.

'Well, it's not exactly suitable for the dinner table!'

Carl could no longer contain himself, and an enormous guffaw burst out.

'Oh go on, little boy,' chided Connie. 'Isn't it funny?'

He was helpless. 'Yeah!'

Connie pressed on: 'It's all right for you. You want babies, you get 'em.'

'Hang on a minute,' Linda interrupted. But Connie was unstoppable.

'You want anything, you get it. You take it. You always have.' She turned angrily to her mother. 'He always has. He should know what it's like to suffer.'

'When have you ever suffered, Connie?' said Bridie.

'I'm suffering now,' she replied quietly. 'Internally.'

Alan caught sight of the conversation, somewhere in the far distance. 'You said not to talk about that.'

'Oh, shut up, Alan. Thanks to you, they all know.'

'S'not my fault, Connie.'

'Isn't it, Alan? Isn't it? Just my luck to pick a husband who's firing blanks. And don't say "S'not" . . . meant to be a teacher, aren't you?'

An uneasy silence settled on them again: the storm seemed to have blown itself out. Carl's amusement lingered as a slight quiver in his lower lip.

Alan felt his colon grumbling and adjusted his position to avoid an unpleasant development. He sensed that everyone was looking at him, and felt obliged to speak.

'We should be off soon. It's quite a tricky drive back to Harlow, you know.'

'Is it, Alan?' asked Carl, sensing a further bout of hysteria just round the corner.

'Oh yes,' Alan continued sagely. 'Some said the M25 would make life easier, but I've always been an A10 and turn off at Broxbourne man myself.'

155

'You're boring people again,' Connie said quietly.

'The real fly in that ointment of course is the B194 at Lower Nazing – '

'We couldn't care less, Alan!'

'I could,' piped up Carl.

'Shut up!' Connie snapped.

Bridie pushed her bowl wearily to one side. 'Why can't you two act like brother and sister?'

''Cos it takes all his energy to behave like a human being!'

'Snob,' Carl retorted.

As hostilities seemed on the verge of full-scale resumption, fate, in the shape of Alan's dicky digestion, took a hand. The hapless geography teacher was propelled from his chair by an enormous fart. Everyone stared at him as he stood, trying to camouflage his mishap with a fit of coughing. Connie's embarrassment was complete: she had not felt so blighted since the time she had returned to the headmaster's dinner table with her frock tucked in the back of her knickers.

'A toast!' Alan almost shrieked. His hand shot to his glass, and suddenly he felt confident that he could turn the incident into the high point of the evening. 'A toast everyone. Come on now, glasses full.' He smiled down at Connie. 'Come on, Connie. I know you're not big on Beaujolais, but muck in. That's it.' They all stood, raised their glasses, and looked expectantly at Alan. He paused for a moment, then raised his glass and announced solemnly: 'To the birthday boy we all miss. To Mark.'

Alan hesitated, with the glass at his lips, as he saw the stare of disbelief. Bridie gently set her glass down on the table and left the room. 'Well, that's why we're all here, isn't it?' Alan queried. 'Twenty-one today?'

'Oh God,' breathed Linda, as she walked out after Bridie.

'Isn't that why we're here?' asked Alan again, puzzled.

Connie's face soured, and then went off completely as she sank back down on her seat. 'Yes, Alan,' she said coldly, 'but it didn't need to be mentioned.'

'He's dead, Alan,' added Carl tersely, and then drained his glass and walked out to the hall.

Carl popped his head round the kitchen door to see Karen and Nicky. Karen sat at the table, watching her younger brother struggling to open a plastic, one-litre bottle of Coke.

'Where's Nana?'

Karen shrugged and then flinched as the bottle dropped to the floor, spilling out a pool of caramel-coloured liquid.

'Why din't you do that for him?' barked Carl. 'Now clear it up.' Nicky laughed at his father's unkindness.

When Carl reached the top of the stairs he saw that the door to Bridie's room was open, and that there was no one inside. He walked on to the end of the landing, and eased open the door to Mark's old room.

He was met by the inconstant gleam from fifty candles. The white, Formica-clad bed-side unit stood in the centre of the room and Bridie was kneeling before it. Relics of her dead son had been arranged on top of this MFI shrine: a black and white photo; a silver Walkman; a white handkerchief; a crimson Swiss Army knife; a tattered, brown stuffed monkey.

Linda stood back against the far wall; a frightened, uncomprehending stare flickered on her face. She glanced up when Carl entered the room. Bridie too, sensed his presence, but she did not avert her eyes from the remnants of Mark's life.

'I wanted a memorial service for him at the church, Carl,' she said in a hushed, cracked voice, 'but they wouldn't have it. They couldn't fit God's poor dead child in.' Carl listened in silence, but the agitation in him was beginning to well up. 'The devil can take away our church, Carl, but faith is buried deep in the heart of us. It will always seek a place for prayer. This is my church now. Come and pray with me in my church, Carl . . . for your brother's soul.'

Carl walked to the centre of the room and circled where Bridie knelt. He looked down at Mark's possessions with mounting disgust. He reached out and prodded at the items. 'This gonna bring him back? Or this? Or this maybe?' He plucked up the monkey.

'Pray with me, Carl,' Bridie pleaded.

'What exactly we meant to do with this?' Carl dangled the toy in front of Bridie's face and then took the knife from the top of the unit and opened the largest blade. 'We meant to slit it open!' His voice rose to a shout as the blade of the knife sliced into the belly of the monkey, and a cloud of pastel-coloured foam stuffing showered down on the shrine.

'We meant to look for some goddammed sign in its guts!' he roared. The disembowelled toy flapped in his hand. Bridie raised her eyes and then snatched it from him. She placed it carefully back on the white unit. The blade of the knife glinted in Carl's hand.

Bridie rose from her knees. She reached out and took the blade between her fingers. Carl loosened his grip. Bridie leaned over and placed the knife next to the monkey. Then she returned her stare to Carl. Their eyes met in steely confrontation for several seconds before her hand cracked across his face.

He said nothing to her. Instead, he looked over to Linda. 'Let's go.' Linda moved to the door, and Carl took her by the arm and led her down the stairs.

Bridie did not watch them go. She kneeled before the shrine, clasped her hands together, and began to pray.

'Our Father, who art in Heaven, who art in everything,
158

and in Heaven with Mark, give us food for pain, and lead us not into temptation, and give us this bread, and daily bread, and amen . . . and lead us. Amen. Amen.'

George Klein had been sitting in the same spot for over an hour. He had resolved very little. If anything, the knot in his brain seemed to be pulling tighter.

The anger had erupted immediately after he had slammed his front door on Con's smug face and ripped the photos from the envelope. He had rampaged round his house in Stamford Hill, screaming abuse at the walls. He had swept the collection of photos from the top of his cherished, unplayed grand piano. He had searched out and destroyed letters he had written to Pat; he had ripped her clothes from drawers and wardrobes, and had strewn them over the furniture and floors.

After about ten minutes, the fury had given way to a deep, brooding melancholy. He had grabbed the bottle of Famous Grouse, gone up to the bedroom, and sunk down on the pink velvet-covered stool in front of the dressing-table.

And that was where he still sat. His hand gripped the neck of the bottle of Scotch. He looked at his weary, drawn reflection in the mirror of the dressing-table, and he saw the toll the alcohol had taken. The photos lay in an untidy pile between Opium and Joy. He drifted back to the first night he had met Pat: the Tangerine Suite in Walthamstow. What a hole that was! His head filled with the remembrance of the sickly, cheap scent she had worn that night; how it had made him sneeze when he snuggled up to the nape of her neck; how Tony had spelled out the word 'Chanel', and told him where he could buy it. . . .

George forced the nostalgia from his head. He wanted to smash those expensive French perfumes. They were the accessories to her crime.

He took the photo from the top of the pile and studied it with disgust. Her face was only inches from Slater's, moving towards it, her tongue moistening her lips to kiss him. And Slater, intoxicated with her smell, animal, devouring, ready to take her, and close his teeth on the pale flesh of her neck, and smile at the pain of her nails scoring his back, and force his cock up the unfaithful bitch and . . .

His powerful hands tore them apart, and scattered the shredded photo on the floor.

Within the hour George Klein was striding across the plush carpet of the lounge in the Park Tower Hotel. His resolve was strengthened; his intent was soberly clear. His objective was the neat circle of softly upholstered sofas in the centre of the room.

Dot Fleming looked up from her magazine and smiled when she saw George standing before her.

'I've been thinking 'bout it,' he said.

'I only have five minutes, George,' she urged. 'Your nice Mr Jamieson is expecting me for dinner at The Caprice.'

'And I've made a decision,' he added definitively.

She glanced round the lounge, and then at her watch. 'Perhaps we better just step up to my room.'

Ten

Two weeks after the dinner at Bridie's, July slipped
unnoticed into August. The sun continued to beat down
uncharacteristically. The dazzling yellow flowers of the
hypericum in Carl and Linda's garden burst open each
morning, only to wither in the space of the same day.
They were not the only casualties in the garden.

Linda stood for a moment and surveyed the wilting
blooms. It occurred to her that they needed watering. She
could not be bothered to perform the task. The garden
held no pleasure for her; the wall which stretched round
it only emphasized the depressing confines of the house.
She did not feel the 'privacy', emphasized by the estate
agent: that wall could not stop the sound of traffic; the
industrial yawn of the waking city; the sirens.

She abandoned her grey reverie, reached down to the
laundry basket at her feet, and took out another damp
item to peg onto the clothes line.

She had seen little of Carl recently. She had almost got
used to it; learned how to cope with her isolation. When
they had met – late at night or early in the morning – they
had spoken little, seldom touched, and asked no questions. They made a conscious effort to occupy different
spaces, and performed their individual tasks individually.

The incidence of him staying out all night had
increased. The 'woman to clean the house' had not

materialized, and if she knocked on the door now, she would have to spill something before there was anything to clean. Linda had turned all her efforts to sanitization. She still hated that house.

She heard the children protesting in the hall as Carl called them to order. The job of taking Karen and Nicky to school was no longer entrusted to Linda. Any pang of resentment she might have felt was cut short by the ring of the phone.

'Can you get that, Carl?' She looked back to the house, but the ringing continued. 'Carl? You getting that?' The answer was the slam of the front door. Linda dropped an armful of white T-shirts back into the laundry basket and hurried into the house. She picked up the portable phone in the kitchen and extended the aerial. 'Hallo?'

'Hallo?' It was Chris's voice. 'Hallo? Linda?'

In a silence which lasted ten seconds, the false equilibrium which had settled on Linda in the past fortnight collapsed like a house of cards.

'Hallo? . . . Linda?'

'Yes. Hallo.'

'I know I shouldn't have called you there, but I had to speak to you.'

Her fingers clawed at the spotless counter-top. How could he still sound so calmly persuasive? Why couldn't he see how she'd cleaned that house; scrubbed every last corner? Couldn't he accept that she'd learned to be bored rather than anxious? Couldn't he just understand why she'd abandoned expectations and filled her life with numb emptiness?

'How have you been?' he asked.

'Errr . . . terrible really, in a way.'

'Yeah.'

What did that mean? Was he just ringing to punish her? 'How 'bout you?'

162

'Well, OK . . .' he replied. 'Well . . . you know . . . Can I see you?'

He had ripped up the rug, and she felt the cloud of grime it concealed settling on her.

'Chris, I can't. Please.'

'I'm going away, Linda. Tomorrow. Back up north. I just . . . Can I see you?'

'I can't . . .'

'I have to see you, Linda,' he pressed. 'Don't you think you owe me that?'

She knew she owed him something, but she could no longer distinguish whether it was pain or happiness.

'Will this be the last time, Chris?'

'Is that what you want?'

'I just want a bit of . . . peace.'

But she went to Highbury Fields, as he had asked.

They sat opposite each other on the bleached grass. She looked up at the angry welt which inflamed his cheek. His expression was governed by the appearance of the injury, not the pain. Now, more than ever, he bore the look of a demanding child. See what you've done to me, Mummy.

'I'm so sorry,' she murmured, and bowed her head again.

Chris was pleased by that opening, and quickly reinforced her perception of him as the 'injured' party. 'Carl might not be responsible,' he said. 'Whoever the gentleman was, I'm not sure he had his heart in it . . . could've been anyone, Linda.' He paused to let her guilt seep deeper.

'It's not that bad . . . It's not why I'm going, Linda.'

'What will you do up there?'

'There's no work in Manchester. I'll probably go back to college, if I can get a grant.'

163

'Can't be a student all yer life. Gotta think of the future.'

'I don't see much future anywhere,' he replied dourly. That was the first truthful contribution he had made to the conversation. 'At least up there, I've got a past,' he continued. 'I can look at things and say "Hasn't it changed? Things ain't what they used to be." Least up there, I can have a good moan. I'm tired of this place, these people, this time.'

Linda raised her eyes to him, and tried to offer comfort: 'All those meetings you go to, all those good causes . . . you'll meet lots of people. Lots of women . . . and they'll all be a lot cleverer than me – '

'I don't want them. Come with me, Linda?'

'I can't – '

'I know you can't. I even know why you can't.' He watched her hands pluck nervously at the grass. 'I know you can't . . . but just do it!' He sensed the tightening in her chest, and the flutter in her breathing. He recognized 'crisis' when he saw it, and used it mercilessly to justify his own inadequacy. 'Christ, I love you, Linda! It's not a crush or a fancy, or something stupid. It's a great big bloody love! Come with me.'

'I can't, Chris – '

'Why don't you just lie to me, Linda? Why don't you look me in the face now, and say you'll be there at Euston Station tomorrow morning, with the kids and a bag? Why don't you just let me walk away from you now, and feel bloody over-the-moon happy? Why won't you let me be that happy for twenty-four hours, Linda? Is that too difficult?'

She stared at him. She bit hard on her lip, searching for a physical pain to banish the mental battering.

'You don't even think you have a choice,' shrugged

Chris. 'You really are one of feminism's failures, aren't you?'

She looked at him, uncomprehending. He stood, considered for a moment, and manufactured the uncharitable wisdom of one who feels himself wrongfully rejected. 'You've built your love on waste ground, Linda.'

He saw a suitable lack of understanding in her eyes, and he began to walk away. 'Never mind,' he muttered patronizingly, 'it doesn't really matter.'

Linda sat there on the grass for another ten minutes. She thought about the washing she had left in the laundry basket. She reminded herself to go round and check on Marty's father.

She felt trapped in the sun like an actress in a spotlight, and she did not know the lines. She prayed for a cloud to take away the accusing glare.

Broderick looked anxiously out of the window of the Angel office. His eyes darted along the line of traffic which was creeping down City Road at a funereal pace. He made a small sound of nervous agitation as he saw a motorcycle policeman arrive to unclog the bottle-neck.

'I hope no one bloody followed me,' he said tersely.

Carl and Con looked up from their seats at the conference table. A dozen photocopied documents were spread neatly before them.

'Someone did follow yer, Mr B.,' Carl stated calmly.

'What!' Broderick swung away from the exposure of the window.

'Someone followed yer,' Carl continued, 'to make sure nobody followed yer.' Carl smiled at the alarm he had caused, and then returned his attention to the documents. Broderick took his courage in both hands and marched across to the table.

'Now look,' he said, trying to appear forceful, 'I don't

see what else I can do. I've given you copies of all the transport contracts we've dealt with in the last three months. Klein's gonna get suspicious if he catches me lifting files again.'

'He caught yer?' Carl queried.

'Last night. Round ten o'clock. There wasn't anyone in the despatch office: I reckoned it'd be safe. But he come in.'

'What did you say to him?' asked Con.

'He crept up on me – I almost jumped out me bloody skin. I told him I was just trying to get rid of some of the backlog that built up in the strike. Said I was taking some stuff to work on at home.'

'And he believed yer?' Carl demanded.

'I think so. He was drunk. He started on 'bout how he understood why I did what I did at the meeting, and how a good man'll always fight for his job and his dignity, and how us old 'uns have to stick together. He even said he's gonna try and get Slater off me back.'

'So what you complaining 'bout?' laughed Carl.

'He's not that stupid. I told yer; he was drunk and it was easy to get out of that time. I can't keep doing it.'

'Did he log any of these jobs himself?' said Con.

Broderick leaned across the table and studied the documents. 'Yes. That one.'

Con read the name from the top of the booking order: 'East London Import Services?'

'There's nothing unusual 'bout that,' Broderick countered, 'they're old clients: he's always handled them.' Con raised his eyebrows slightly and gave Carl a look which demanded privacy.

'That'll be all for now, Mr Broderick,' said Carl. 'We'll be in touch.'

'I hope not.' Broderick turned and walked quickly to the door. Carl's voice interrupted his swift exit.

'Just one more thing, Mr B.' Broderick felt his knuckles whiten as he gripped hard on the door handle. 'Does George Klein get drunk a lot?'

'Only when his wife's playing him up. That's no secret.'

Carl nodded and Broderick snatched at his chance to escape. Con chuckled as the door closed. 'You got something?' Carl asked eagerly.

'Oh I think so,' Con replied, and his face broke into a self-satisfied grin. 'You no doubt recall, I told you how affectionate Klein was towards Bobby Chalker? Much more than Slater was.' He slid his chair back from the table, got up and began to pace the room like a predatory barrister about to pounce on a weeping witness. 'Slater would launder the odd wad of dirty money for Chalker,' he expanded, 'but for any other favours, Chalker had to go to Klein. And occasionally, we needed legitimate-looking transport for illegitimate purposes. And Klein obliged. Of course, he didn't want Slater to know – he'd go spare – so it was always logged in a false name. Always the same name.' He paused.

'East London Import Services!' Carl exclaimed in triumph.

'Exactly. East London Import Services does not exist, Bobby's long deceased, yet here it is again.'

'So whad'you reckon?'

'That Klein hasn't got much imagination. And, that's why he automatically thought of the name he always used when he was up to something underhand that he didn't want Slater to know about.'

A tremor of excitement swept through Carl. 'What the hell's he playing at, Con?' Con returned to the table and took up the three stapled pages that related to East London Import Services.

'Well, it says here that they have a lorry booked, the second Friday in each month, for the next three months.

Starting on the eleventh of August.' He worked his mouth into a smile of sadistic delight. 'That's the end of next week.'

'The end of next week,' echoed Carl. 'Now I wonder what's gonna be in those lorries.'

'There's one sure way to find out,' said Con.

Eleven

Carl's hand wiped away the condensation from the centre of the bathroom mirror, and he admired his clean-shaven face. For most Londoners, the last week had dragged in the slow torture of soaking humidity and broken, sweating nights. But for Carl, it had flashed past with breathtaking speed. The passing of each day pushed him closer to his obsession: to settle with George Klein for the injustice that man had perpetrated. The eleventh of August was marked in glowing, neon letters in Carl's mind.

He left the bathroom and dressed with all his usual care. If anything, he had become more precise, more fastidious, more consciously self-disciplined, since Broderick had delivered the tell-tale document. Above all, he had become more single-minded: the target was in sight now, and everything else had become secondary. Russell's repeated warnings that the East End protection was continuing to erode were only garbled whispers in Carl's ears. The other boys were swept along in the wake of Carl's ambition.

He looked over to Linda. She was still in bed, with her eyes firmly closed. Carl knew she was awake: she had taken to 'sleeping late', to avoid the anguish of seeing her children taken away from her each morning. Carl called out to her: 'You'll have to take the kids in this morning.

I've got business.' He did not wait for a reply; he knew she had heard.

He trotted down the stairs, took his keys from the table in the hall and made for the door. The phone rang. He made a detour to the living-room and snatched up the receiver. 'Hallo,' he said brusquely.

'I'm sorry, I know it's terribly early, but I was hoping to arrange a meeting with you, Mr Galton.' Carl did not recognize the woman's soft, West Coast accent. 'I represent – '

'Go stick a pin in another bit of the phone book, love,' he cut her off. 'I don't want none.' He slammed down the phone, annoyed at the stranger's intrusion. He flicked on the answering machine and walked out into the already-simmering Tuesday morning.

Carl drove down through Holloway and Highbury, moving quickly against the steadily increasing tide of rush-hour traffic. He followed the Balls Pond Road to Dalston, continued along Dalston Lane, and then turned into Amhurst Road. He reached Clapton Square by half past eight. He parked the Porsche at the top of the square, behind a skip which was overflowing with the debris from 'yuppie' restoration. He walked the last hundred yards to Clapton Mews.

'Mews' seemed an inappropriately grand title for the narrow, cobbled alley of lock-ups. But Carl reassured himself that the yuppies in the square would soon be wheeling their double pushchairs down here, and speculating how nice these little boxes could be, painted white, with hanging baskets of geraniums outside. Perhaps he had inherited something worthwhile from Bobby Chalker after all.

Carl reached a lock-up near the bottom of the mews. The spray-canned number on the large wooden doors was the only thing which distinguished it from all the others.

170

Carl gave a ra-ta-tat-tat bang on the door. A few seconds later, the door swung open and Jo Jo's face smiled out.

The only light in the lock-up came from a grimy casement window, set in the sloping, corrugated roof. The ungenerous interior was almost completely filled by the rusting hulk of an ancient-looking Ford Transit. Carl edged his way along the side of the vehicle and saw Freddie, Russell and Mario gathered round a map set on an upturned tea-chest. Their faces were tense and expectant. Carl surveyed the group, smiled, and congratulated himself for being so conspicuously over-dressed.

'The runt thinks we're breaking out of Colditz,' jibed Freddie. Carl turned to inspect Jo Jo closely. The boy was wearing a pair of oil-stained overalls which were four sizes too big, and what looked like a thick, black, woolly hat. He was sweating profusely. Carl shook his head slightly, but was determined to waste no more time. He moved to the tea-chest and looked down at the map. London lay spread out below him.

'Right, this is what we do,' he said, as his index finger descended on the City. 'Slater and Klein's depot opens on the main road here. This is Murry Street. The solicitors' on the corner of Tower Bridge Road's got a plate glass window. We can park 'bout twenty-five feet back and watch for the dodgy lorry to leave without being seen ourselves.'

'How do we know which one it is?' said Russell, unconvinced. Carl shot him a withering look.

'Broderick says it's the first one out.'

'What if it's not?' Russell challenged, being deliberately difficult.

'What if pigs piss champagne, Russ?' snapped Carl. He returned his attention to the map and continued. 'Broderick says it's booked to go out at six a.m. on Friday morning. We rendezvous at the office at five. Jo Jo drives

171

the tank with Mario.' He glanced up at the Transit. 'We're behind in Freddie's car. We follow the lorry. OK?'

Freddie, Jo Jo, and Mario nodded, but Russell looked quizzically at Carl. 'Excuse me for being a thick nigger,' he said, 'but . . . what's the plan, master?'

Carl did not need to refer to the map. He continued: 'The lorry makes its pick-up. We follow it till it gets somewhere quiet. Then Jo Jo overtakes, brakes hard, and we close in behind. We get out of our vehicles, Russ, poke a shooter down the driver's throat, and we ask him nicely if he'll open the back. Depending what's in it, we smash it up or nick it.'

Russell stared incredulously. 'Ain't that rather . . . basic?'

'Yeah,' said Carl, 'I s'pose it is.'

'It's foolproof!' gasped Jo Jo.

Something was bothering Mario. Not much did, but when it did, it was obvious. His face contorted, out of proportion with the problem. 'Don't we have to change the plates on that thing?'

'This ain't a telly programme, Mar,' sighed Carl. 'We din't nick it; we bought it. Least, someone we made up bought it. Let's see if the bugger still goes, shall we?'

'All right!' Jo Jo's enthusiasm swelled further. He reached up to the woolly hat and tugged at the roll of material. The others stared at him in disbelief as his head was swathed in a complete balaclava, with only two small holes for the eyes.

'Jo Jo?' said Carl quietly.

'Yeah?'

'We're about a hundred yards from a main road.'

'Yeah.'

'A main road in the middle of London.'

'Yeah.'

'A great big city with lots of people in, Jo Jo.'

172

'Yeah.'

'Now we're only doing this to see if you can find the gears. We don't want to draw attention to ourselves, do we?'

'No. Carl?'

'Yes, Jo Jo.'

'Lemme get this right. I pull in in front of the lorry.'

'Yes, Jo Jo.'

'Then I stop. Quick, like.'

'Yes, Jo Jo.'

'What if it hits me?'

'You are gonna use your skill and judgement to make sure it don't. Otherwise, you will be deaded.' Freddie snorted with laugher. 'Now let's shift it,' ordered Carl, peeling the wool up over Jo Jo's eyes.

Mario scrambled dutifully to open the wooden doors, while Freddie and Jo Jo jumped up into the front of the Transit. Jo Jo adjusted the rear-view mirror. Behind him, in the lock-up, he saw that Russell had taken Carl to one side. He turned to Freddie. 'Con was right 'bout Russ,' he said, hushed.

'Do what?' Freddie was more concerned with finding another foot of seat-belt to stretch round him.

'Old Irish,' Jo Jo emphasized, 'he was right 'bout Russell. Said he was a proper Sandra. He is. Right old whining Sandra.'

'He said he was a proper Cassandra, you dip shit.'

'Well, same thing, innit?' Jo Jo looked pensive. 'Who is she anyway, this Cassandra?'

'I dunno,' Freddie said impatiently. 'Some bird, I s'pose.'

Jo Jo glanced behind again. 'Come on,' he urged. Freddie reached over to the ignition and turned on the engine.

'Don't worry 'bout 'em, Jo Jo. Let's just get the bloody

173

thing out into the street, eh?' Jo Jo stamped his foot down on the accelerator and separated Carl and Russell with a cloud of carbon monoxide.

'Steady on!' Freddie roared.

Jo Jo looked unrepentant. 'Just getting her warmed up a bit.'

'She's warm. Now just get her out. And, Jo Jo,' Freddie warned, 'be bloody careful: she's sharp in first.'

Jo Jo ground half an inch from the cogs of third and reverse, before he eventually turned to Freddie for assistance. Freddie eased the gear stick into first, cocked his granite jaw, and shook his head.

Jo Jo's face was a study in concentration as he eased his foot off the clutch millimetre by millimetre.

'Give her a chance,' urged Freddie. Jo Jo gave her more than that. He raised his left foot and the Transit shot out into the mews. Freddie's hand flew to the gearstick and dragged it into neutral, but it was too late; neither of Jo Jo's panic-stricken feet could find the brake, and with a shuddering crash, the Transit found the wall opposite.

Freddie clutched at his stomach, where the seat-belt had cut into him. Half a pound of bacon, four sausages, and three fried eggs were looking for a way out. He smiled at Jo Jo with the sincerity of the Mona Lisa after a six-hour sitting. Jo Jo was shaking, but, as usual, he tried to make the best of his inadequacy. 'Well,' he said, 'least we know she goes.'

'Yep,' Freddie replied. 'Now let's see if she goes backwards, shall we?'

She did go backwards. She jolted all round Clapton. The insurrection in Freddie's stomach did not calm down until he was sitting in the passenger seat of Carl's Porsche, powering smoothly back to the office at the Angel.

'You reckon he's gonna hack it?' said Carl.

Freddie gave his usual, non-committal shrug. 'Let him take it out again tomorrow. See how it goes.'

'You two are priceless, man.'

'Bollocks. I'll dance on the stupid sod's grave.'

Carl pulled up outside the office. The Transit had beaten them back. He glanced up to the third floor. 'What the hell's going on here?' Freddie followed Carl's look and saw Jo Jo waving frantically at the window.

'Got his first erection?'

'I don't think so, Freddie.' They jumped out of the car and ran into the building.

The door to the reception was open, but Margie was not at her desk. The two boys hurried into the main office. They stopped sharply, just inside the door, and surveyed the scene.

The blinds had been ripped down and torn to shreds. All the chairs had been overturned. The computer screen had been reduced to jagged splinters of glass. The video and TV were gone. A long, deep score cut down the centre of the mirror-like surface of the conference table. Margie was sitting on the floor by the window. She was whimpering quietly, as Russell comforted her. Jo Jo and Mario stood shocked by the destruction. Con stared at Carl from the far end of the room.

Russell looked up. 'She din't get a good sight of 'em.'

Freddie took a step towards him. 'What the . . . it was broad bloody daylight!' Carl put a hand on Freddie's arm and restrained him.

'Leave her alone,' he said. 'Take her somewhere. Go on. Jo Jo? Take her somewhere. Get her to a doctor.' Russell helped Margie to her feet and Jo Jo supported her as they walked to the door. Margie let out a huge sob as she passed Carl.

'They hit me! One of 'em did.'

'Ssshh,' Carl soothed. 'Don't you come back till you

175

feel like it. You hear?' She nodded as she left. Carl immediately turned his attention to Con. He marched towards him, his eyes set dark and threatening. 'And where were you, Mr Nobody?'

Con stammered slightly. 'I – I . . . went out . . . to get a sandwich.' He raised a small brown paper bag, as evidence for his alibi. Carl snatched the bag from Con and was about to hurl it against the wall, when he caught Russell's accusing eye. Roughly, he shoved the bag back in Con's midriff, righted one of the chairs and sat. Russell did not want to miss this opportunity to say 'I told you so.'

'There's obviously a lot of little hooligans out there with the same eye to the main chance as us, Carl. We been losing Bobby Chalker's gaffs one by one. Oh, you might not be interested in 'em – you think the East End's a health hazard, don't yer?'

'Yeah. I do.'

'Well, those little shit-holes paid for this place. The pennies on the pavement, what you can't be bothered to pick up, well they bought yer new Porsche, Carl. The dumps in Dalston and the sewers down Hackney Road . . . they gave us a good wage, din't they?'

'We're better than that.'

'They're not a bank account, Carl! They don't pay if we don't get down there and see 'em right! And if we don't, some one else bloody will. Whad'you reckon happened here? They heard we got soft and they came to stick the boot in.'

'Bollocks.'

'They're even snapping at our heels all over Islington! Ain't they, Freddie?' Carl glanced at Freddie for confirmation. Reluctantly, Freddie nodded in agreement.

'I guess we got unreliable,' Russell concluded. 'Too busy worrying 'bout Slater and Klein.'

*

176

Carl sat at the desk in his study at Cranley Gardens. The room had been transformed from the flowery monstrosity it used to be. Now it was decorated in high-tech, minimal style: the black, white and chrome gave it a hard, clinical atmosphere.

Carl had moved the answering machine upstairs. Some of the boys had been less than diplomatic recently, and he did not want Linda to hear their messages. He reached out and depressed the play button on the sleek, metallic unit, and then settled back to study the sound of his own voice.

'Hi. This is Carl. Can't speak to yer now. Leave yer message after the beep.' He flicked off the message and considered for a moment. He pressed *record* and spoke into the microphone.

'Hallo. This is Carl Galton. I'm sorry, I can't take your call at the moment, but you can leave yer name and any message for me after the beep.' He waited for the 'beep' and then played the message back.

'Hallo. This is Carl Galton. I'm sorry – ' Carl quickly turned off the tape when he heard a gentle tap at the door. 'Yep.'

Linda pushed the door half-open and stepped just inside the room. Her hair fell untidily across her face. She stood for a moment, apologetically, and then in a small voice she asked: 'Am I disturbing you?'

'Yeah. But it don't matter.'

She nodded her head. 'We need to talk.'

'Do we?'

'Yes, goddammit.' The veil of sweet submission fell away.

'Then get rid of that thing, sit down, and talk.'

Linda looked awkwardly at the cigarette in her hand. Carl opened the desk drawer, removed a pristine, black ceramic ashtray, and offered it to her. She walked up to the desk, stubbed out the cigarette, pulled up a chair, and sat down next to him. She took a piece of crumpled paper from the pocket of her jeans, and passed it to Carl. 'They're threatening to cut us off.'

Carl inspected the official letter from North Thames Gas. 'So pay it.' He tossed it back across the desk.

'I don't have any money,' she replied. Carl put his hand to his forehead and sighed. 'We can't afford this house, Carl.'

'Where the bloody hell has it all gone?' he snapped.

'On paying your champagne tab at Cheers, on your car, on your clothes, on this bloody awful house!'

'I'll get you money, don't worry 'bout it.' He turned his head away from her, expecting this conversation to be as brief and clipped as all the others they had had recently. But she did not get up and leave this time.

'What's happened to us, Carl?' she said sadly.

'I dunno, darlin'. You tell me. Got anything to tell me? Anything I should know? Got any secrets swimming round that pretty little head of yours?'

'No – '

'Oh come on. I bet you have. Go on. Tell us. Tell us. Come on, Linda, tell us . . . Eh? Eh?' He sneered accusingly, and then began to shake his head. 'And you wonder why I don't talk to yer . . . I'm busy.'

'We're dying in this house, Carl.'

'You are darlin'. Not me.'

'I need to talk to you!'

'What!' he screamed.

She began to speak, to confess, stumbling and distressed.

'There was somebody . . . I met . . . somebody. Not somebody. Chris. The one who works . . . worked . . . at the nursery. I mean I . . . I met him without the kids. That's what I mean . . . Oh God . . . I mean he was nice to me, that's all.'

'Was he?' said Carl with cool, detached superiority.

She forced herself on; trying to cut a path through the thickening cloud of tension between them. 'I think he liked me a lot . . . I know he did. And I liked him, but nothing really happened . . . Don't look at me like that, Carl. I'm only telling you 'cos . . . it weren't an affair, or anything like that. It weren't like that.'

'No?'

'No,' she repeated.

'No, it was, errr . . . it was a lot worse than that, weren't it?' She leaned towards him, but he gave her no opportunity to explain further. He had promised himself something, when this time came, as he knew it would. And Carl very rarely denied himself. For the first time in their relationship, he hit her.

Linda's hand flew to her cheek. The pounding canoned through her head and then turned her body to jelly. She rocked for a moment and then slipped slowly from the chair to the floor. She rested on all fours, and gulped for breath. She could not cry.

'Yes, I think it was a lot worse than that. Get up,' he snarled. One hand reached up for the support of the desk, and she dragged herself shakily to her feet.

'Why did you do that to me?' Her voice came cracked and quiet, from miles away.

''Cos you're a whore. You should be used to it.'

'Our children!' she pleaded.

'I hope they heard. They should know what you are. That way, they'll understand why I might have to take 'em away from yer one day soon.'

'I love them.'

'You don't deserve 'em.'

'I love them, damn you!'

'Din't think that when yer popped the pills.'

'You don't understand, Carl . . .'

179

'No. Explain it to me. I'm doing me best by you, Linda, and you are giving me grief all the time.' He stared hard at her. 'I think yer cracking up, darlin' – you know that? And God it hurts me to see yer like this. See, you don't know this but . . .' He paused for the maximum effect. '. . . I've walked out of this house and cried, Linda. Cried.' He did not take his eyes off her: he was waiting for the surrender.

'Come here,' he said. She did not move. She was not playing the old game; not dragging out the seconds till the moment when she fell into his arms, admitted her own illogic, and let him win. That would never happen again.

'I watch you sometimes,' she said bitterly, 'when you're getting ready to go out "on business". You stand in front of the mirror. You're so careful 'bout everything. Yer clothes, yer hair . . . It's just like you was going to meet a lover. And sometimes . . . I wish you was.' She turned on her heels and walked out of the room.

Carl sat quite still for a moment, and then reached forward to the answering machine. He pressed the button to record and spoke into the microphone in a measured, unruffled voice.

'Hallo. This is Carl Galton's answering service. There's no one available to take your call at the moment. Please leave your name, the time you called, and any message, after the tone.' He played the message back to make sure he had said *your* and not *yer*. Satisfied, he switched the machine to *answer*. He was startled by the immediate ring of the phone. The message played. Carl monitored the caller.

'Linda? S'me,' Kathy bellowed down the phone. 'Oh, I hate these bloody things. Look, yer better call me quick, right? Yeah. 'Bye.'

The machine clicked off.

*

It was too early in the evening for the regular crowd to be in Cheers. But all the boys were there when Carl arrived. They exchanged pleasantries and chatted idly about girls and buying shares in BAA, but soon the conversation turned to the decision they had gathered to consider.

'We ain't got a clue what might be in that lorry,' said Russell.

'Klein could just be doing an old mate a favour,' Mario added.

Carl looked pained. 'Why would Klein wanna hide anything from Slater, 'less it's bent?' he demanded. More and more, he was coming to resent having to justify himself to the others. 'You can't have it all ways, Russ. You say we've been sat on our arses doing nothing. You say things are getting out of hand. And now we got a chance to make something happen, you still got a face like a turkey at Christmas.'

'Bullshit,' grated Russell. 'We was earning, Carl – '

'Peanuts! We gotta move up.'

Russell realized that Carl was in no mood to argue and lowered his stare to his glass. Carl pressed on, to ram home his superiority. 'Any time we been on our uppers before, we went out and smacked it to someone, Russ. That's free enterprise innit? All the better that Klein's the one we smack.'

Freddie's appetite was conjuring up a vision of mountains of pasta soaked in bolognese sauce. He attempted to force a decision. 'So we go on Friday?'

'Any objections?' asked Carl. Russell searched the faces for support, but was disappointed. Even Mario – good old smiling, nodding Mario, the man who could see five sides to every argument – even he knew which way this wind was blowing: it was the icy northern blast of Carl's ambition, and it was as well to take cover. The brief silence signalled Carl's success.

181

'All right!' Jo Jo's face lit up and he clenched his fists with determination.

'I don't think so, Jo Jo,' said Carl softly.

'What?'

'You couldn't park a mini,' Freddie scolded.

The younger boy gulped back a protest. He tried to be reasonable. 'Yer not throwing me out, are yer, Carl?' Carl did not answer, but the disinterested way he raised his glass and sipped his drink was enough to spark Jo Jo's furious indignation. 'Well . . . well . . . so where you gonna be then, Carl? Sat in a flashy motor behind, eh? And who says s'you what decides everything, eh? . . . Eh? . . .'Cos we was all in this together, right, and yer know what? . . . Eh? . . . Yer know what? I am well sick of being coated off by you. By the lot of yer!'

Carl looked down calmly at Jo Jo, and then, without raising his voice, he said: 'The way I see it, you're a child. You can't do nothing for yerself – you never have. And if we was stranded on a desert island, then you'd wash my socks, and cook my dinner, and pick up my mess, while I thought of a way to get off. So if I toss you a sweet, be grateful, say thank you – don't spit it back in my face, little boy.' He stared at Jo Jo for a moment, and then swung round to the bar.

Jo Jo felt the eyes of the other boys searing into him. He caught the snicker on Freddie's face, and looked close to tears. Carl turned back to him. Jo Jo lowered his head. 'I can do it,' he muttered.

Carl's face broke into a smile as he saw another exercise in power successfully completed. He reached out and put his hand on the back of Jo Jo's neck. He pulled the deflated boy to him, and wrapped his arms round him. But the embrace was not affectionate; it was full of bravado and self-importance.

The grin on Carl's face disappeared as the front door of

Cheers opened and two boys entered. He released Jo Jo and fixed a hostile stare on the new arrivals. One by one, the other boys began to turn towards the door.

The first of the two newcomers was a tall, slim boy of about twenty. He sported a bleached-blond crew cut, green nylon bomber jacket, skin-tight faded jeans, and twelve-hole Doc Martens. The second boy was dressed identically, but the shadow on his shaved head was darker, the body thicker set, the face more tired.

It was quite a transformation, that second boy. But even without the hair, without the designer clothes, there could be no mistake. It was Marty.

He made no show of having registered the presence of Carl and the others. He shepherded the taller boy to the corner table, in front of a large mirror by the door. His movements seemed unco-ordinated and his speech slurred. 'There. Look at that. Perfect. Sit yerself down, Kev,' he said. Kev was well aware of the attention he and Marty were being given and looked uncomfortable. 'I'll get 'em in, Kev,' Marty offered, ''cos this is my place, right?'

'Yeah, I guess so.' Kev's voice was low and unenthusiastic.

Marty walked unsteadily to the bar and almost fell against it. 'Couple of Pils please, David.' The barman shot a glance at Carl, who was almost within touching distance of Marty.

'Not tonight, Marty,' said David.

'Oh.' Marty's face looked disappointed, and his already diminished energy seemed to drain even further. He turned and picked his way shakily back to Kev. He flopped down into a chair and leaned back. His mouth opened slightly and he blinked his eyes as the room went out of focus. Kev nudged Marty's arm and nodded to the door.

'No, s'all right, Kev,' said Marty, trying to pull himself together. 'We'll just sit here for a bit and enjoy the . . . atmosph . . . atmosphere. Great, innit?'

'Let's go now,' Kev hissed.

'No. No, please,' Marty pleaded. 'I been to all your places, and all Pete's places. I want yer to see my place. This is my place, Kev.' His eyes fixed on a half-empty glass of lager which had been left on the table. 'Look, see? Someone's left a drink for me. David din't mean that, see?' He picked up the glass and pressed it close to Kev's face. 'Here yer go. Drink that, Kev. Looks like lager.'

Kev pushed the drink away roughly and the beer spilled down Marty's chest. He said: 'You're embarrassing me, you tosser,' and then walked quickly out of the bar.

'I din't mean to,' said Marty, quiet and sad. 'I'm sorry 'bout that . . . Catch yer later, eh? Yeah . . . yeah.' His head, lolling back, cracked sharply against the wall.

'So the fairy flew home.' Carl walked over and stood, collected, in front of Marty. Marty strained his tired eyes to focus again. 'You're pissed,' said Carl.

'Yep.'

'You're high as a kite, too.'

'Mmmm.'

'This place has gone downhill, David. You shouldn't let scum in.'

Marty smirked. 'Why not? You're here.' He began to laugh, quietly at first, but growing louder with an angry, suicidal defiance. Carl dismissed him with one slow shake of the head and turned to rejoin the other boys, who stood mute and shocked by the unfolding spectacle.

Marty's laughing stopped abruptly. He grabbed at the glass and smashed it on the edge of the table. As Carl looked round, Marty held out the glass to him.

'Go on, Carl. You know yer want to. When have yer ever not done something yer wanted to?'

A young couple slid by Carl and out of the door, dismayed by the sudden eruption of violence. Carl returned to Marty's table. Their chests were both heaving with tension, as Carl reached out and took the fractured glass from Marty. He held it for a moment and considered how easily it would be for those jagged peaks to slice through flesh, to disfigure and mutilate.

Carl drew back his arm and then hurled the glass into the mirror. He saw his own reflection shatter. He said: 'You can send me the bill for that, David . . . you can charge me for the glass, too.'

The glass had struck the mirror like a bullet; the pattern of cracks snaked out from the point of impact, like the finest threads in a spider's web. Marty's head was crowned with this splintered halo. Carl watched him as his eyes fell shut, and then turned and walked out to the street. The other boys filed after him. They each cast a glance at Marty as they passed.

Russell was the last to leave. He paused in front of Marty. Marty sensed his presence and opened his eyes. He tried to smile.

'He won't do it for yer, Marty. Get some sleep, man. Yer look terrible.'

Kathy jigged nervously as she watched Linda peer through the letter-box of Bill and Marty's flat. The trickle of dry blood from Linda's mouth and the darkening bruise on her cheek had provided Kathy with a distracting talking point when they first met, but there was no escaping the accusing finger now.

Linda turned and said angrily: 'I promised Marty! How could you let me down like that, Kathy? I only asked yer to look in on him twice. Good God, he could be dead!'

185

'I was gonna come yesterday, Linda,' Kathy squirmed, 'honest I was. But Elaine come round and I had all me chores . . . and the day just sorta went.'

Linda fired off another glowering look, and then began to call through the letter-box. 'Bill? Bill?' She raised her voice to a shout: 'Bill? You there?' She banged on the door with her fist.

'I reckon we oughta call the police,' Kathy suggested tentatively. Linda considered for a moment, and was about to agree, when she heard a voice call down the stairs inside the flat.

'Who is it?' Bill gasped.

'Bill, it's Linda. Can you open the door?' There was no response. 'Come on. Can you open the door, my love?' she urged.

'Hang on,' he replied weakly. Linda and Kathy heard his footsteps pad slowly and unsteadily down the stairs. There was a fiddling noise from the lock and the door slipped open. They moved quickly into the small hall to support Bill, as he sagged against the wall.

'Come on, you're all right, my love,' breathed Linda. 'We're here now. Come on, come on.'

'Bugger me,' Kathy exclaimed. 'It stinks in 'ere!'

'I messed meself,' moaned Bill, and he began to sob with embarrassment.

Kathy could not hide her revulsion. 'Oh no!' Linda slapped her sister's arm and turned to reassure Bill.

'It don' matter, luvvy. Don' cry now. Let's get you back upstairs.'

Bill's body was racked with sickness and exhaustion. Coming down the stairs had drained him; he was little help to them as they tried to get him back up. When they finally arrived at the upstairs hall, Linda and Kathy were both sweating heavily. They paused for a moment to catch their breath, and then negotiated the last leg by virtually

186

carrying Bill into his room. He let out another enormous sob as they eased him down on the bed.

Linda shook her aching arms and said: 'I'll get a flannel and a towel. You try to find some clean sheets.' Kathy nodded.

They hurried out to the hall. Linda was well acquainted with the geography of the flat; she moved efficiently to a small cupboard set low in the wall, pulled open the door and took out a towel. Kathy hovered by her. 'That bed's had it, Linda,' she suggested. 'Why don't we put him in Marty's room?'

The stench hit them like a hammer as soon as they opened Marty's door. Kathy reeled back from it and groaned. 'What's that smells?' she cried as she clapped a hand over her nose and mouth.

Linda waved towards a small, uncapped, brown-glass bottle on the bedside table. 'Poppers. Oh God, God, God!' The initial blast of amyl nitrate had fuzzed their brains; for a few seconds the raw, biting chemical was their sole concern. But now they began to take in the story told by the rest of the room.

The carpet was invisible beneath a sea of discarded clothes. Old photos had been scattered like confetti. Homosexual pornographic magazines lay open on the bed and floor. Ripped-up newspapers added to the degradation, and there was a second unpleasant odour, emanating from a plate of half-eaten food which was rapidly going off in the heat. Linda stood frozen and mute in the doorway, as Kathy ventured back into the room. She kicked the clothes from her feet, crossed to the bedside table and picked up the bottle of poppers.

''Wos it for?' she asked.

'Don't sniff it, you daft cow! Put the top on it!' Linda rushed back down the hall and into Bill's room. 'Bill?

Bill?' He opened his eyes and looked mournfully up at her. 'Bill, is Marty back?'

'What? Yeah.'

'How long's he been back?'

'Dunno. Couple of days.'

'Well why ain't he looking after you!' she cried. Bill's eyes fell slowly shut, and he began to shake his head. Linda stared at this burned-out hulk of a man, who was caught up in something he did not understand. She had always thought of him as 'a bit of a cantankerous old sod', but now her eyes were filled with genuine pity. She took a corner of the sheet, gently wiped the beads of sweat from his forehead, and then hurried back to Marty's room.

Kathy was slumped on the bed. Her eyes felt like they were dangling on elastic stalks; her heart was pounding in her ears. 'I don't half feel funny,' she moaned. Linda marched past her and threw open the window.

'I told yer not to sniff it,' she said. 'Now pull yerself together. Can yer drive Carl's car?'

'Linda, he'll kill – '

'Bollocks!' Kathy looked stunned: she could not remember the last time Linda had sworn like that.

'The spare keys are in the vegetable crisper in the fridge,' Linda continued. 'Don't ask me why, they just are. Get the car and bring it back here. I'm gonna call an ambulance.'

'Won't Carl be at home?'

'Of course he won't. He's taken the kids to me mum's, and then he's going down Cheers. He says.' Linda took the house keys from her jeans and threw them to her sister.

'What we need the car for?'

'Just get it!'

188

Kathy jumped up, regretted the effect the sudden movement had on her head, and left. Linda watched her go and then went and sat among the rubbish on the bed. She sorted idly through the magazines and photos. She was surprised when she came across pictures of herself, and then of Carl. She began to study the photos more carefully. Buried under a pile of torn newspaper she found the record of a day she remembered: Brighton beach in August 1983. Marty, Carl and herself, posing on the promenade while an obliging passer-by took a snap. She remembered that as a perfectly happy day, and she had always loved that photo. But it had changed now: Marty's smiling face had been scored out with a biro.

Linda cast the photo aside and picked up a copy of a twenty-page paper called *Capital Gay*. It was folded open at the section advertising all the gay pubs and clubs in London.

As Linda scanned the list of venues, she began to understand the years of pain which had exploded in that room.

The ambulance arrived ten minutes after Linda put through the call. A further ten minutes passed, before the Porsche shuddered and hiccuped along Southgate Road with Kathy at the wheel.

For the next hour and a half, Linda and Kathy, armed with the copy of *Capital Gay*, scoured the gay clubs and pubs of North London in their search for Marty.

Linda had forgotten the pain in her jaw. She was methodical and efficient; working systematically in an arc from Hampstead to the East End.

They had already made six calls when they pulled up at the London Apprentice. They had received predictably similar receptions at every venue so far: a mixture of curiosity and hostility from the sparse Tuesday crowds.

Kathy was beginning to tire of this little game. She hesitated as Linda opened the car door.

'I don't wanna go in another one, Linda. They all look at me funny. Like they're not sure whether I'm a man or not.'

'Stay here then. I'll go.'

'You reckon it's safe on yer own?'

'It's a gay bar, Kathy. How much safer can I get?'

Linda got out of the car and walked purposefully to the door of the pub. She pressed the buzzer on the intercom and the door swung open. The burly doorman opened his mouth to dissuade her, but she was in no mood to negotiate. She said: 'I'm just looking,' and pushed past him.

Kathy looked down at the mind-boggling array of switches and knobs on the dash of the Porsche. She determined to work out once and for all where the indicators were. For her first effort, she was rewarded with a demonstration of the windscreen wipers. Her second choice was no more successful: she gave a little jump in the seat as the stereo blared to life. She slapped off the switch and looked round her to see if anyone had witnessed her mistake.

Daylight had gone now, but by the glare of the street-lamps Kathy saw a group of figures in the narrow road which ran along the side of the pub. She looked intently towards them. For a moment there was a glimmer of recognition. A shape, a shadow, a way of walking. She got out of the car and took a few paces towards the group. She peered down the road. She could see clearer now. A group of about ten young skinheads were jostling and taunting a hunched, frightened figure. She recognized the victim.

Kathy ran back to the door of the London Apprentice. She pressed the buzzer and the door opened again. The doorman gave an astonished look and wondered if the pub's advertisement had been posted to *Ms London* by mistake.

'S'cuse me,' Kathy ventured, 'you know the girl what just come in . . . well, could yer . . . d'yer think yer . . . never mind, I'll get 'er.' The doorman was pushed aside by a woman for the second time in one night.

Kathy stopped just inside the door and strained to pick out Linda in the sparse crowd of men. She spotted her sister on the far side of the bar.

'Linda!' she screamed, and was immediately the object of everyone's attention. But her embarrassment was soon dispelled by the sight of Linda rushing towards her. Kathy grabbed her by the arm and dragged her out of the door. It was all becoming a bit much for the doorman. He just smiled at them and said: 'All right, girls? I'll leave it open, case you wanna come back.'

'What is it?' asked Linda.

Kathy pointed to the group of boys in the road. 'I'm not sure it's him.'

They began to walk towards the boys. Linda saw them pushing at Marty, taunting him, spitting on him, and hurling abuse. Marty whimpered slightly as he was forced back against a wall, and then tried to laugh it off. But the laugh was a desperate, pathetic sound; a thin howling noise.

'Marty?' Linda called out, as she broke into a run.

The skinheads all turned to identify the intruders.

'That you, Marty?' Marty stood stock-still, but the other skinheads backed off slightly as Linda approached. She slowed to a walk and he saw her shocked face.

Marty glanced round at the other boys and then clasped both hands to his shaved head. The skinheads began to drift back, and within a few seconds Linda and Kathy found themselves surrounded by a wall of sneering aggression. Kathy looked round anxiously, but Linda's eyes were fixed on Marty. 'What's happened to you?' she said.

A powerful, harsh-faced boy in a Union Jack T-shirt pushed through his cordon of lieutenants. 'You sly, dishonest little tyro, Marty. This is a good-looker, innit?'

'Two little darlin's.' The blond boy, Kev, moved up to his leader's shoulder. 'Don't let the little fat one get on top – she'll squash yer.'

'Oh nuts!' Kathy spat back.

Linda looked into the face of the gang leader and said quietly: 'Who are you?'

'Oh excuse me for not introducing meself,' he answered with exaggerated sarcasm, 'My name's Pete Morris. Ain't Marty told yer 'bout me? I poke his tight little arse for him.' He pressed his face closer to Linda. 'Whad'you do with him, fish? Is it nice? Is he lovely? Like he is with me? P'raps we could make a night of it.' As he began to run the stubble of his chin along her shoulder, she flung out her arm and caught him painfully in the eye. 'You bitch!' Morris rasped.

'Don't you touch me,' she warned.

Morris did not take his eyes off her as he pressed his mouth to Marty's ear. In a loud whisper, he said: 'You better make her suffer for that, Marty. You better think of me when yer up it. Tell 'er 'bout me when yer in it, Marty. Tell the bitch.' He began to back away. ''Bye, lover. 'Bye, girlie.' The other boys drifted after him, each murmuring 'bitch' as they passed Linda and Kathy.

Morris broke into a run, and then jumped up on the bonnet of a parked car. He turned back to Marty, stamped his foot on the groaning metal and let out a banshee-like scream, before jumping back down in the road and disappearing into the darkness.

Marty shivered in the silence. Linda reached out to him, but he cowered away from her. 'Marty!' she implored, but he rolled along the wall, avoiding her touch, and making a noise like an hysterical, sobbing child.

'Stop it!' she shouted.

'Don't look at me! Don't! Go away!' He beat at himself with his fists and threw himself hard against the wall. Linda grabbed at one of his flailing hands. For a moment, he struggled to escape her, but then all life seemed to seep out of him and he sank slowly to the ground, and curled into a ball.

Linda knelt beside him. Slowly and gently, she wrapped her arms around him. He trembled, and his cheeks were scored with silent tears.

'Oh, Marty,' Linda breathed, 'what's everyone done to you?'

Twelve

A dull note rang out from the coke can and it bobbed beneath the oily surface of Regent's Canal. A second pebble struck the can, and Marty turned his face to Linda and forced a smile. His gaze flitted along the line of tranquil, compact cherry trees which lined Colebrooke Row, and then moved reluctantly back down the bank which guarded the canal. Linda sat on a solid wooden bench on the canalside. Her expression was demanding an explanation, an excuse, anything other than the present melancholy silence in which Marty was wallowing.

In the heat of the unrelenting midday sun, Marty felt a shiver run through him.

'It was here,' he began, 'the first time he killed someone, yer know?' His voice was almost whispering to her; fearful that the breath of wind would catch a secret, or a confession. 'May of been the only time. I dunno.' He stared down into the rainbow slick which lapped the edge of the canal. 'He din't die here. But then that don't matter, does it? . . . Was the first time I called it wrong with Carl. Never thought he'd do that.'

Linda leaned forward, and Marty raised his eyes to the cloudless sky. 'A bird, pigeon or something,' he said.

'What bird?' she questioned.

'No. Pigeons don't swim. Just crap everywhere. I hate that, don't you? Must of been a duck. Flew off the water there.' He gestured to a spot near the Packington Street bridge. 'Made a bloody terrible noise. Claarrgh! Like an echo. Noise of the gun. It frightened me.'

She strained to disentangle the garbled account of the time when Toddy came for them. Marty was lost in the trauma of that night. He said: 'He din't wanna talk 'bout it after. He said the bloke was gonna kill us. He was probably right.'

'Don't make excuses for him, Marty.'

'Oh I mean it, darlin'. Must of been then when he realized I let him down, see. I was walking the other way. Running away . . . You gotta stick by yer mates. Can't trust people after that . . . If the bloke was gonna kill us, then Carl saved my life.' His chin sank back on his chest. 'I was never strong like him. That's why things din't work out for me and Carl . . .'

He felt her heavy stare. 'I don't mean . . . we never . . . Oh God, I miss him, Linda. Ain't that funny?'

'Why did you let those blokes treat you like that, Marty? Last night?'

'Dunno,' he replied, quiet and embarrassed.

'You must know – '

He rounded on her angrily. ''Cos I wanted to! 'Cos no one gives a shit what I am, so I'll do what I like, and if it makes you sick, well good! If you don't like it, sod yer, and everyone else who's told me how I'm meant to be and what I'm meant to be!'

Linda shook her head and rose from the bench. 'I din't deserve that, Marty,' she said, and moved to leave.

Regret at his outburst coursed through Marty. He felt suddenly exposed and abandoned, and lost. 'Linda?' he cried. She stopped.

'What?' she asked stonily.

'Where yer going?'

'Home. I'm not strong like him. I have to be careful, or

195

I get hit.' She paused and looked Marty up and down.
The skinhead 'uniform' had gone, but what was left was
not the young man she had known. He had grown thin in
the past few weeks, and the skin on his face was stretched
and pallid. His eyes were sunken, unhappy, and evasive.
She said deliberately: 'Last night I cried, Marty. Not 'cos
of what you are; not 'cos I found out yer gay. I cried 'cos
I thought of all the years you must of known, and how
alone yer must of been, and 'cos none of us were any
help. And now I'm trying to understand, and yer won't
let me. How much more guilt d'yer want?'

'Ask Bridie; s'in the book.'

'Go visit yer dad, eh?'

'Stick by him, Linda,' Marty muttered.

'What?'

'Carl needs yer.'

'No he don't.'

'S'fate, Linda. You two was meant for each other.'

He stared full at her. For a brief moment she thought
she saw a smile. She thought it signalled the end of this
assignation and a determination on Marty's part to get on
with his life; to rehabilitate the negative force which
dragged him down, to reverse the atrophy of self-pity.
But the flicker on his face soon melted away to bitterness,
and she felt accused. It was as if that face was blaming
her for its sadness. She approached him.

'I thought I achieved something last night,' she said. 'I
took yer home and put yer to bed like a baby. In a room
I cleaned for yer – '

'I'm useless – '

'Why do you – why do men, think they got a right to
spend the whole of their bloody lives reliving their childhood? Catching up on the bits they missed? I'm not
allowed to do it. But now, right now, Marty, I know what
I am. I'm the cleaning woman. I clean up after kids. And

what chance do I have with the two I've got at home? What chance with my son?'

'Linda – '

'I clean him and protect him and love him. Carl plays with him. And Nicky thinks that man is God. And yer know, one day, that kid will hate me . . . The same way you do.'

'I love yer for Christ's sake!'

'Like Carl does? You're both the same. You, Carl, and all the rest of 'em. You love me and Kathy, and Bridie and yer mum, 'cos we let yer pin medals on each other. 'Cos we let yer love each other . . . You'd be ashamed of that if we weren't around.'

Marty nodded slightly, but his mind had switched off under the attack.

'I love Carl,' Linda continued. 'Ain't that funny after all that? P'raps I ain't got anything else. But the last few weeks . . . the last few weeks, I seem to spend me whole day thinking how I can get me kids away from him. I think he's gonna die, but that might make it worse . . . You tell me, Marty, how do I stop him dying a hero in my son's eyes?'

Freddie sensed that Carl had one thing and one thing only on his mind as they bustled down the corridor to the office at the Angel on Wednesday afternoon.

'Russell's going over the top a bit,' Freddie said. 'We've lost the hamburger joint, and the Tiger Café in Upper Street. But that's about it. We was busy with other things and Theo stepped in. We can get 'em back.'

'S'just careless, man,' Carl scolded quietly.

Freddie tried not to be too harsh. 'They was places you was meant to deal with, Carl.'

Carl ignored the mild rebuke and steered the exchange

197

back to his one ambition. 'Did Jo Jo take the van out again?'

'He'll be OK.'

They turned into the reception to see Margie force a weak smile. The incident of the previous day had left her visibly shaken, but she had forced herself back into the office, mindful that Carl's generosity might not stretch to sick pay. Her evidence for that assumption fluttered in her hand.

'The cheque for the office rent,' she whispered, 'the bank sent it back.'

Carl took the cheque and accompanying pompous letter. 'What yer whispering for?' he queried. Margie put a finger to her lips and gestured through the open door of the conference room.

Carl looked up to see the back of a slim woman, with cascading mahogany hair which matched the colour of the table where she was seated. Carl gave a little chuckle and shake of the head. Since they had moved into that office, he had been pestered by enough photocopy companies to realize that they would use any means to make their product seem more attractive than Xerox. Perhaps a touch of nubile femininity was the latest trick. Still, the back was sufficiently interesting to make him curious for a sight of the front.

Carl screwed up the bounced cheque and tossed it into the waste-bin as he walked into the conference room. The woman heard his step. 'Mr Galton,' she announced, as she swung round in the chair.

Carl's face was illuminated with its fullest, most appealing charm as he took in the sophisticated vision that had turned to meet him. He eased shut the door behind him, and contemplated a new-found interest in continuous-sheet stationery.

The woman spoke with the same silky efficiency that

governed her dress. 'My name's Dot Fleming. We've spoken briefly on the phone.'

'Have we?' Carl cursed the distortion of Telecom for disguising that deep, purring voice.

'You hung up on me. Perhaps we could talk now. I have a proposition you may be interested in. Heavens, it's warm, isn't it?'

'P'raps you'd like to take something off.' Carl could not disguise his suggestiveness.

'Like the day?' she replied, easy in the knowledge that she could beat this little one at his own game without extending her current level of perspiration. She took in his propositioning look, and then moved swiftly to the purpose of her visit. 'Let's get down to business, shall we?'

'Xerox?' Carl guessed. She gazed at him quizzically. 'Well, p'raps it's high-class office cleaning. Or maybe yer wanna come round and talk to the plants for fifty a week. Marry some Brit, did yer?'

She began to lose patience. 'Mr Galton. I hate plants; they belong in the outdoors. The only thing I have ever cleaned is myself, and I am married to the most successful company lawyer in New York. Happily.' She picked a calfskin briefcase from beside the chair and flicked round the combination lock. She took a plain black file from the case and slid it across the table to Carl. 'Before we go any further, perhaps you ought to take a look at that. It might at least get you onto the right track. I'll just sit here by the window and catch the wind. OK?'

Carl saw no harm in allowing her to decorate the office for a while, so he nodded and opened the file. It consisted of a dozen pages, some filled with columns of figures, some with schedules and guarantees. The presentation was glossy and commercial, but the content was a mystery to Carl. Less than five minutes passed before he tossed the file back towards Dot.

'Well?' She looked up expectantly.

'I don't understand a word of it,' he replied honestly. 'S'full of garbage.'

'I'll try to make it clearer,' she said, with more than a hint of patronization. 'We're setting up a network of contacts in major urban centres. I'm looking for someone to deal in East London. It will be distributed – '

'Hang on a minute, love,' he interrupted. 'You ain't told me, and that thing don't tell me, what *it* is. Or who you are, darlin'.'

'Who I represent does not matter to you, and what *it* is, you'll find out.'

'Stuff it, love. You ain't told me nothing.'

Her expression was remote and dispassionate. She longed to snatch up her things and walk coolly out of that office, but the constraint of necessity prevented her.

She made one last attempt to clarify. 'If you'd read the document carefully, instead of looking for the pictures, you would have seen on page three that a bank account has been opened in your name. It does not contain a fortune. More an incentive. I could close it with one phone call. But if you accept, then my clients would view that as a binding contract. Some initial investment capital is required on your side. The amount in the account will not be sufficient. As to what the product is . . . well, I don't see the attraction of it myself, but millions do. Perhaps they have boring lives.'

A light was beginning to grow brighter in Carl's head, and for the first time in weeks Slater and Klein had drifted into the shadows. He stared hard at Dot. 'You're a fascinating woman.'

'And I have a fascinating weapon in my purse. The flirting was amusing for thirty seconds, Mr Galton. Don't push it. I always aim for the balls; if you miss one, you usually hit the other. Do we understand each other?'

'I'll have to consult my colleagues,' he stated untruthfully. He felt no need to consult them at all, but felt he should display a measure of professional, business acumen. That's what they do, isn't it? Consult their colleagues?

'Of course.' She seemed relieved that the meeting was nearing its close. 'Now a meeting has been arranged for tomorrow. I know it's short notice, but then you're a difficult man to track down. I'll be setting out the price packages in which my clients are prepared to deal, and outlining the discount benefits for large investors. But I can tell you now that we are offering a thirty per cent discount on your first order, by way of an introductory offer.'

Carl considered that she spoke with the same tone as the woman who had brought Freeman's catalogue and its thirty-six weekly payments into his mother's life.

Dot got up from the chair and sealed the briefcase. 'The address is on the back page of the presentation,' she added. 'Oh, and Mr Galton, don't bring a tribe. We don't want to turn this into a hoodlum's day out.' She walked to the door, poised and spotless. 'I'm rather looking forward to it. Tony Slater tells me his house can be beautiful in the summer.'

'Slater's mixed up in this?' Carl asked incredulously.

'Of course. It was Tony who gave me your name. My clients are buying his and George Klein's company. Goodbye, Mr Galton.'

Carl rose respectfully and gave a slight nod of the head as the vision left. Then he sat down and began to take in the magnitude of the proposition she had just made. Within minutes, the mind which had focused, heavy and determined, on two middle-aged men in the transport

201

business began to spiral upwards and drag him into a fantasy of wealth and power.

It was a private fantasy: he did not 'consult his colleagues'.

At three o'clock on Thursday afternoon Carl's Porsche swept up the gravel drive of Slater's house.

Carl had judged it necessary to be accompanied, and had decided that Con was the person for the job. After all, he had visited the house before, had snooped unseen round the grounds to record Pat's adultery on film. He knew the lie of the land. It also amused Carl to imagine the look on Klein's face when his 'spy' walked in.

The two boys got out of the car and surveyed the opulence of the surroundings. The sprawling Elizabethan farmhouse sat comfortable and solid in thirty landscaped acres of Essex countryside. A high, red-brick wall meandered round the perimeter of the land. It was broken at three points by imposing carbon-coloured gates: visitors did not seem welcome. The lath-and-plaster front elevation of the house had been painted pink, and looked out over finely manicured gardens, giant topiaries and a mock-baroque fountain which depicted dolphins and water nymphs. From the paved terrace on one side of the gardens, the lawns sloped down to a large man-made lake. On the far side of the lake there was a small boat-house, where the thatch had long since rotted away and been replaced with more functional tiling. In the meadow beyond, a flock of geese strutted noisily round a half-constructed bonfire.

Carl turned to Con as they entered the house. 'It's a long way from Bobby Chalker,' he breathed.

The collection of Mercs and Porsches in the drive had informed them that they were not the first to arrive, and as they walked through the oak porch and into the dark, stone-flagged hall, they heard voices drift towards them from a large reception room.

Perhaps Carl had expected spats and violin cases, Cagney and Raft, gunmen in birthday cakes, and Italian accents. The least he had expected was that these people would look criminal. What he saw was quite different and left him visibly surprised.

There were about thirty besuited men in the plush, spacious room. The ones that did not look like lawyers had the odour of the educated car salesman. There were no olive skins, sweating stubble, or heavy, hairy hands wiping dribbles of Chianti from chins. Slater, Dot, and Jamieson stood in a trio on the far side of the room. The talk was of the quality of the Chablis.

Carl was doing his best to compose himself and not to appear out of his depth when a familiar voice floated across the chatter. 'Hey, Carl!'

A forty-year-old Jamaican, slightly gone to seed and squeezed into a Burtons bargain, walked over to Carl and Con.

'Hey, Gandy,' Carl responded. 'How's that place old nigger villains go to die?'

'Tottenham is fine, me boy. Very fine. I hear Islington is not so very good.'

'We're not interested in insurance no more,' said Carl, admitting no weakness. 'What you doing here? Ain't yer afraid yer'll miss a riot?'

Gandy looked round the collection of immaculate suits. 'I come to do business, man. But I don't see no one I know. And this lot is using words I thought was diseases.'

Con had drifted over to the crowd. Carl stared out perplexed, as he caught the cynical Irish drawl. Con's newly met acquaintances greeted his wit with controlled amusement. The laughter grated on Carl's ears. How could that little bastard find this all so easy?

Con was launching into another example of his warped personal philosophy. 'I found Trinity College, Dublin, an island of erudition in a sea of ignorance. But then, that's the nature of Ireland. Catholicism is a brilliant wife, but agricultural labour a banal husband; the children of that marriage were always likely to be inconsistent.'

Carl scoured the room with lowered, defensive eyes. There was one person missing: Klein.

'Can we get on please, gentlemen?' Dot called, and the gathering shuffled itself to attention. They began to file out into the hall; and into a second, smaller room, where rows of folding chairs had been set out. Carl followed the flow. When he arrived at a seat with his name on, he sat and looked round for Con. The Irishman had melted away.

Slater escorted Dot into the room and then slipped back to the hall, closing the panelled door behind him.

Con left the shadows beneath the stairs when he saw Slater walk out into the garden. He peered out into the bright sunlight, just in time to glimpse Pat Klein disappearing behind the sculptured hedges. Slater was walking in the same direction.

Con waited till Slater was out of sight and then hurried upstairs. He stepped noiselessly down the hall and tapped gently on the last door. He got the response he had hoped for. Nothing. He glanced back down the hall and then ducked into the room. He stole two items of jewellery from the room: a plain gold necklace, and a brooch in the shape of a ballerina. Presents from George.

Con managed to conceal himself in the garden like a chameleon for the next hour. He emerged into public view again when the door to the meeting swung open and the participants began to wander out to the terrace.

Two trestle tables had been erected. The snow-white cloths gleamed through an over-generous array of salads and cold meats. A row of round, canopied tables ran parallel with the buffet. Slater sat at the far table and contemplated a peacock which strutted down the slope to the lake.

Carl wandered along the tables. He approved of Slater's overt and grandiose hospitality. Slater saw him approaching, rose with obvious indifference and began to descend the steps from the terrace to the lawns.

Carl followed him. The meeting had hardened his understanding of the magnitude of this little offer, but he wanted further confirmation from Slater. Besides, he disliked being ignored.

'Nice garden,' Carl called, as he trotted down the steps. Slater turned, feeling obliged to treat this boy with at least a modicum of social grace. 'Pity you got no one to share it with,' Carl added.

Slater felt the jibe and tacked away from it. 'You used to be able to see the road. Through there by the lake,' he said in a matter-of-fact tone. 'So I moved a tree.'

Carl tried to look suitably impressed. 'It's very natural.'

'I think it's what God would have done if he'd had the money.'

'That's good,' Carl laughed. 'D'you make that up?'

'No.' Slater gazed out to the horizon. 'No.'

'That was a good day at the races, Tony, weren't it?'

'I've known better.'

''Course, I knew you was up to something then. The feathers was flying round old Bobby Chalker, weren't they? You must of had a terrible time, what with all this going through.'

Slater stared at the cocky, grinning face. He said: 'Can't you have a conversation without scoring points off people, Carl?'

Carl detected the weakness and pressed on. 'Worth all the bother, though. I mean, I can see you must be making

205

a packet out of this deal. Well, 'course you are; your little company's perfect for old Ms Fleming's mob. S'no trouble to toss a few extra parcels in all those vans shooting round the country . . . I'm just a bit confused 'bout what "the goods" are. She still ain't said.'

'To be honest, I don't care. It doesn't take much imagination to narrow it down to four types of the same thing. Probably all four at various times.'

'Ain't a fine upstanding man like you bothered by . . . the morals of it, Tony?'

'Yes. Any more questions?'

'Why yer doing it then?'

'Money.'

'You don't need it!'

Slater cast a glance down to the lake. The shimmering reflection of the water seemed to wake a memory in him. His voice became sullen and resigned. 'I bought this house for my wife. She was sick. I thought it would make her better. The day she died, she told me how much she hated it . . . People still climb over the wall sometimes, so I'll build a higher one. You see I like it here, Carl. I've worked twenty years for all this. I'll take as much as I can from the world and then I'll shut the gates on it.'

'So twenty years ago you was just like me,' said Carl smugly.

'I was never just like you. Anything I earned illegally was invested in the future. And in the last ten years, I've committed no crime. At least none that isn't accepted business practice.'

'So what the hell's going on here, then?' Carl gestured to the party on the terrace.

'I don't know,' Slater replied with a shrug. 'Ms Fleming is the legal representative of the American concern which is buying CPC. I don't know what she said to you. I wasn't listening. I wasn't even in the room.'

'And that makes it right?'

'That makes it none of my business.'

Carl tired of the moral argument. He sensed he was not going to win. He pointed to the bonfire in the meadow. 'What you gonna burn, Tony – apart from yer fingers, that is?'

Slater knew now, if he did not know before, that Carl's malice was persistent. He said: 'Next week is Redfield Fayre. It's an old pagan celebration of midsummer. It got hijacked by Christianity during the Reformation. You know the Reformation?' Carl shook his head. He did not care either. 'The festival had died out, really. When I bought this house I revived it.'

'Sounds like big fun,' Carl noted sarcastically.

'It's not whirring mechanical things that make people scream,' Slater countered. 'It's a procession and a feast, and games. And a lot of mess to clear up the next morning. But the local villagers like it. This is the manor house, you see: they expect it. And sometimes you have to do what's expected of you, Carl.'

'Maybe I'll come down and have a look. Why don't yer invite me? Why don't yer educate me?'

'There'll be another houseful of people next Wednesday. Come down if you like. Bring your wife, if you like.'

'You mean that?' The offer had surprised Carl.

Slater pushed his hands into his pockets and began to saunter away. 'I'm not out to make an enemy of you, Carl. I really couldn't be bothered. It's just an invitation. It's just common courtesy.'

George Klein was working late again that Thursday night. More and more he had come to feel like a traitor when he was occupied in the depot. The drivers and mechanics seemed to stare at him with grim-faced distrust these days. Broderick may have magnified the issue of redundancies, but it had not been complete fabrication: the tear was in the cloth, and it could only get bigger. Klein had tried to maintain his slap-on-the-back bonhomie, but his heart was not in it. They knew that. Their wives and children knew that. Klein felt as if he were selling people's lives, instead of a company.

The alternative to the depot was the office, and with it, exposure to Slater's cool efficiency. The alternative to the office was home, and the constant reminders of how that efficiency had prised away his wife. For George, it was a choice between being stabbed, shot, or poisoned. At least in the depot he knew his job; he had twenty years of conditioned manual response to fall back on.

George leaned back on the filing cabinet in the despatch office and stared at Con's sneering, bony face. He silently cursed the web of events and circumstances that tangled up his life and denied the contentment of ignorance. He took an envelope from the inside pocket of his sports jacket and tossed it down on the desk in front of Con. He said: 'That'll be the last. I don't need you for nothing any more.'

Con's eyebrows twisted as he frowned. 'Oh. What a blow to my finances.'

'Go back and work for that little Hitler, Con. You two deserve each other,' spat Klein.

Con adopted a pose of studious reflection and then manufactured a smile as he crossed to Klein. 'You've been so very generous, Mr Klein,' he whined with sickly servility. 'So much so, that I decided to do something for you. Off my own back, as it were. To give you the peace of mind that only absolute certainty can bring.' He reached in the pocket of his suit and removed the ballerina brooch. He placed it carefully on top of the filing cabinet. Klein looked on with numb fury.

'She was there,' Con confirmed, 'with her lover in Arcady. So sad. Does it carry very special memories – '

'Shut up you filthy little parasite.' Klein snatched up the brooch. 'Now get out.'

Con fingered the necklace in his pocket as he sidled to the door. The brooch was a sharp enough knife in the old fool's guts. He rather fancied the necklace for himself. He paused briefly by the partition which separated Klein's office from the reception. For that split second he was well enough obscured for Broderick not to notice him when he entered the reception.

'That's the last one out, George,' Broderick called. 'East London Import. I'm off now.' But instead of turning and leaving, he stood frozen to the spot as Con emerged from behind the partition and smiled at him.

The boys sat hunched round a table in Cheers. As usual Carl was the centre of attention. The others had taken the news of the approach by Dot and the conference at Slater's with varying degrees of disapproval. Their reactions ranged from Freddie's feeling of mild rejection, to Russell's outright astonishment and hostility.

Carl was saying: 'I'll tell yer why we are gonna hit that lorry, Russell. Nice Ms Fleming is offering us a deal. She's even offering thirty percent discount. What we gonna pay with, eh? You got a house to sell? Some bent mortgage company owns mine. But Klein's got something going on. It's ten to one on he's carrying her stuff for her. We hit the lorry, and then we get a hundred per cent discount.'

'Thas brilliant, man,' gasped Jo Jo.

'And if he's not,' Carl added, 'well, what he's got in that lorry's gotta be worth something.'

Russell rolled his eyes to the ceiling and launched into his fifth attack. 'This ain't a little bit of this and that, Carl.

We could go down for life! You want that? I say it stinks. And I say drugs stink. I don't wanna see some little idiot dead on an overdose. We always said drugs was for morons, Carl.'

'Klein screwed us!' Carl replied angrily.

'What the hell are we making a career out of here?' Russell queried.

Carl snapped back impatiently: 'I don't wanna pension out of this, Russ. If we're right 'bout that lorry, then we can kiss goodbye to Ms Fleming's "organization" and live in luxury. Do we hit the lorry?'

There was no further objection. Carl leaned back in his chair and smiled. 'We hit the lorry,' he said firmly.

'It left twenty minutes ago.'

Five heads turned at the sound of Con's breathless voice.

The door to Broderick's flat splintered and cracked under the weight of Freddie's powerful shoulder. He and Mario ran in through the shattered frame and scattered in search of their man. Mario hurried down the corridor to the bedroom and kicked open the flimsy two-ply door.

Broderick stood stricken, like a rabbit in headlights. Two half-packed vinyl suitcases lay on the bed beside him. 'I don't . . . know nothing . . . honest . . . I don't know . . .' he whimpered desperately.

Freddie walked slowly into the doorway, and took an automatic pistol from his pocket. Broderick's roller-coaster thoughts sensed the worst, and in an instant he committed himself to one last chance of escape. He darted back through the French windows to the balcony, and jumped.

He crumpled as he hit the ground twenty-five feet below. He felt the shooting pain in his left thigh, and the agonizing throb in his knee, where the sinews and ligaments had wrenched away from the bones. He saw Freddie and Mario peering down from the balcony and tried to heave himself to his feet. His left knee dangled like the shattered fetlock of a racehorse and he collapsed back to the hard earth.

Broderick's heart leaped into his mouth as he saw the architect of his downfall stroll from the shadows of the building. 'You been telling porkies,' murmured Carl. There was an adolescent laugh and Jo Jo approached from the opposite direction.

'Klein changed the booking today. Honest he did . . . I didn't know . . . I . . .'

Carl squatted down next to the wrecked life which was squirming on the grass.

'Let me have a look at that knee for yer, Mr B.'

'Please . . . please. You promised me money and you didn't . . . My job's all I've got. Please! He would have known it was me. I couldn't tell . . . please.'

'No really,' Carl reasoned. 'I done me knee once playing football. I know 'bout these things.' He placed his hand lightly on the swollen jelly that used to be Broderick's knee. Broderick screamed out with pain.

'I reckon you torn all the ligaments, Mr B. Same as what I did. But worse. You put any pressure on it and it's agony.'

Carl paused and stared hard into Broderick's terrified eyes. 'Now where's that lorry gone, Mr B.?'

Thirteen

A bank of cloud slipped across the moon and dragged its shadow over Freddie's Cadillac, which was parked on the cliff road above Newhaven. Freddie lowered himself to sit on the front bumper of the car. He lit his fortieth cigarette of the day, tossed the screwed-up packet onto the grass and gazed over to where Carl sat observing the docks.

Russell wandered back from the road and leaned against the wing of the car. He yawned, took a swig of beer from a can of Pils and then crushed the metal container in his grip and threw it over the cliff.

'Jo Jo was spooked,' said Russell quietly.

'Dunno why we put up with the stupid tosser,' Freddie hissed.

Russell lowered his elbows onto the bonnet and settled his head on his forearms. 'He's no different from the rest of us,' he remarked wearily. 'Carl'll get us all killed trying to prove a point. We don't know what we're doing here. What do we know about? Dressing up on Friday night, acting hard once in a while . . . when we can be bothered to get up early enough.'

Freddie looked up sternly. 'You shouldn't be here then.'

'I won't be after this.'

'You can go now. Stick yer thumb out. Go on, you're a

big boy.' Freddie gave a little satisfied smile. 'You got quite a patter, ain't yer, Russ? Must be working on that stall – conning people that a bit of old junk's an antique.'

Russell eased himself away from Freddie's accusing gaze.

'Who's yer best mate, Russ? No one special, is it? Just whoever's getting their hands dirty for yer. You can toss cold water on anything, can't yer? But yer always want a lick of everyone else's lolly.'

The truth was as unpalatable to Russell as it was to Carl. But he was saved by the green light.

Carl's cat-like stare pounced on the lorry as it pulled out of the dock complex. He jumped to his feet. 'Let's go,' he commanded.

They quickly jumped into the car and sped down the cliff road. They caught the lorry as it was pulling onto the Lewes Road. It was easily recognizable: white thirty-five-hundred weight with the red CPC logo. Freddie closed in behind, checked his mirrors, and then accelerated past. Carl and Russell screwed round in their seats. One driver.

About a mile along the deserted, winding road, the Transit sat parked on a verge. Jo Jo stretched his arm along the back of the driver's seat and glanced at Mario, who was dozing in the back.

'S'quarter past two,' he said, anxious for more comforting company.

Mario lifted his tired eyes and glared at Jo Jo. 'Could be hours yet. Have a kip,' he barked, bad-tempered through lack of sleep.

'I can't!'

'You'll wake up when Carl gets here. Now shut up, will yer?'

Jo Jo saw the heavy lids fall shut. He began to drum with his fingers on the seat back, but Mario ignored the distraction and lolled back against the wall of the Transit.

213

'I can't sleep sometimes, yer know . . .'

The response was not immediate, but it came eventually. Mario forced open his eyes, took a deep, irritated breath, and realized that Jo Jo would not tolerate being left alone with his thoughts. 'Why not, Jo Jo?'

'Just can't . . . Just lay there thinking 'bout how people go to sleep. I don't understand what happens to yer, see? More I think about it, the worse it gets. Till I don't wanna sleep. Till I'm frightened to . . . Thas all.'

The headlights of the Cadillac interrupted Jo Jo's morbidity. 'Here comes something,' Mario warned.

The Cadillac flashed by with the horn blaring. Mario hoisted himself upright. 'Let's go,' he urged Jo Jo.

Jo Jo's fingers fumbled with the ignition key.

'Come on!' Mario repeated.

'All right man!' The engine sparked to life and Jo Jo shoved the gear stick into first. The Transit shuddered into a stall as Jo Jo tried to pull away.

'For chrissake!' Mario pressed close to the sweating Jo Jo.

'Shut up!' The engine roared again. Jo Jo's face was taught with concentration as the Transit moved off. Mario scuttled back to the rear window. Behind them in the distance, he saw the headlights of the lorry.

'That must be it,' he breathed.

Freddie had parked a further mile down the road. He watched with Russell and Carl as the Transit approached, followed closely now by the CPC lorry.

'Here he comes,' said Freddie, hushed and expectant.

The Transit passed the Cadillac barely fifty yards in front of the lorry. 'Jeez, he's shifting!' gasped Russell, as the lorry flashed past.

'Get after 'em!' Carl shouted.

Freddie screeched out into the road and accelerated as

hard as he could, but the Cadillac had seen better days: it had been bought for status, not speed.

Russell leaned over from the back seat. 'He'll catch him at this rate.'

'Shift it, Freddie!' said Carl hoarsely.

The sweat on Jo Jo's face and the trembling in his voice was growing as his eyes flitted to the rear-view mirror and he saw the lorry closing fast. Mario shifted uncomfortably in the back of the Transit. 'He's coming up quick, Jo Jo. Put yer foot down!'

'It is down! Where's Freddie? Why ain't he hooting?'

'The bloody thing'll be on us, Jo Jo! Come on!' Mario beat his fist on the wall of the van. 'Don't let him pass yer!'

'What'll I do? Where's Freddie?' The lorry was less than twenty feet from the rear of the Transit now. The face of the driver was illuminated by the ghostly glow of the diffused headlights. Mario could see the determination on that face.

'Where's Freddie?' Jo Jo screamed again.

'Keep going!'

'How much longer can I bloody keep going? Shall I hit the brakes?'

'No! He's too close, man!'

'He's gonna pass!' Jo Jo saw the indicator flash, and the headlights of the lorry slid out of his mirror. The panic took control. His foot slammed on the brake. Mario was thrown forward and then jolted back as the lorry slammed into the right rear of the Transit. The impact spun the van full circle; it toppled onto its side and the back doors were forced open. Mario was flung out onto the verge as the vehicle skimmed along the grass and struck a line of pine trees.

The driver of the lorry was fighting to keep control, but the impact with the Transit had thrown it off line and it

215

could not negotiate the next bend in the road. It ploughed through the barbed wire fence which guarded the steep slope down to a field. The fence posts were dragged up in its wake as it somersaulted down the slope. The sliding back door flew up like a roller blind, and a shower of importation crates sprayed out behind the doomed vehicle.

The metal of the lorry frame groaned in surrender as it reached the bottom of the slope. It toppled over three more times before coming to rest on its side.

There was no movement from the cab. For a moment there was silence. But the billowing white smoke from the engine gave warning of what was about to happen.

The explosion lit the countryside like a giant flare, a fireball shot from the bed and flew in a tongue of flame across the field. Within seconds the air was thick with acrid smoke.

Mario was crawling, shocked, across the road when the Cadillac's brakes screamed the other boys' arrival. They jumped out of the car and scattered in three different directions. Russell ran quickly to Mario and carried him to the soft grass of the verge. Mario's face was grazed and bruised, his clothes ripped, and his body shivering with fear.

Carl ran quickly to the edge of the slope and looked down at the incinerated lorry. His fixation had gone up in flames. He had no thought for the driver, or for the injured Mario. He was racked with angry disappointment. He had been cheated again and his frustration gnawed relentlessly at his brain.

He had no thought for Jo Jo either.

When Carl finally turned to the devastation on the other side of the road, he saw Freddie walking slowly and unsteadily from the spot where the Transit had come to rest.

216

Freddie had always said that he would 'dance on the stupid sod's grave'. He could now. His face was streaked with tears.

Russell's voice rang sour and fatigued across the office at the Angel. 'We was on the news, yer know?'

A small electronic chime on Freddie's watch announced midday. Carl raised a can of beer and drained half the contents in one go.

The nine hours since the crash had ticked away like the last moments in the condemned cell. Their faces were gaunt and unshaven, numb and expressionless. Only Con's eyes flickered with animation as he watched the scene from the corner of the room.

Freddie ran his finger along the gash in the centre of the table. Carl looked up at him and offered him the can. 'Want some of this?' Freddie shook his head, got up from the chair and wandered to the window.

Carl's thoughts had traced an erratic arc since Jo Jo's death. His grief was not for the boy. In fact he had found himself developing a brooding anger at Jo Jo's imcompetence. That anger soon grew to resentment for anyone around him. He stared round the faces and wondered why they could not share his certainty, his ambition, his strength. How could any fault be laid at the feet of a man without failing, like himself? Nothing would have gone wrong if they had shared his single-minded dedication. Would it?

And Marty. Now there was the bastard who had started the dissent. There was someone Carl had relied on. That's where the treachery of fate began. That's where the blame lies. . . .'

'Queer boy Marty's the first thing I'm gonna deal with,' growled Carl, as his thoughts forced themselves into words. 'D'you believe that, eh? Someone yer used to call

217

a mate? I reckon we'd still be raking it in if it weren't for him. Me own bloody wife saw him with a bunch of scum and tried to keep her mouth shut.'

'Sure,' said Russell. 'That explains everything.'

'Shut up,' Carl snapped. 'Where the hell is Mario?'

Russell glanced up from the table. 'Well, last night he was running round with you. He's been running round with you most nights . . . that's why his mum and dad have got a new cook. I saw him 'bout an hour ago. He's still shaking. But he's got no job and no money, 'cos we ain't been paid, have we? So he's tried to pull himself together and gone to do a pick-up at Casey's Wine Bar.' Carl looked up, surprised. 'A pick-up for Theo,' Russell added.

Carl's face sank back to blank disinterest. 'I don't care.'

'Don't it twist yer guts, huh?' Russell queried. 'Yer know what "crack" is – what people take when they can't get high on cocaine no more. If yer believe what they said on the news, we watched a million quid's worth of the stuff burn! . . . Just what gets you high any more, Carl? Did that do it?'

'Slater and Klein don't know it was us,' Carl said, trying to believe his own logic. 'They don't know Jo Jo, do they, Con?'

'I don't think – '

'So how can they know it was us, eh?'

'How long's it gonna take 'em to find out?' said Russell.

'We'll get things back together. We still got a deal with the Yank bird. We just gotta get some cash.'

Russell got up from the table and took his aching limbs to the door. 'Which bank shall we rob, Carl?'

Carl stared hard at him, and said: 'You gonna go work for Theo too?'

'I'm going as far as these little nigger feet will take me,'

218

Russell replied. 'Like I said, Carl, I think we're in big trouble.'

Carl considered him gone and searched for other support. 'Like I said, Freddie, we'd have all the cash we need if that queer bastard Marty hadn't shopped us to every hood in town. That's what he's done yer know – '

Russell's temper snapped and he shouted at Carl: 'Stupid arse silly Jo Jo is dead, and all you can do is whine on 'bout Marty!'

'He let me down!'

'We all did, Carl. You go on thinking that. You'll feel better.' Russell slammed the door to reception behind him as he left.

The bang shook Freddie; took him back to the exploding lorry, the crash, Jo Jo . . .

Freddie gazed at Carl with wide, uncomprehending eyes. He said in a whisper: 'Why'd he have to get himself killed, Carl?'

Con slipped his hands into his jacket pockets. He gave an almost imperceptible sigh and decided that time was running out for these boys. He would have to look elsewhere for amusement.

Less than an hour later, Con was standing in the depot at CPC. Klein stood in front of him, agitated and fuming with it.

'Of course I'm sure it was him,' Con said. 'They were practically in tears. I hadn't realized they had so much affection for the stupid little boy.'

'I hope you didn't know they were planning this,' threatened Klein.

'How could I have? I would have told you, Mr Klein. I always worked for you. Your welfare was my welfare . . . Oh and by the way, I did hear Mr Broderick's name mentioned today. For the first time, of course . . . I'm really not sure he can be trusted.'

Con smiled and congratulated himself. The manoeuvring, and all the entertainment that had brought, was over. Now the end-game was in motion. He eagerly anticipated one last climactic thrill from his machinations.

Slater sank back into the chair behind his desk at CPC. He looked anxiously for a reaction from Dot as Klein blustered on.

'The driver's dead. Broderick was the only other one who knew about it and he's – '

'Apart from five little maniacs in Islington,' said Slater bitterly.

'Broderick's done a bunk. They can't trace it to us,' Klein added.

Dot dropped her calm indifference. 'But there's a chance. And until there isn't a chance, the deal's on hold.' She looked knowingly at Slater. 'The perfect company is beginning to appear a little frayed at the edges, Tony.'

Klein hovered by the door, nervous and embarrassed. Slater stared up at him. 'Why did you do it, George, after all we agreed?'

Dot answered for him. 'Because he wanted to get a deal. Just like you, Tony. We needed that shipment. And there were others on the way, incidentally. You obviously don't know much about creating a market. I've been patient with you. I stood outside this office and watched a riot going on. I've been hanging on the phone to New York all morning, trying to explain to the consortium how and why their tax-free dollars went up in smoke. I don't care how strong the wind is; this tree don't bend any more.'

She rose and walked to the door. As she passed Klein, she said quietly: 'I trust you'll deal with the little boy who got us into this mess.'

Slater watched her leave and then turned angrily on

Klein. 'I warned you to stay away from Bobby Chalker, George. In 1963 I told you not to buy a hot van for fifteen quid.' He left his seat and walked briskly out into the open-plan office.

Klein banged his fist against the door-frame and then called after Slater: 'You told me to give up everything I worked for, Tony. Sweated for, for you!' His voice boomed across the floor and the activity of twenty office staff petered out in deference to the bosses' drama. 'Well, I did this for me. And if it makes you squirm, well then something good's come out of it.'

'I told you,' repeated Slater, as he walked away.

Klein roared back. 'And if you've got anything else to tell me . . . well . . . tell it to my wife. You taken her from me too, ain't you? You think I don't know? I've got pictures, Tony. When did that all start? When she was holding your hand and saying "There, there" the day Jacky died?' The pain of rejection cracked through Klein's voice. 'The only thing I had that . . . the only way I was better off than you. And now you've got her too. You're a greedy bastard, ain't you, Tony?'

Marty ripped the shirt from hangers in his wardrobe. He patted frantically at the pockets and then cast the clothing aside. He moved to the pine chest beneath the window, wrenched out the drawers and began to rifle through them. Disappointed, he turned and almost dived down to the floor. He dragged a pair of tattered 501s from beneath the bed and snatched out the contents of the pockets. Loose change scattered onto the floor, along with the object of Marty's frenzied search: a small, clear-plastic bag containing a tab of LSD.

Marty rolled onto the bed and smiled, his face illuminated by the evening sun. He tapped the soles of his DMs together. The skinhead uniform was back. He dangled the packet in front of him for a moment and then swung his legs round onto the floor and sat up. His eyes met Carl's.

Carl had washed, shaved, and changed. Despite his tiredness, he still conjured up an image of cool, collected elegance. He laughed dismissively and cruelly.

'How d'you get in here?' asked Marty.

Carl held up a key. 'Gave it to Linda, remember?'

'Oh yeah.' Marty attempted to act and sound as bored and uninterested as possible. He took the white tab from the packet, stuck out his tongue, and popped the drug into his mouth.

'That what one of yer queer mates give yer?' said Carl.

'More than you ever did.' Marty began to chew on the tab.

'You look high enough already to me. How stoned out of yer head d'yer have to be to let some bloke spunk it down yer throat?'

Marty nodded his head. 'That what you wanna do, Carl? 'Course I know yer like to shoot it into birds' mouths, yer told me.' He got up and tried to push his way past Carl, but the other boy grabbed him and forced him back against the wall. 'You let go of me,' Marty snarled.

Carl gripped tighter, and shook Marty harder. He could feel the vibration of the floor as Marty's head repeatedly struck the wall. 'Think I don't know what your game is, queer boy? What'd I do to you, eh? Who'd you take up to my office to smash the place up, queer boy?'

Marty's body twisted with pain as he hit the wall again. 'I ain't done nothing to yer,' he moaned.

'Wanna know how sick yer make me?' Carl screamed. 'Just 'cos yer can't get yer end away with me!'

'Oh, sir – '

'Shut up!'

Marty knew this could not go on. He felt every bone in

his back would snap if it did. He summoned up all his reserves of strength and pushed Carl off. Carl fell back against the bed and Marty escaped down into the street.

Marty rushed out of the front door of the builders' merchant and swung it shut behind him to make pursuit more difficult. He ran about twenty yards down the street and then turned to see Carl emerge through the door. Carl was not running after him, as he had expected, but just walking slowly to his car.

'Gonna kill me, Carl? That make you feel like a real man?' Marty was beside the red Porsche now. He turned his head and spat at the car. 'Or maybe that does, eh?'

Marty stopped, and the anger in him turned to confusion when Carl spoke. The voice was sad and pleading for explanation. 'Why d'yer walk out on me, Marty? . . . Why d'yer leave me on me own, when I needed yer? . . .'

They stared silently at each other, and then Carl began to walk towards Marty.

A black Cortina was doing sixty in Southgate Road.

Marty did not move.

That made him an easy target.

The bullet struck him in the stomach.

Carl heard the car approaching, and he heard the shot. He did not see where it hit. He looked round, panicked. 'Get in the car!' he screamed to Marty.

Marty fumbled open the passenger door, and Carl jumped in the driver's side. The Cortina was coming back, Carl ducked down in the seat as a second bullet shattered the side window of the Porsche. Marty slumped into the car and dragged shut the door. Carl started the engine and spun the wheels. The Porsche sped off. Carl glanced in the rear-view mirror to see the Cortina swing back out of Northchurch Road about a hundred and fifty yards behind. 'They won't catch us,' he said breathlessly. He turned sharply into Downham Road and accelerated.

223

He depressed a button near the gear stick and the passenger window rolled down with a quiet whirring. Carl took the Smith and Wesson from the glove shelf and tossed it into Marty's lap. 'If they do get close, use it.'

Carl expected some response; at least a nod. He looked over to Marty and saw the stream of blood. 'Oh God,' he murmured. He beat his fist on the steering wheel. 'Oh Christ no, Marty!'

The horror came cold and hard: Carl knew that bullet was meant for him.

Fourteen

The next morning came stonier and greyer than any had for months. It had rained in the night. Torrential and angry.

Carl opened his eyes to an unfamiliar landscape: a broad sloping heath, crested with a row of trees which lay on the far side of a newly tarmacked main road. A string of racehorses, powerful and coltish, making their way home after the morning gallops. Closer to him he saw three disused petrol pumps, a decaying outbuilding, a rusting metal sign assuring passing motorists that they could 'Be sure of Shell'.

A sandy-haired boy of fourteen moved directly into Carl's vision, wheeling a BMX bike. Carl stared at him blearily.

'You want this car washed?' demanded the boy. 'There's a hose still working over there. I could do it for you.'

Carl groped to get his bearings, to force his brain into reluctant action. 'What?' he said, disorientated.

'It's filthy. I'll do it for two quid. I won't do it for less.'

Carl rubbed at his eyes, as the boy leaned closer to the open car window. 'He's dead, ain't he?' the boy remarked casually. 'I seen a video. They looked just like that.'

The sun stabbed through the clouds and shot a shaft of light into the car as Carl turned quickly to his left. It was not a dream. He had lived the nightmare through the night. Marty's head rested on the back of the seat, his eyes stared lifelessly, cold; there was a trickle of dry blood on his chin.

'You want this car done or not?' the boy insisted.

'No,' Carl answered softly. 'No.'

'It's bloody filthy. You oughta be ashamed of yourself.'

Carl called to the boy as he began to wheel the bike away. 'Where is this?'

The boy looked utterly disgusted. '*This* is Royston, mate.' He turned and wandered off, muttering: 'Don't even know where you are. You shouldn't be allowed to drive that car, you shouldn't.'

Carl jolted himself awake. Royston. Where the hell was Royston? A10? Yep, that was it. That was the road. Driving all night to go thirty miles! In circles, turning back on himself, and back again. Another circle. Anywhere to get away from this nightmare!

And Marty. Oh God. Oh God. . . .

Carl looked numbly over to the heath and tried to fix his eyes on one spot, one tree, to focus, to decide, to expel these thousand battling emotions and make a decision.

He saw a narrow road, turning off the A10 and cutting a black scar across the lush green grass. He started the car and headed for that road. He drove up to the top of the heath and pulled in to a muddy verge, next to a small bridge. A swollen stream flowed noisily off the chalk escarpment.

Huge, white clouds were scudding across the pale sky, emerging like specious smoke signals from the coppiced crest of the heath. Above the sweating horses. Above the weeping carpet of grass.

Carl heaved Marty's inert body from the car and into his arms. In this deathly embrace, Carl struck off into the

226

woods. Marty's head bobbed, as Carl half stumbled over the exposed tree roots which punctured the thick carpet of leaves; a carpet which lay undisturbed from season to season in this secluded spot. Carl faltered and fell against a tree, almost dropping Marty, but just managing to regain his balance. He paused for a while and squatted by the tree to catch his breath. He leaned back against the smooth beech trunk and slowly slid down to the ground, all the time still cradling Marty.

Carl sat there for some time, rocking slightly, like a disturbed child with an immense rag doll. Occasionally, Marty's head lolled back over Carl's encircling arms. Each time, Carl gently gathered it and nestled it between his arm and chest. The fatigue came like a wave, and washed over Carl. He let his eyes slip shut. His arms relaxed slightly, as he began to drift into sleep. Marty's hand fell down from Carl's shoulder and brushed against his cheek. Carl's eyes flickered open and shut as he felt the motion of the fingers across his unwashed face. After a few moments the hand slid away, Carl's eyes closed firmly and he relaxed his grip on the body.

Carl woke with a start as Marty rolled away from him and rested face down in the leaves. He jumped up and moved to Marty's side. He rolled the dead boy over and began to dust away the small pieces of leaf and dirt which had stuck to his face.

'I'm sorry, Marty,' Carl breathed. 'I din't mean to drop yer.' He looked down at the wide, staring eyes. 'You oughta close those eyes, Marty. Sleep now.' He moved his hand to close the lids, but hesitated. He followed Marty's unseeing gaze up to the canopy of tree branches and leaves.

Carl sank down on the ground next to Marty, looked up to the sky and moved his mouth into the slightest smile. He said: 'That's neat. Can yer hear that? It's

227

raining, but s'not falling on us.' He closed his eyes and listened.

A few drops of rain pierced the cover and struck Marty's face. 'I gotta leave yer here, Mart,' said Carl quietly. 'S'quiet. No one'll bother yer here. You'll never get old, man.'

He opened his eyes and turned to Marty. He saw a droplet which had fallen in the cavity of the dead boy's eye. Now it trickled down his cheek. A perfect tear. 'I forgot all that stuff yer told me, Marty. Forgot it already. I know yer better than yer know yerself.' He shuddered with guilt. 'I shoulda taken yer to a hospital. I know that. But they was after me, Mart. They was gonna kill me.'

They lay there for a while. The natural colonnade of trees rose immovably black against the whitening sky. The two prostrate figures looked small and helpless in the forest.

The rain soon stopped its mesmeric patter on the leaves and Carl got to his feet. He covered Marty's body with leaves and made his way back to the Porsche.

He drove into Royston as the town was waking. He bought a shovel from a hardware shop and then found a telephone box and called Freddie. He said little to satisfy Freddie's sleepy curiosity. They arranged to meet in the office at one. Carl was about to hang up, when he added a warning that Freddie should keep his head down: whoever had fired those shots was still on the loose. Carl was alert enough to know that.

Carl picked his way carefully through the trees to the spot where he had left Marty. Tiredness seemed to be dragging him down, rooting his feet in the earth. He pressed on in search of atonement, or at least, in search of propriety.

He dug for what seemed hours before the hole was deep enough. The soft, peaty earth fell in on itself,

228

reluctant to form a grave. Finally, Carl stood and wiped the sweat from his face. Behind him, the rising sun made bars out of the woods. It would do. It would conceal.

He took Marty by the arms and dragged him to the shallow grave. He placed the corpse gently in the earth and began to cover it. When the interment was complete, Carl scraped leaves over the loose soil, and then sagged back against a tree, exhausted.

'I oughta say something for yer, Marty.' He paused, deep in troubled thought. 'I dunno what to say.' After a few seconds, he began to sing, quietly and unsure.

> Stand up, stand up for Jesus,
> Ye soldiers of the cross,
> Lift high his royal banner,
> It must not suffer loss.
> From victory unto victory
> His army he shall lead . . . lead,
> Till every foe is vanquished,
> And Christ is Lord indeed.
>
> Stand up, stand up for Jesus,
> The strife will not be long,
> This day . . . this day . . .

He clasped his head in his hands and began to sob pitifully. 'Oh Christ! I'm sorry, Marty. I've forgotten the bastard thing!'

Carl snatched up the shovel and began to run in the direction of his car. As he passed the untidy picket fence which marked the boundary of the protected woods, he lashed out with the shovel. He beat maniacally at the fence, becoming more violent as he saw it disintegrate. 'I've forgot the bastard thing!' he screamed, and hurled the shovel into the stream.

The journey back to London was a white-knuckle ride

for Carl. The houses and farm buildings which dotted the edge of the road flew in and out of his vision, hypnotizing him one minute, cracking into his brain like a whip the next. The horizon pulsed and the vibration of the car was magnified a thousand times; shuddering his body, dislocating his thoughts.

When he arrived back at Cranley Gardens, he found the house deserted. The French windows to the garden were half open and the fine net curtains billowed in a breath of wind. Carl's face was shadowed with anxiety. What if they were here? Hiding, waiting, ready to fire the bullets into his wretched, tired, immobile body?

The ring of the phone hit Carl's ears like a deafening clang of church bells. He jumped back and pulled the pistol from his pocket. The shot was automatic, and the machine exploded into a cloud of splintered plastic.

Five seconds passed like eternity, before there was a small click, followed by a familiar sound. 'Hallo. This is Carl Galton's answering service. There's no one available to take your call at the moment. Please leave your name, the time you called, and any message, after the tone.'

Dishevelled and spent, he began to climb the stairs. He called out for Linda. There was no one in the house.

He washed away Marty. He washed away Jo Jo. He cleansed his doubt and locked it in a secret, secure place in his mind. When he emerged from the shower, his face was scrubbed, enlivened, smoothly and aggressively charming again.

Glo had changed little in the bedroom in the seven years since Linda had left it.

There were posters of Adam Ant and Abba. Neat piles of *Jackie* and *19*. A pin-board, covered with photos of Linda and her friends; in the bottom corner, a booth picture of Linda and Carl, smiling, pulling faces. A

'Happiness is . . .' mirror still struggled against the floral wallpaper. On the dressing table, a collection of small porcelain jars and dishes, which once held make-up and pins. A ceramic pot in the shape of an apple, with a large bite taken out of it. A single bed in the centre of one wall, and beside that, a blow-up mattress and a put-you-up. An open suitcase on the floor, full of Linda's things: make-up, shoes, clothes, toiletries. Just beyond that, crammed into the corner, a collection of stuffed toys, now gathering dust. On the bedside table, a wine glass, half full. An ashtray. A pad of paper, with the one word *Dear* written on it.

Kathy pulled back the covers of the bed and tucked them in neatly. She took Linda's nightdress from the bed and held it up against herself. She admired herself in the mirror for a moment, laughed and folded the nightdress. She crossed to the window and pulled back the net.

Carl was still there, sitting in the drizzle on the rustic bench in the small, manicured front garden. Beyond him, the street stretched out, straight and regular: each house a precise outward representation of the formal normality which had been constructed within. A blankness of suburbia; unemotional, suppressed, grey.

Kathy saw Linda, Glo and Stan approaching the house. Linda carried two bags of shopping from Sainsbury's. Glo wearily pushed Stan in his wheelchair. They hesitated at the gate when they spotted Carl, then Glo took the bags from Linda, sat them on Stan's lap and continued into the house.

Kathy let the curtain slip back into place, and Carl and Linda were translated into softer focus.

Linda crossed to the bench and sat down next to Carl.

'Where are the kids?' he asked.

'They're in the house. I couldn't get far on the house-keeping, Carl. Besides, you'd go to the ends of the earth to get yer little ones back, wouldn't yer?' She turned and smiled. She saw a desperate emptiness in his eyes. 'I just din't wanna stay in that house on me own, Carl. Not again. That's all. Really, it was nothing else.'

'I thought yer'd left me, Linda.'

'No – '

'I thought yer'd left me, darlin'.'

'I ran away from here seven years ago. To you.' She paused and put one hand to her brow. 'I tried to leave yer, Carl. But there's nowhere to go.'

'Come home, darlin'.'

'All right.' He was visibly taken aback by the speed of her reply. He had expected to have to cajole and persuade. 'Well, that's what yer want, ain't it?' she added.

'Don't yer want some time to think?'

'No.'

'You can – '

'No. It's obvious for me. I din't think 'bout marrying yer. I just did it; it was easy. Why should I think 'bout *being* married to yer?'

'I'm sorry I hit – '

'I made yer. Sorry, you,' she corrected.

'But – '

'No, really. I'm the one who's sorry. You're a good man. You must be. I'm lucky.'

'I need you, Linda,' he breathed.

There was a sudden minute crack in the protective armour of dumb submissiveness which she had constructed. 'I'm late,' she said quietly. He stared at her for a moment, as if he did not understand. 'I'm pregnant, Carl.'

'You sure?'

'Oh yes . . . Why are you smiling? I'll get the kids.'

He jumped up from the bench and placed his hands on her shoulders. 'No, not yet. I'll pick yer up later, right?'

He smiled warmly, enfolded her in his arms and kissed her tenderly. She watched as he jogged off down the street to his car. She waited for the realization. It came to him when he reached down to unlock the door of the Porsche.

Carl stared back at Linda. The smile had vanished from his face. They were both thinking the same thing: Chris.

Carl trotted up the steps of the house in Bethnal Green and rang Con's bell. He muttered impatiently, glanced over his shoulder and then rang again. The door opened and Con peered out circumspectly. Carl pushed past him into the hall.

Con pushed the door shut and leaned against it. He watched as Carl began to ascend the stairs to the bedsit.

'Marty's dead,' said Carl. 'I had to leave him out in the country. I reckon whoever it was, was after me. Come on, I got things to do.'

Con did not move to the stairs. Instead, he walked over to the first door which ran off the hall. Carl turned and gazed down the stairs. Con motioned him to enter the door on the ground floor. Carl's unease erupted again as he wandered down the stairs and in through the door. Con followed him and locked the door behind them.

They had entered a small lobby, which had been converted into a library. The walls were completely lined with books on black lacquered shelves. Con passed Carl and went through a second door. 'This way,' he beckoned. Carl followed him into a large, pristine kitchen. The walls were a grey, paint-effected mottle; there was a circular glass table surrounded by four, green metal, gothic-backed chairs. A glass vase with a dozen white lilies. Fifty bottles of wine, racked inobtrusively in one corner.

'This is very nice, Con,' said Carl, uncertain why they were there.

233

Con quickly clarified the situation. 'I'm afraid the nasty little attic bedsit was something of an understatement. You see, I own the whole house. Each floor is different, you know. I occupy them according to my mood.'

They moved on to the living-room, which was decorated with the same exquisite taste as the rest of the house: sparse, minimal, with a restrained flourish of baroque. Bright bands of light were cast onto the floor by the slatted wooden blinds. There were moulded architraves on doors which had been extended to the ceiling. Two matching sofas in plain, pale fabric faced each other across the room. On the walls were the photos Con had taken of Slater and Pat, blown up and framed. A sheet of thick aquamarine-tinted glass rested on a steel girder base to form a low table between the sofas. There were two books on the glass: Horst and Bruce Webber. An architect's drawing-board stood in the bay window.

Carl's eyes were drawn first to the photos. 'Nice snaps,' he quipped, trying to sound relaxed.

'They're not snaps you fool, they're art,' Con said forcefully. Carl's head swung round to Con. 'They say it comes out of suffering,' the Irishman added.

'Quite full of yerself today, Con. Never dared speak to me like that before.'

'You never cared to get to know me.'

'How long you had all this?'

'About three years. I had it re-done last August. Do you like it?'

'You're a nutter, ain't yer?' Carl said coldly.

Con tossed his head back and laughed with intense amusement. 'Perhaps,' he chuckled, 'I just loved my mother. Or was it my father? Or was it my brother? And yes . . . they were after you. Mr Klein was very upset.'

'How long yer been telling him everything, Con?'

'I've always told him what I wanted to tell him, other-

234

wise you would have been dead in a ditch months ago. I always work for myself, Carl. The only truly free people in this world are those who can convincingly carry off the role of slave. And you really believed I was terrified of your mindless violence! That's funny.'

He flopped down on the sofa and studied Carl's confusion. 'I got this place by siphoning money off Bobby Chalker, and did very nicely thank you when he died. Oh, I got all the decent stuff . . . I was far too clever for that idiotic beast Stalky. Your first guess was quite right there. I was worried for a time. But you got rid of him for me in the end.'

The extent of Con's duplicity was seeping like acid into Carl's brain, burning and scarring. He walked over to the window, trying to collect his thoughts, to work out a suitable punishment. He noticed a set of blueprints on the drawing-board.

'Oh yes,' said Con gleefully, 'those are the plans for the warehouse you thought Klein had stolen from you. Mine too, I'm afraid. Don't be too disappointed. George Klein is an odious relic of a dead world. He deserved your hate.'

Carl stared out through the window. 'Who you gonna screw up next, Con?'

'You were quite hard work. I deserve a break. My taxi should be here soon. I'm taking a long holiday. By tomorrow, my path will be marked by the stars of the southern hemisphere.'

'You couldn't go far enough,' growled Carl, as he clenched his fists and turned. There was no fear in Con's expression. Perhaps it was because he held a gun in his hand.

The soft Irish drawl did not waver. 'Don't worry, Carl. I'm not going to kill you. But you know that. I don't need to. If Klein doesn't get you, then the police will probably trace Jo Jo, or dig up Marty, wherever he lies rotting. And so I win again, because I think you'd prefer me to shoot you here, than rot in prison. That would be hell to you. To have the next twenty years of your life mapped out by someone else. . . . You should still be grateful to me, though. I'm a spirit which has touched your life, and illuminated it with intense pleasure and dreadful pain. That's a joy most people never experience . . . You can go now.'

Con ushered Carl to the front door and out into the street. As the door slammed behind him, Carl gazed up at the sky and thought it seemed stained and sickly. It might just have been the haze of pollution. He looked down to the street and saw a girl on a bicycle. He remarked to himself that she was the most beautiful thing he had ever seen. He walked off to his car and kept his appointment at the office.

Freddie took the news of Marty's death with silent grief. Good old reliable Freddie. In the past forty-eight hours his nerves had been stretched taught, and the body that once glowed with power seemed deflated and suddenly frail. His life and mentality was based on certainties: that he was stronger than anyone else, so they would get out of his way and make his passage easy. The intangibility of fate confused and dulled him.

Carl glanced up from the table. 'You crying?'

Freddie did not turn his face from the window. 'Yeah . . . I am.'

'Will yer do something for me?' Carl asked quietly.

'What?'

'Go home, man.'

'Then what?'

'Just wait for me to call. And look after yerself, Freddie.' Carl paused as he saw Freddie wipe the tears

236

from his cheek. 'Go on. Get out of this place 'fore the bailiffs arrive.'

'What we gonna do, Carl?'

'Be hard.'

'Go down fighting, eh?'

'Oh we're not going down, Freddie. See, I been thinking 'bout it on the way here. And the way I figure it, everything's just fallen into our lap. We are going way, way up.'

After Freddie had left the office, Carl sat there alone, for some time, and tried to reconstruct a shattered fantasy.

'I'm warning you lot: keep yer eyes shut.'

Linda and the children obeyed Carl and felt their way gingerly into the hall at Cranley Gardens. He marched them down to the kitchen and positioned them in a group near the open back door.

'You can open them now.'

The garden was full with a hundred vases of cut flowers, and beside each vase a candle burned. Karen and Nicky ran into the garden and squealed with delight. Linda stared out at the flickering display; chattering tongues of flame, hardening against the evaporating light of the day.

'I bought you some flowers,' said Carl. 'I thought you might be pleased.'

She smiled. 'I am.'

He bent his head down and kissed her lightly on the neck. He pressed his face into her full, soft hair, and drank in its fragrance. 'What yer thinking, darlin'?' he said in a whisper.

'We should plant some next year. These are beautiful, but they'll be dead next week.' He turned away from her, hurt and annoyed by her response. She pulled his face back round to hers and kissed him. He wrapped his arms

237

round her and her face sank onto his chest. She shuddered slightly with a sadness, to which she would no longer allow him to be witness. Holding each other close, they walked out into the garden.

They moved out of the triangle of bright light cast through the kitchen window and into the gathering gloom at the far end of the garden.

Carl called to the children: 'Hey look, you two. I've got something for yer.' He reached down to a small box on the lawn. A lighter flicked, and a sparkler fizzed to life in Carl's hand.

'It's not firework time!' said Linda, with a grin.

Soon, they were each holding a sparkler in their hands, tracing brilliant patterns of concentrated light in the air.

The horror came back in dreams that night. Feverish and struggling against the twisted shroud of linen sheet, Carl screamed out in the darkness: 'Marty!' She tried to hold him, to comfort him and calm him. She did not see the dead leaves blowing across the bed. She did not hear the wind in the beech trees, or watch the thick crimson tide gush from his stomach. But she felt the gripping, twisting pain in her guts, when he finally lay back quiet and still, and breathed: 'Marty's dead.'

Fifteen

Children were playing on the grassy area behind the nursery on Highbury Fields. Inside the school, Nicky's head rested sullenly on his mother's lap. Linda stared intently at the young woman teacher who had summoned her so urgently.

Val could tell this was going to be difficult. She felt the hostility in Linda's eyes. She leaned over and tried to attract Nicky's attention. 'Coo coo, Nicky? Don't you want to go and play with the other children?'

Nicky raised his head six inches and shook it violently. Val smiled weakly and patted at her neat little spiky haircut. She judged that it would be as well to get on with things.

'You see, he's quite different with you,' she began. 'I mean . . . I'm not, you know I'm not . . . a counsellor or anything, but we do make a practice of discussing these matters as and when they arise. You see?'

Linda was not sure what she was being asked. She maintained her blank stare.

Val pressed on. 'It's not just a question of general unruliness – you expect that in most young boys – it's that he . . . well, I don't want to sound alarmist . . .' Her hesitation ensured that she would. 'But there's really no other way I can put it. Nicky actually assaulted two other children. Really rather badly.'

Linda wished she could tell this woman a thing or two about assault, but she satisfied herself with a more relevant comment. 'He's worried 'bout his sister going to proper school.'

'I'm sure it's a difficult adjustment . . .' She paused as she heard a peal of laughter from the playroom. Linda, too, turned to see the source of the amusement. When she saw Chris's face, she wondered what the third disaster of the day would be. He caught her eye and smiled. How dare he bloody smile, she thought. He turned his attention back to another young woman teacher.

'Karen is always very protective towards him. He'll obviously need some time to reassimilate,' reasoned Val.

Linda was not listening. 'What?'

'Oh, I'm sorry . . . ummm . . . get used to being on his own, might be a simpler way of putting it.'

'I'm not stupid, Ms Rhodes,' said Linda coldly.

'No, of course . . . No . . . But it could equally well be that in her protectiveness, she actually managed to camouflage a lot of his errant behaviour. I know that sounds complex . . . psychologically that is . . . but some five-year-olds are capable of a fair degree of sophistication, Mrs Galton.'

'Yes? . . . You want me to take Nicky out of the school.'

'No. Not at all. Well . . . no, not necessarily. Look, please don't be offended when I say this . . . but I feel obliged to ask if . . . well, if everything's all right at home.'

Linda and Chris exchanged another look. His expression flickered dangerously close to pity. Linda turned away and gave a slight laugh.

'What I mean is . . .' Val was struggling.

'It's none of your business,' snapped Linda.

240

'When we spoke on the phone, I was under the impression that your husband would be here too . . .'

'He's picking us up any minute.'

'Well, great. Perhaps we could all sit down and have a chat.'

'I don't think he'd like that, Ms Rhodes. He don't like people called Ms. I'll take Nicky out of school.'

Val got up and tried hard to disguise her relief. 'Such a pity. Such a bright little boy. It doesn't seem . . . I don't know . . . not right.'

Linda looked up sharply. 'I'm not a charity case, Ms Rhodes. Please don't waste any of yer valuable time feeling sorry for us.'

Linda heard Chris distractedly bid farewell to the other teacher. She felt Nicky's head rise from her lap, and his body screw out of her embrace.

'Daddy!' Nicky yelled, as he ran across to the doors and was swept up into Carl's arms.

'There's my man,' said Carl as he gave his son a hug.

Nicky stretched out his finger and pointed to the playroom. 'There's Chris,' he said.

Carl turned and looked. 'Yes, there's Chris. Hallo, Chris.' He made the name sound like an illness.

On the warm evening of the same day, Linda and Chris found themselves sitting at a table outside the Valiant Charger public house on the corner of Highbury Fields. The crowd spilled out from the busy bar, and packed the forecourt area.

Linda was saying: 'It's Mum and Dad's twenty-fifth anniversary the day after tomorrow, so we're all meant to go down that dingy social club and sing along to "The Anniversary Waltz". Mum'll dance with Ron, then the band'll play the "Conga", and she'll push Dad round the floor in his wheelchair. Everyone else'll tag on behind and

241

say "What a laugh," and "S'marvellous really how she's stood by him." Carl'll take pictures of 'em. Same ones he's taken for the last seven years. Mum'll kiss Dad on the cheek and look at the camera. And Dad, smiling, not knowing where he is, or why, or which way is up. Then we'll have another drink and reminisce for a bit, and at the end of the evening, Mum'll say it was lovely and then she'll cry. She'll say it's because she's happy. But really, it's 'cos she's waiting for him to die. And he could live another twenty years.'

She paused and sipped at her drink. She looked round the crowd, and her eyes lit on a group of three business-men having a drink after work. One of the men was short and porcine; he stared back lasciviously at Linda. 'Why did you have to come back, Chris?' she asked.

'Things didn't really work out up north. I'm going to Spain. I've got an old mate there. He works for a car hire place. He said I could stay for a bit. Get my head together, you know?'

For a brief moment she looked amused. 'Mate,' she said, stretching the *a*. 'That's how yer say it. Maaate.'

'Sorry?' he said, feigning ignorance.

'Bit of a mess, ain't yer,' Linda replied, and for the first time he sensed indifference in her voice.

'I suppose I am, Linda. In some ways. I saw some good friends up in Manchester. Helen and Russ. Terry, Jan.'

'Never mentioned them to me.'

'They were the people I was at college with. We were going to buy some land together up in Northumberland. Go and live on it. Grow our own food.'

'So why din't yer?' she demanded.

He floundered for a moment as he searched for the best way to avoid the truth, to avoid saying it was yet another self-indulgent pipe dream that withered through his lack of responsibility and commitment. 'Property didn't mean

242

that much to us then,' he offered. 'I don't think we wanted it badly enough. Anyway, they're all settled now. I haven't seen most of them for years, but it was nice. You don't need to see real friends that often. You know you'll always be close.'

'Bullshit.' She was not fooled this time.

'What?'

'Bull. That's what yer full of, Chris. Bullshit.'

Before he had a chance to reply she rose from the table and marched off purposefully across the park. For a moment he was stunned by her assertiveness, but then he began to chase after her.

'Linda! Please. Linda!' he called.

She stopped and rounded on him angrily. 'What?'

'Please don't go. Not like that. Look, I know how you're feeling – '

'What do yer know about me? I'm just an ordinary girl, Chris. And you're just another little boy who gives me wet looks and tears, and thinks that makes me feel useful. It don't work any more, 'cos I know now. I'm useless.'

'Don't say – '

'I can't even drive a bloody car! I can't cook. Having babies frightens me. Don't yer believe all this rubbish yer read 'bout the beauty of childbirth. Pull yer bottom lip over yer head. That's how much it hurts!'

'Where are you going?'

'To another pub, for another drink. That's where. And then . . . home. I've got things to do. Things what won't get done without me. S'got nothing to do with politics, or demos, or how . . . how women in the Labour Party make you lose yer hard-on. S'more like a load of wet washing.'

She made to go but he grabbed her by the arm and pulled her back. 'Can't we even get a friendship out of this mess?' he pleaded.

'Carl picks my friends.'

'I'll write.'

'I came here so you wouldn't write! So yer wouldn't phone my house again, like this afternoon. The clean-up woman came to clean up the little mess you dropped in her life.'

'It takes two, Linda,' he said bitterly.

'No. You did it all on yer own. 'Cos yer don't know. I'm an ordinary girl. You wonder why I ain't got a clue when yer rattle on 'bout feminism, and my right to choose? It's 'cos ordinary girls still have husbands who don't like other boys looking at their wives.'

'Helen was right about you. She said some women are so far gone, they enjoy being victims.'

His cruelty bit into Linda. She slapped him hard across the face. 'Don't you ever talk to anyone 'bout me,' she rasped.

'You'll stay with him, won't you Linda? Put up with all the shit "for the sake of the kids"?'

'I din't have to marry him. I could of said no. But the alternative weren't up to much, and he was so beautiful to me, d'you know that?' He made no response. She lowered her head and continued quietly. 'He's given me half a fairy story, Chris, and after seven years I've found out a happy ending ain't part of the deal. Well, so what? Don't you dare call what happened between you and me "love". You know as well as me that it didn't even come close.'

She turned her back and walked away. She left him with his pity and masochism.

She went home to get on with what was left of her life.

When Linda arrived back at Cranley Gardens the house appeared to be in darkness. She turned the key in the front door and pushed warily inside. The light from the open fridge in the kitchen darted down the hall. Linda saw Carl lying on the kitchen floor, in only a pair of shorts, his head resting on the bottom shelf of the fridge.

He heard her come in. 'I told yer not to go out on your own,' he called softly.

She began to walk towards the kitchen. 'I know. I'm sorry.'

'Where yer been?'

'Ask me something yer don't know,' she murmured.

'Why d'yer go to him?'

'Ask me something yer don't know.'

She stumbled slightly on the step down to the kitchen. She was frightened he would smell the alcohol on her breath. She slipped off her shoes and settled down on the floor, next to Carl. He did not alter his position.

'I forgive yer,' he said.

She leaned forward and took a beer from the fridge. 'Do yer?' She slurped at the froth which bubbled up when she pulled the ring on the can. 'Want one?'

He shook his head. 'We're going away tomorrow.'

'It's Mum and Dad's anniversary the day after.'

'We'll be back.'

'Where we going?' she asked.

'Surprise. But yer gotta look pretty. D'yer love me?'

'Ask me something yer don't know, Carl.'

He stared up at her. She put her hand to his mouth and slowly clenched the fingers into a fist. The hand dropped down and beat lightly on his chest. He continued to watch her, hawk-like. She raised her hand again, and let it drop. Harder this time. He smiled, and she laid her hand flat on his stomach, knowing she could never hurt him.

Carl closed his eyes as Linda ran her hand back up to his mouth. She prised his lips apart and gently inclined the can so that a few drops of beer fell on his face. He spluttered slightly and stayed her hand. 'No, don't,' he warned.

245

'Sssh, sssh, sssh,' she breathed, as she let a few more droplets fall on his chest. She lowered her head and licked the beer from his smooth skin. Her hand travelled slowly down to the waistband of his shorts. His eyes slipped shut once more. Suddenly she emptied the can down his shorts. He let out a startled cry as she jumped up and ran for the stairs.

He set off in pursuit. 'You'll pay for that my little wench!'

'Carl no! Don't!' she screamed.

It was the only time their laughter filled that house.

The next day, they set off in the late afternoon. Carl had appeared in a blue silk suit, which Linda had never seen before. She dressed as formally as him: a grey linen jacket and pleated skirt. As they walked out of the house they could have been mistaken for the perfect young executive couple.

He drove out of London, through Leyton and Woodford. The Porsche had been cleaned and polished. It powered smoothly along the M11. Despite her persistent questioning, he would not reveal their destination.

They turned off the motorway at junction eight and followed the road for Great Dunmow. About three miles down the road Carl slowed and joined the rear of a queue of traffic, delayed by a set of temporary traffic-lights which marked roadworks. On the verge, close to the impatient, revving engines, a middle-aged couple had parked their car and erected a picnic-table. They sat in a cloud of carbon monoxide and nibbled at sandwiches and sausage rolls. They poured lukewarm tea from a thermos flask and ignored the rolling wheat fields which stretched behind them.

Carl looked over at the couple and said: 'People are ridiculous. If they know how it's gonna be, how they're always gonna have nothing, well how can they carry on? They can't all think they're gonna win the pools. How can they be that bored? They say I've lost God. I believe in God. I ain't frightened of him. How bad can God's punishment be? Can't be worse than a nice cup of tea and a little sit-down.'

Linda gazed out at the couple. 'I hate leaving Kathy to look after the kids all the time,' she said.

'It's not exactly the kind of thing I can turn up at with a couple of kids, Linda.'

'And I thought this was my special treat, Carl.'

'It is.'

'Chance for us to spend a bit of time together?'

'I thought that might be nice.'

Linda glanced again into the side mirror of the Porsche. 'So why is Freddie following us?'

Carl moved uncomfortably in his seat. 'P'raps he just likes us,' he replied in a steely voice.

They drove on, through Great Dunmow to Redfield. They circled the village green and pond and Carl pulled up outside a whitewashed pub. He jumped out of the car and ran back to where Freddie had stopped, a hundred yards behind.

Freddie's face looked out questioningly. 'I din't bring nothing with me,' Carl said, hushed.

'What?'

Carl clicked his fingers impatiently and then made them into the shape of a gun.

'Oh sure,' said Freddie, understanding the demand, and reaching down to produce a gleaming Smith and Wesson 645. Carl forced Freddie's hand back into the car.

'Gimme a break,' Carl hissed. 'Linda's in the car.'

Freddie rooted through the Cadillac's glove compartment and pulled out a soiled AA envelope. He slipped

247

the gun inside and offered it to Carl. Carl nodded and smiled with sarcastic sweetness.

Pat Klein shook out of her husband's grip and continued along the galleried landing on the first floor of Slater's house. Klein staggered against the stair rail as he reached out to grab her back. He was much the worse for drink.

From down in the shadows of the hall, Slater silently observed their tortured progress.

'Don't you touch me,' Pat barked back at George.

'Get your things. I'm taking you home,' he slurred.

She scowled at him. 'You're drunk. You stink with it!'

He beat his fist on the banister. 'S'only 'cos I love you, Pat.'

She began to descend the stairs. 'You bore me.'

'Get your things. Please.'

'You're pathetic.'

Klein lurched dangerously near the top step. He thrust out a hand and dragged himself back upright. 'He don't want you round any more than me. You're all right for a quick screw, or a dirty weekend, my love. When nobody knows about it. When he thinks he's got one over on me. He's called me mate and screwed my wife!'

'Shut your foul mouth!' she cried hoarsely.

'He don't want you, can't you see? It's nothing to do with you. You think he'd want an old whore like you if you weren't my wife?'

Slater stepped out of the darkness. 'That's enough, George,' he said stonily. Pat rushed to his side.

'Tell him,' she implored her lover.

'What?' Slater asked.

'That you love me. And that you want me to stay. Please tell him.'

Klein began to totter awkwardly down the stairs. 'Go

on, Tony. Tell me. You make me feel like a fool all the rest of the time.'

'Tell him!' Pat shrieked.

'I have a houseful of people,' Slater chided, 'and you sound like a fishwife. And as for you, George, well, I don't remember inviting you this year.'

He turned and strode out through the porch. Pat ran after him. Klein could not run but he managed to stagger to the door. He stood there and began to laugh. 'Look what the lord of the manor's bought for himself, Pat. We're just the dirt from his past, love. You think Mr Respectable wants to be seen in public with a tart on his arm?'

Pat tugged at Slater's sleeve as he marched across the gravel to the terrace. 'Please tell him, Tony,' she pleaded, close to tears. 'Please.' But Slater's attention was quickly wrenched away from the domestic trauma.

Carl's Porsche swung in through the gates and drove up the drive.

Klein was shocked back to near-sobriety. 'He's got a bloody nerve,' he gasped. Carl got out of the car and approached Slater. 'What the hell's he doing here?'

'Shut up, George,' ordered Slater.

'I believe we was invited,' said Carl suavely.

'You better piss off now, son,' spat Klein.

Slater turned to chastise his partner. 'Don't be so rude, George.'

'What!'

'Of course you were,' Slater said to Carl. 'The procession through the village starts at ten. The housekeeper will show you and your wife to a room. It's very warm. I'm sure she'd like to freshen up.' Carl nodded to Slater, glanced pointedly at Klein and then walked back to his car.

Klein made his way unsteadily to Slater's side.

'What do you suggest, George?' questioned Slater severely. 'Stick him on a skewer and roast him on a spit? Lace his cheap champagne with arsenic? Or perhaps we could just execute him on my lawn?'

'Oh no, Tony. We mustn't get blood on your lawn,' With that, Klein barrelled his way back to the house.

'Tony?' Pat asked quietly.

'Tell him what, Pat? That I love you? You told me you didn't want that. You told me you understood my grief. You said it wasn't adultery; it was help from a friend. The one thing it never was, was love.'

As the sun settled, red and lazy, over the lake, Carl walked back into the small guest bedroom he and Linda had been allocated. He had been fuelled by the ease of his arrival, and his confidence was beginning to swell once more.

Linda was sitting hunched on the edge of the bed. Carl strode past her and crossed to check his appearance in the Edwardian oval mirror, which stood on a marble-topped wash-stand.

'This house is neat,' said Carl, impressed. 'I want it. Come on, let's go.'

Linda clutched at her stomach. 'I don't feel well, Carl.'

He turned to her with a look of agitated frustration. 'Don't start, Linda.'

'You go.'

'I brought yer here to enjoy yerself, not sit locked up in a room.'

Her features were flushed with resentment and pain. 'Oh? I thought yer might have come 'cos you wanted to. 'Cos yer want something out of these people, whoever they are. You didn't tell me the first time I met them.'

'Here we go – '

'You can't stop, Carl, can yer? Worse than a drug

addict. I dunno why we're here, I dunno who these people are. Our best friend is dead – '

'You don't understand,' he barked.

'Don't tell me more lies!'

A sudden agony gripped her. Her breath shortened, and she was bent double on the bed. Carl knelt before her and jerked her chin up with his hand.

'I never told yer lies, darlin',' he said cruelly. 'You wanna talk about lies? How 'bout what's in yer belly. That a lie?' She let out an anguished cry and flailed out her arms to him, begging for help. 'Wos that got yer, darlin'? Guilt, is it?'

'It's yours!' she moaned. 'I hurt, Carl. Please!'

He rose and stood over her. 'Not as much as me, darlin'. Don't worry. You don't need a headache, darlin'. I ain't gonna touch yer.'

She did not see him hurry out of the room. The shooting pains spread lightning sparks before her eyes, the fire inside strangled her breath.

'Please get me a doctor.' He did not hear. She could no longer say those words out loud. They were a prayer.

Sixteen

Broad pink streaks cut across the iron wall sky.

Pat Klein swilled the ice round a large gin and tonic and tidied her lipstick with her finger. She raised a smile when the sound came from the village.

'It's beginning,' said Pat. 'Did you hear the roar? The giant must've gone up.'

Linda's head lifted an inch from the mound of pillows. She stared towards the bedroom window. Her face had been wiped clean of make-up. Perhaps it was the sudden loss of blood that had caused the darkness beneath her eyes. She listened. She heard only the clink of Pat's nails on the glass. 'What's it like?' she asked.

Pat returned to sit on the edge of the bed. 'Oh, bloody great ugly thing.' She reached out and dragged a straggling hair from Linda's face. 'They call it a "dancing giant". It's 'cos the men can hardly carry it. So it wobbles. It scares me, if you want to know the truth.'

Linda's head fell back and she gazed out across the hard, white linen. 'I'm all right now, Mrs Klein, if yer wanna go.'

'You are not all right and I've seen it all before.' Pat saw Linda's appreciation flickering into those sad eyes. She had heard the girl's strangled scream, seen the writhing agony. That body may be calm now, but the mind was still fighting against the tranquillizers. Looking down at her now, Pat suddenly realized how young the girl was. She said quietly: 'Why did he bring you here?'

'I don't know, Mrs Klein. Are they gonna kill Carl?'

'What? Luvvy, my husband's downstairs, rancid as a newt. He couldn't kill time. And Tony . . . well Tony doesn't kill people. He eats them. Limb by limb.'

'I don't understand.'

Pat bowed her head and ran out a hand to smooth the bedding. 'Stick around twenty years; you still won't.'

Linda dragged herself a fraction from that languishing torpor and tried to talk to the woman. Their alliance was fragile: based on being discarded accessories. There was no commitment. The honesty came from a mutual realization that they had no active part to play in the drama that swirled round them. They were simply observers. Choice was the privilege of others; opinion was not part of the deal.

'I was just a little shop girl from Balham,' said Pat, 'riding all the way up to Walthamstow on the bus with my friend Jacky to go to dances at the Tangerine Suite. That's where I met George. And Tony. It was like it was "their" place. They were on the up. They had a little car hire business. Tony held the money and George spent it. Mostly on me, it seemed. Tony was always the first to leave and George was always the last. Tony polished his Cresta and took us for picnics in the country. George went through six cars in as many months.' She paused, and smiled with gentle incredulity. 'Tony always seemed to treat Jacky like a little sister. We none of us could believe it when he said they'd got married. She never asked him for anything. And he bought her everything. A couple of years ago, when we went out to dinner with them, she knocked over a glass and he made her cry just by looking at her. I never saw them out again together.' She breathed a small laugh. 'When I started sleeping with

253

Tony . . . it didn't seem wrong really. I never loved George, you see. I loved "them". And now, it's not my marriage that's broken down . . . it's theirs.'

The door cracked open. Carl walked into the room with calm measured strides. He held a bowl of soup in his hand. He stopped at the end of the bed and stared at Pat. His face was expressionless, but his entrance was enough to tell Pat that her presence was no longer required. Pat glanced round at Linda as she left the room. The girl's face was frightened and frozen; an animal close to death.

Carl sat next to Linda and raised a spoonful of the soup to her mouth. He said flatly: 'Swapping lover stories?' She let her jaw drop and then close again on the spoon. The action was mechanical and obedient to his silent demand.

He offered her a second spoonful. The warm liquid felt creamy and tight in her throat.

'It's all right,' Carl said in the same monotone. 'I know yer made it happen. But that's all right, 'cos I know why yer did it. S'cos it weren't mine. So I s'pose that was right. I don't wanna pay for a kid what's not mine.' He placed the bowl on the bed beside her. 'Eat the rest of that, it'll do yer good. Soup's good for yer. You look awful. Where are the tranquillizers the doctor give yer?' She opened her left hand. It was white where she had been clutching so hard. He took the bottle from her and removed two pills. He placed the pills next to the soup bowl and slipped the bottle into his pocket.

'Take one, or two,' he said. 'They'll do yer good. Sleep.' He rose from the bed and left the room without further comment. Linda's hand closed around the pills and tried to crush them to powder.

From the doorway of the small study downstairs, Pat Klein stood and studied every contour of her husband's alcohol-flushed face. George Klein was slumped in an

254

armchair, snoring loudly. Pat approached him noiselessly. She saw the twitch of his moustache and the glistening beads of sweat on his wide forehead. She smiled slightly as she wondered what might be under that thick wedge of bristle on his top lip. She realized for the first time that she had never seen him without it.

'I wish I could say I was sorry, George,' she said in a hushed, wavering voice.

Klein's eyes opened wearily. 'Whad'you say?' he mumbled.

'I said I'm going to get in my car and go home, George.'

He shook his pounding head. He said: 'Tony. With him . . . is it . . . are yer . . .'

She sighed and clutched her bag tightly. 'I was just a bright shiny thing in the street when you picked me up, George. Over the years I got to feeling like a Christmas decoration that had been left up too long. Tony just took me down and dusted me off a bit. That's all. It doesn't matter any more.'

'Will yer be there when I get back?' he asked.

'What happened to our imagination, George? We can't even whip up a halfway decent tragedy any more.'

'Will yer be there?' he insisted.

She opened her arms in surrender. 'You called me an old whore, George. Still got a cheque-book, haven't you?'

To the eerie, hollow beat of long drums, the procession had wound its way along Redfield's High Street to the top of the village and was now passing through the gates of Slater's estate.

Floodlights, mounted high up on skeletal scaffolding towers, beat down on the crowds which milled along the tree-lined drive.

Villagers in the costumes of Greenmen, wood spirits, led the procession, carrying cresset torches and sweeping the path with flame. Behind them, a sinewy figure, in the costume of the Devil, danced and darted into the cheering onlookers, brandishing a horsebladder, occasionally dropping to all fours and slithering like a reptile along the grass and grit. Masked musicians and dancers followed in an untidy, colourful throng. Some had faces blacked and menacing, while others disguised their identity with the bright, iridescent feathers of peacocks and pheasants. There were animal-hide headdresses and horned beasts.

The revellers yelled at the crowd, taunting with abuse, dragging onlookers into the heart of the procession, jostling and intimidating them. The roar of the spectacle steadily increased as a hundred, two hundred, three hundred bizarre figures filtered through the gates.

Rising dark and menacing at the rear of the line a giant, some thirty feet high, danced onto Tony Slater's land. It was clad in sackcloth, and held an enormous scythe in its right hand. The gaunt, sculpted face stared ghostly and grim as it was struck by the beams of light.

Carl pushed his way through the crowd and laid a hand on Slater's shoulder. 'This is brilliant, man!' he cried, with uncontained, agitated enthusiasm. 'I want one of those things to stick in me back garden! I want one!'

'I bet you do,' said Slater.

'Who pays for all this?' Carl asked, impressed by the magnitude of the affair.

'I do.'

'So who organizes it all?'

'I do,' Slater repeated. 'I'm the pageant master. I told you, this festival had died. My money revived it. Perhaps you've got a short memory. I'm a traditionalist.'

Carl shrugged dismissively. 'Tell me 'bout the war sometime.'

Slater's expression cooled. 'I'll tell you about the giant.

256

It's a confrontation between man and his own mortality. Doesn't it put the fear of God into you now?'

Carl opted not to rise to Slater's bait. He had not come here for another lecture on morals. 'Where's the virgins?' he quipped.

'When this festival first started people only lived till they were thirty-five. Virginity was a waste of the community's resources. Just like you.' Slater was not prepared to continue this false etiquette. He added: 'You shouldn't have come here, Carl. But then you need to gloat, don't you?'

Carl feigned innocence. 'I come 'cos yer invited me. And din't we set up a little deal last time I saw yer?'

'Not with me.' Slater paused to register any discomfort in the boy. There was none that he could see. Carl poised himself like a hungry hawk sizing up its prey. The smile did not leave his face.

'The last time I saw you,' Slater went on, 'you told me you thought I was just like you. I denied it. But what if you were right, Carl? How many people might there be in this seething mass, just waiting to stick you one, because . . . because . . . I'm just like you?'

For the first time since he had arrived at Slater's, Carl felt the swell of disquiet. He had rolled unaffected over the pain and trauma with Linda, but now he saw a threat to his intention, to the supremacy he had concocted in his head.

Slater saw the disconcerted look he had wanted. He said: 'What's wrong, Carl? Lost your minder?' Carl scoured the crowd for Freddie's face. When he turned once more to reinforce his threatened position, Slater had slipped away into a tide of villagers which was following the procession across the terrace and down onto the lawn before the lake.

Carl cursed, enraged that Slater had abandoned him,

257

and impatient for the moment when he could turn the screw on that man.

It was over an hour before they confronted each other again. The giant had been carried to the meadow on the far side of the lake; it stood propped up by the bonfire with the crowd humming and rippling round. Across the still water came the echoing cry: 'Burn him, burn him.'

Carl was standing on the terrace, alone and frustrated, when Slater appeared through the trees. The lord of the manor wandered along the ranks of trestle-tables which had been laid out on the lawn and laden with food. He nodded approval to a group of white-coated waiters and went to give a half-turn to a suckling pig roasting on a spit. The skin of the skewered animal cracked and oozed grease as the handle cranked round. Carl saw the self-congratulatory look on Slater's face, he saw the way the man smiled at his own benevolence and it fuelled his contempt. The only parties Carl ever went to were the ones he gave.

Slater glanced up to the boy. He saw an expression which demanded attention: a child who nags for the toy and screams and shouts and stamps his feet if he does not get it. He walked calmly to the base of the stone steps which led up to the terrace.

'I was waiting for yer, Mr Slater,' Carl called down. Slater began to mount the steps. 'Thought p'raps yer might have considered my position more carefully.' Slater smiled sweetly as he passed but did not halt his progress to the house. 'I've got something to tell yer, Mr Slater, and I want yer to listen to me.' Carl's voice rose and his composure snapped when Slater failed to react. 'Listen to me!' he screamed furiously.

Slater stopped and turned. He spoke quietly, seemingly unruffled. 'You think everyone owes you something, don't you? You think the world owes you a future. Too many people told you how good it was in the sixties. It weren't that good for me; I worked my backside off. I'm the one who deserves a decent future. You just deserve a chance. And you've had your share of that.'

'Peddling drugs ain't decent, Tony. It's bent.'

'Everything's bent now. But not everything's as obvious as you.'

Carl laughed away another dose of morality. 'Huh! Well, it weren't my lorry, Tony. And Broderick din't work for me . . . half the police in the country are looking for him, ain't they? And I weren't interviewed by the CID. And it weren't my nice country gaff where the Yankee lady met all those nice gentlemen. You keeping up?'

Slater nodded. The child had played its trump card.

'So p'raps we do still have a deal,' Carl concluded.

'What if I told you she'd cleared out after your little escapades? Got cold feet? No one gets a deal.'

'Whatever. I'm sure we can still work something out. A good deal, Tony.'

'I suppose you've got someone up in town, waiting to post a letter to New Scotland Yard if you don't come back?'

'You guessed!' Carl cried in triumph.

'We've all seen that film, Carl . . . Tell me one thing. What is it that fascinates you about me?'

'I started being mad at Mr Klein. But now . . . I want what you've got.'

'All of it?'

The booming howl of approval rose from the crowd in the meadow as the bonfire and the giant were engulfed in flames.

Slater said: 'They're going to play games now. I may not see you again tonight. I know where to find you. I'll be in touch.' Then he turned and walked into the house.

For several minutes, Slater and Klein sat silent in the study. The shouts from the window floated across on the wind and punctuated the silence.

Slater got up from his chair and ran his finger along a row of the well-stocked bookshelf. He read the titles to himself: *Reader's Digest*, collections of Shakespeare and Bernard Shaw, a guide to Impressionism, Dick Francis thrillers, photo books, book club titles. He said: 'I didn't need to read all these books, George. Everything I've learned, he sees as . . . knick-knacks in my conversation. He reads magazines on warfare and weapons. He thinks money is respect. I never thought it would be that easy.'

'We've got to get rid of him,' Klein breathed.

'Oh, there's the old villain talking. Let's just add another murder to the list. Won't even make the papers these days.' He swung round, and Klein saw that his expression was strangely bemused and mournful.

'What have we come to?' Slater said quietly.

'If you don't know, then I'm damn sure I don't. You're the one who says you've always dragged me with yer. You're the one who said how good the last eight years have been to us.'

'I admit it. I cheered and shouted louder than anyone in '79. And the past couple of years, well, you couldn't wipe the smile off our accountant's face. We're rich men . . . But Jacky always said she felt like the housekeeper here. She said the people in the village would never like us, because they were used to aristocracy at Redfield Manor. They could respect that. They could only be jealous of us.'

Slater sank back in the Dralon-covered armchair and continued to dissect his melancholy: 'It's hard to argue with our boy Carl. Selling the company to those people is wrong. I can pretend I don't know who they are, but I do. I felt cheated when I saw how business and politics had turned into a racket, worse than anything my old dad ran on the streets of East Ham. I thought I was owed one last big pay-off, before I shut the door on the bloody awful world, George. I should've known someone like Carl could come along and say "Gotcha." '

Klein said hopefully: 'We can carry on, Tony. I remember the first time you saw those offices in Aldgate. You said yer loved the way the sun shone off the glass and blinded yer.'

Slater had lost himself in jagged memories of his wife. 'I remember a picnic. In Epping Forest. When we first got the Cresta. You and me, and Pat and Jacky.' He dragged himself back to the even more unpleasant discomfort of the present and said: 'Do you see what he's done, George? We've let him drag us back to the gutter. You carry on. I'm going to cultivate my garden.'

Slater looked hard at Klein. 'You know who to call, George,' he said purposefully. 'After all, you tried to get rid of him before, didn't you? . . . Arrange it, will you? But not here, please God. Not tonight. Tomorrow.'

Carl and Linda sat on the edge of a small coppice which topped a grassy hill. She looked pale and *distrait* in a white rosette of a dress. Her hair was bunched, neat and compact. Carl stretched his arms over his head, fell back on the jacket of his black silk suit and soaked in the sun which had escaped the bank of low, charcoal cloud.

Linda stared into the dark, impenetrable coppice and said: 'I'd like to go home now please.'

Carl's eyes squinted open. 'We're only here 'cos yer wanted to be. S'posed to be tripping the light with yer mum and dad.'

'I changed me mind, Carl. I want to go to the party now.'

He jumped up, dusted down his jacket and reached out

his hand. 'Great. We should of been back hours ago. Come on. We might just catch the end.' But she made no move. She gazed down at vast pools of shadow, gliding silently over the Essex countryside. She felt the sun's meagre warmth on her cheek and felt sorry for the people who were trapped in that darkness, waiting for the light to reappear and invigorate them. She wanted to shout out to them that the sun was cool today. She wanted to tell them not to get their hopes up. Not to expect too much. She was lost in the flimsiest fantasy.

'What is it now?' Carl demanded. 'We've done the car's hot, you din't sleep, the pub was too full, the field's dirty. What is it now, for chrissake?'

'I want to go away,' she said dreamily.

'We are away! You just said yer wanted to go back!'

'Listen to me,' she said, suddenly clipped and resistant. 'I want to go away. Not for a holiday. Not for a few days. For ever. To another country, where we don't speak the language, where we'd have to learn together, where we don't know anyone. I want us to sell up and start again. Together. Do something together.'

Carl's selfish cruelty beat her down. 'I'm fed up with this. You'll go away, darlin'. They'll put yer away. Yer watch me slog my guts out to make something for us . . . whoever gave me nothing, eh? And then yer run off at the mouth 'bout ripping off to some bumscrew country and living in a mud hut.'

'Listen to me, Carl, and I'll never say this again . . . Let me go. I don't want another man. Ever. I won't go far and yer could see the kids . . .' Her plea dissolved into the fresh, summer air. Her head dropped and she picked nervously at the edge of the dress. 'Yer can't, can yer?' she muttered.

'You are mine, Linda. Don't fight me.'

She looked up at him. Her thoughts flashed back to the

time two days earlier, in the kitchen, in the heat, beating his chest. She could never hurt him. 'I can't fight yer,' she said hoarsely. 'You wore me out, Carl. We crammed so much good and so much bad into such a short time. We got no secrets any more. I thought it would take a lifetime to be this disappointed. But p'raps our lives were meant to be short.' She winced slightly as a cramping pain gripped her stomach. She turned her head, to hide the pain from his restless glare.

She reached up a hand to him. 'Help me up, please.'

Chris pushed the envelope halfway through the letter-box at Cranley Gardens. He stopped to consider for a moment and then jumped back with surprise as it was yanked into the house. He heard a mischievous giggle from behind the door and then saw Karen's laughing eyes peer out through the letter-box.

'Hallo, Chris.'

He squatted down and shook his head at her. 'You little bugger.'

'You're a little bugger!' she squealed as she opened the door.

'You're not on your own?' he said.

Karen hushed her voice to a tiny whisper. 'Aunty Kathy's upstairs lying down. I don't think she's very well. She ate three bars of chocolate.'

'Where's your mum and dad?' he asked, slightly nervous that Carl might also be in the house.

'They went away. Mum cried when she said goodbye. Come and look at Nicky's tortoise. Kathy says it's dead.'

He backed away a step. Why wasn't she there? Why couldn't it have been her who pulled the letter from his hand, smiling forgiveness, asking him to read it to her, listening to the well-rounded apologies, absolving guilt, salving conscience, rekindling the vision of romance that would sustain him? But she wasn't. She could read the note and throw it in the bin, uncaring, unobserved. He would never know her reaction.

'Please, Chris.' Karen took him by the hand and pulled him into the house. He wondered what kind of suicide he was committing. Christ! What if they came back? Karen pushed the door to and led him down the hall.

'I'm only going to stay for a minute,' he said, as they walked out into the garden.

Nicky was kneeling at the foot of the rockery, peering inquisitively into the tortoise shell. He said chirpily: 'Hallo, Chris. What yer reckon?'

Chris picked up the shell and pronounced the tortoise very dead. Nicky looked puzzled. 'Then why's it still in there?' he asked. 'Aunty Kathy said the angels took it.'

'Well, she didn't mean that. I'm sure your mum'll buy you another one.'

'I don't want 'nother one,' Nicky said firmly. 'They're no good. Yer can't play with Torty. I want a Mr Exterminator.'

Chris smiled. 'I've got to go, kids.'

'Can't we bury Torty?' said Karen.

'Your dad'll dig a hole for it,' Chris replied.

Nicky took the shell of the dead creature from Chris. He said: 'Let's throw him over the wall.'

'No!' shouted Karen.

Chris thought he should arbitrate over the disposal of Torty. 'Have you got a box?' he said, lifting Nicky into his arms.

Karen smiled. 'I know where's one,' she cried and ran off into the house.

Karen hurried up to her bedroom and tipped a pile of Nicky's Smurfs from Torty's future coffin. She heard Kathy stir in the next bedroom and then ran back down the stairs. As she jumped the last three steps into the hall, the doorbell rang. Three short, sharp blasts.

Karen wrenched open the door. She looked up to the gun in the stranger's hand. She said quietly: 'You want my daddy?'

The tall man's eyes widened and he took a deep breath. He forced off his hesitation, pushed past Karen and sent her scrambling on the floor. She wailed out a long, anguished cry.

The gunman ran into the living-room, then the kitchen, then the garden . . .

Nicky screamed with terror and ecstasy as Chris threw him high in the air. The first shot smacked deep in Chris's shoulder and jerked him forward. Nicky toppled through his grasp and fell to the ground. The second shot struck Chris's spine. His body twisted in a violent spasm and he shuddered into the garden wall. He sank down, contorted, like a broken doll, dead.

Kathy's screams filled the house as the gunman ran back to the street.

Carl's Porsche stood in the car park of a Little Chef. The watering hole stood just off the M11, in the grey waste-land between the country and city.

Linda's stare was fixed on the horizon, where the pylons and gas holders formed the border of the city. She heard his footsteps crossing the pitted tarmac. A small package of aspirin landed in her lap. She felt his warm breath on her neck.

'Medicine for my pretty baby,' came his voice, sweet with charm and control. 'Why d'yer have to make things so complicated, darlin'? Fill yer head with rubbish? Everything's simple, Linda. I love you. That's simple. We'll always be together. That's simple. The first time yer saw me, yer knew that. Life's full of opportunities, if yer make 'em. You didn't marry a nobody. I'm a very special man, darlin'.' She felt his hand brush her temple. 'The one you was made to love. I'll always be part of you. You don't need those pills. See, I can even make yer headache go away.'

She had found the gun in the glove compartment.

The noise it made terrified her.

Also available from Methuen

John Burke

THE BILL 2

There is tension at Sun Hill Police Station, and
not just between the police and the villains.
Detective Inspector Galloway's marriage is on the
rocks, Sergeant Cryer is trying to hold his team
together and the word from on high is to cut costs
but not to drop standards.

But outside, on the streets of the East End,
crimes are being committed, and whether it is
staking out bank robbers, searching for missing
school girls, clearing up after a multiple collision
or arresting obstructive animal liberationists, the
private preoccupations of the force at Sun Hill
have to take second place to the strange and often
grim business of policing their patch.

Top Fiction from Methuen Paperbacks

☐ 413 55810 X	**Lords of the Earth**	Patrick Anderson	£2.95
☐ 417 02530 0	**Little Big Man**	Thomas Berger	£2.50
☐ 417 04830 0	**Life at the Top**	John Braine	£1.95
☐ 413 57370 2	**The Two of Us**	John Braine	£1.95
☐ 417 05360 6	**The Good Earth**	Pearl S Buck	£1.95
☐ 413 57930 1	**Here Today**	Zoë Fairbairns	£1.95
☐ 413 57620 5	**Oxford Blood**	Antonia Fraser	£2.50
☐ 413 58680 4	**Dominator**	James Follett	£2.50
☐ 417 03890 9	**The Rich and the Beautiful**	Ruth Harris	£1.75
☐ 413 60420 9	**Metro**	Alexander Kaletski	£2.50
☐ 417 04590 5	**Sometimes a Great Notion**	Ken Kesey	£2.95
☐ 413 55620 4	**Second from Last in the Sack Race**	David Nobbs	£2.50
☐ 413 52370 5	**Titus Groan**	Mervyn Peake	£2.50
☐ 413 52350 0	**Gormenghast**	Mervyn Peake	£2.50
☐ 413 52360 8	**Titus Alone**	Mervyn Peake	£1.95
☐ 417 05390 8	**Lust for Life**	Irving Stone	£1.95
☐ 413 60350 4	**Depths of Glory**	Irving Stone	£2.95
☐ 413 41910 X	**The Agony and the Ecstasy**	Irving Stone	£2.95
☐ 413 53790 0	**The Secret Diary of Adrian Mole Aged 13¾**	Sue Townsend	£1.95
☐ 413 58810 6	**The Growing Pains of Adrian Mole**	Sue Townsend	£1.95

All these books are available at your bookshop or newsagent, or can be ordered direct from the publisher. Just tick the titles you want and fill in the form below.

Methuen Paperbacks, Cash Sales Department,
PO Box 11, Falmouth,
Cornwall TR10 109EN.

Please send cheque or postal order, no currency, for purchase price quoted and allow the following for postage and packing:

UK	60p for the first book, 25p for the second book and 15p for each additional book ordered to a maximum charge of £1.90.
BFPO and Eire	60p for the first book, 25p for the second book and 15p for each next seven books, thereafter 9p per book.
Overseas Customers	£1.25 for the first book, 75p for the second book and 28p for each subsequent title ordered.

NAME (Block Letters) ....

ADDRESS.. ....

....